THE

DISTANCE

FROM

THE HEART

OF THINGS

Houghton Mifflin Literary Fellowship Awards

E. P. O'Donnell, *Green Margins*
Dorothy Baker, *Young Man with a Horn*
Robert Penn Warren, *Night Rider*
Joseph Wechsberg, *Looking for a Bluebird*
Ann Petry, *The Street*
Elizabeth Bishop, *North & South*
Anthony West, *The Vintage*
Arthur Mizener, *The Far Side of Paradise*
Madison A. Cooper, Jr., *Sironia, Texas*
Charles Bracelen Flood, *Love Is a Bridge*
Milton Lott, *The Last Hunt*
Eugene Burdick, *The Ninth Wave*
Philip Roth, *Goodbye, Columbus*
William Brammer, *The Gay Place*
Clancy Sigal, *Going Away*
Edward Hoagland, *The Cat Man*
Ellen Douglas, *A Family's Affairs*
John Stewart Carter, *Full Fathom Five*
Margaret Walker, *Jubilee*
Berry Morgan, *Pursuit*
Robert Stone, *A Hall of Mirrors*
Willie Morris, *North Toward Home*
Georgia McKinley, *Follow the Running Grass*
Elizabeth Cullinan, *House of Gold*
Edward Hannibal, *Chocolate Days, Popsicle Weeks*
Helen Yglesias, *How She Died*
Henry Bromell, *The Slightest Distance*
Julia Markus, *Uncle*
Jean Strouse, *Alice James*
Patricia Hampl, *A Romantic Education*
W. P. Kinsella, *Shoeless Joe*
David Payne, *Confessions of a Taoist on Wall Street*
Ethan Canin, *Emperor of the Air*
David Campbell, *The Crystal Desert*
Ashley Warlick, *The Distance from the Heart of Things*

THE

DISTANCE

FROM

THE HEART

OF THINGS

ASHLEY WARLICK

Houghton Mifflin Company

BOSTON   NEW YORK

For information about permission to reproduce
selections from this book, write to Permissions,
Houghton Mifflin Company, 215 Park Avenue South,
New York, New York 10003.

For information about this and other Houghton Mifflin
trade and reference books and multimedia products,
visit The Bookstore at Houghton Mifflin on the
World Wide Web at http://www.hmco.com/trade/.

Library of Congress Cataloging-in-Publication Data
Warlick, Ashley.
    The distance from the heart of things / Ashley Warlick.
        p.   cm.
    ISBN 0-395-74177-7
    I. Title.
PS3573.A7617D57   1996
813'.54 — dc20   95-36108   CIP

Printed in the United States of America

QUM 10 9 8 7 6 5 4 3 2

Book design by Melodie Wertelet

The author is grateful for permission to reprint lines from "Kudzu,"
from *Poems 1957–1967*, by James Dickey, copyright © 1978 by
James Dickey, published by Wesleyan University Press. Reprinted
by permission of University Press of New England.

~ for my father ~

. . . The night the kudzu has
Your pasture, you sleep like the dead.
Silence has grown Oriental
And you cannot step upon ground:
Your leg plunges somewhere

It should not, it should never be,
Disappears, and waits to be struck

Anywhere between sole and kneecap
For when the kudzu comes,
The snakes do, and weave themselves
Among its lengthening vines,
Their spade heads resting on leaves,
Growing also, in earthly power
And the huge circumstance of
concealment.

"Kudzu," JAMES DICKEY

THE

DISTANCE

FROM

THE HEART

OF THINGS

〜〜〜〜〜〜〜〜〜 Edisto River starts somewhere up about Batesburg, South Carolina, starts itself up like a forest fire or a thread of cancer, pulling down through the flats and the orchards, through the hogs and the Herefords and the smell of rotten peaches in the sun. It will be cancer that finally puts my grandfather Punk in the ground, cancer like fine barbed wire they'll keep pulling from his cheek and jaw for too many years of tobacco. He used to grow his own in the back parts of the pastures, down where the river snakes over his land. He cured it himself with burning cow dung.

What he'd do was harvest the stalk when the leaves were full and green, leaves enough to dress a child head to toe, and he'd bundle them by the dozen in the rafters of his smokehouse. He'd rub each leaf with ash from the last cure, set fire in the floorboards with cedar kindling laid to tent a cow pie and shut the door up tight. Those leaves would smoke until his fire sweated itself out, three, four days. But all that was when he had his cows, back when he'd send us into the pastures with feed sacks to collect up those cow pies, dry as wasps' nests.

After the cows, he bought his tobacco at the Dixie Home Store, like everybody else. He'd buy it and complain about how sweet it was and how they used maple syrup and tonka beans as additive, and how good tobacco didn't need additive to make it smooth. He'd complain the Redman was stale, aged too long, and the grind not fine enough. He'd complain, but he chewed it anyway.

〜〜

The bus I ride lists back and forth slow over the asphalt, crossing the river bridge just at sunset. A spread of light cuts through my window and across my face, warms my skin from temple to collarbone, and I watch as this same light blooms on the river, reflects back to me in yellow and gold and strokes of heat. Punk's farm starts here, right where this water and this highway lope across each other. It's no longer Herefords and Black Angus, chicory and pokeberries and pastureland, but miles and miles of vineyards making rhymes across the hills. It's June, and the grapes are still hard and green on the vine.

Punk sold fifty Herefords for Niagara and Scuppernong vine stock when I was still in grade school, up and did it one afternoon without sign or signal. Miss Pauline, Punk's wife and my grandmother, gave him a piece of her mind, cussed him in such a way as no other soul on earth could and still draw breath.

She said, "Punk, you are a flat-crazy son of a bitch," and there was more, but I'll not tell it here.

Miss Pauline, herself, is an entrepreneur. She has her own business, Miss Pauline's Boutique, and she understands things that make sense and things that don't and where exactly they overlap in her husband. The day Punk picked up his stock shipped down from the nursery, hickory posts and cables for trellising all in the back of his truck, he pulled by her store like he was head of a parade. He threw open the front door to the Boutique and set foot inside for the very last time.

He said, "Hey, Miss Pauline, it's your crazy son of a bitch come to roost on your own slat porch."

He's a caution. His was the first vineyard in South Carolina, and even as Punk Black was Punk Black, more than a few people shook their heads and laughed.

Two years later, he brought in sixty thousand dollars selling his grape to Taylor Winery in Fredonia, New York. Nobody laughed then. He expanded, planted Concords and Catawbas to fill out the season, and when I was in high school and still at home, there wasn't a summer's day I couldn't head out to his barn and find a camp of migrant fruit pickers, tussling over something. These are the facts of his business, the figures, the moments I'll have to remember when I keep books for Punk.

Punk says, "Mavis, honey, you're gonna make me a fine bookkeeper one day. Yessir, this fancy education will return to me tenfold."

It was Punk who paid my four years at Appalachian State. He gave the money willingly and never once did he ask me about my grades, ask about my studies. Five thousand dollars a year, every year in my bank account.

He'd say, "Most of that's for the school, a little extra for your pretty self."

Punk's that kind of man.

Appalachian is the school Miss Pauline graduated from and the school my mother might have gone to if she'd not had me. There is a certain weight to this, a legacy of sorts to carry out. It's like knowing you're the only son in a family line and having only daughters of your own. Thoughts like that can be heavy on a body, can make a person see their situation as a part of something bigger, something older and wiser and testing of themselves. I liked that feeling when I was at school, liked knowing I was connected up to larger workings, a lash in a long chain, part of a constellation. I like weight placed on me. It feels good.

This bus comes out of the Appalachian Mountains, the Blue Ridge Travels Line. It's old, silver, chugging, and yesterday broke down in the rain, left me and twenty others on the berm of the highway with our bags over our heads, raspy and worn down. The kindness of Blue Ridge Travels put us up for the night at a roadside stop near Bessemer City. I've been in roadside motels before with my boyfriend Harris and by myself when I would travel here or there. I've come off a bus tired and anxious with wait or destination, and I've crossed my arms 'neath my head and slept like the dead called home. But last night I was beside myself, alone and fidgeting and walking the floor in my new high-heeled shoes.

It was dark when we checked in, but too early in the evening to go to sleep, that time that's both day and night, when all I wished for was a deck of cards, a good book, or a dog to walk. I was tired with myself, tired with standing up, so tired of stretching my legs out beneath me it almost hurt. I wanted to be still, but I couldn't. I wanted to run the whole rest of the way home, but I couldn't do that either.

My motel room was red, and the carpet was shag, a picture over the big bed of a girl with eyes like blue spades. I walked that room, stretched out my legs, and opened all the drawers, the closets, and the bathroom. There was a Bible in the night-stand, a body hair on one of the towels, a roach in the ice bucket, which made me cringe in spite of myself. I've seen dirt and crawling things before. I've found bugs in my lunch bag or pressed between my books, skittering 'round the toolshed when the light comes on. But those were roaches at home, bugs in familiar places, and this was different. Anybody could have been here before me. I considered standing up the whole night through, but my body got the better of me.

I laid myself out on the big bed fully dressed in my best, folded my hands at my rib cage, and tried to make my limbs go dead still so as not to wrinkle. I'm making this trip in good clothes, careful clothes, new stockings and a short black dress, high heels I walked in for a week to get it right. I'd planned on coming back to Edisto looking polished, like a new penny, smart about myself. I'd planned on coming back sooner; it just didn't happen that way.

I closed my eyes and tried not to be disappointed at my

delay. I tried to fall asleep so that the night could pass quickly and I could wake to the same bus, the same chugging engine taking me closer and closer to home. But it wouldn't happen; I couldn't sleep, and there were still hours and hours of wait ahead. When I took off my dress, I ironed it on a clean towel across the bureau top for a board.

Then I rinsed out my underwear in the sink, my stockings too. I'd brought no change of clothes with me in my canvas bag, so I made a pastime of undressing piece by piece and fixing myself to dress all over again when the time came and the bus was ready to go. I ironed and stacked and shined and rinsed. Finally, I stood naked in that motel room with nothing left to take off, stood naked as if I were comfortable there and this was a just fine way to spend the night I'd been waiting on for so long. If I could have gotten my hands on a chambermaid's cart, I would have cleaned that entire motel room, sheets to shower.

I wasn't going to pout. I was going to stay busy.

I propped my feet on the edge of the bed and smoothed lotion on my bare calves, cupped my knees and ran it down over my ankles, under the arch of my feet. My fingertips tapped at my shins, played that ridge of bone. This was not my lotion, but a bottle from Harris's apartment I'd packed up with my things. Maybe I took it by mistake, or maybe I saw it every day and began to think of it as belonging to me, or maybe I took it because it was Harris's and I wanted it to belong to me. They all come from the same place, these mistakes and thoughts and wants, and it doesn't really matter which turned my mind at the time.

Harris had taken me to the station to catch my bus home, watched me board, and even stood on the platform and waved as we left Boone. But there was no kiss, no tears or flowers or promises to write every day. We had words in his car, minutes before leaving; not a fight really but something that passed over us and cast things off balance like a great gust of wind. He doesn't understand why I'm coming home, and I don't understand why I must explain myself. I thought of him last night like a tickle in my throat, something that needed soothing, and a phone call might have done just that.

But instead I called home. I told Miss Pauline not to wait up for me, told her to make sure my mama didn't worry, but we didn't talk long or about anything other than me and my broken-down bus. I don't want to talk to her on the phone anymore. I've been two years away from Edisto at school, two years without seeing my mama or Miss Pauline or Punk or anybody in my family. I was unable to hush my fluttering brain, let-down and restless and full of thoughts that would not lie quietly.

I could say I'd kept away from home. I could say I'd been kept away, and in some sense both would be true. There have been things for me to do without that place, those people, in my foremost mind. But what I'd not thought about once I finally steered myself toward home was the sheer amount of time it would take me to get there.

And so last night, with the sound of Miss Pauline's good-bye still in my ears, with my wistful, anxious self about to set to flight or shatter, I realized something. I am about to enter a moment in burgeon, wide open and flat out. I am traveling back home to my family, sprawling and uncommon and longed for as they are, and those hours in that bare red room were to be my last in harbor with myself.

It was enough reason for quiet, almost enough for content.

I slept in the middle of that big red bed with all four pillows, two under my head, one to my side, and one in my arms held close.

It was a calm and dreamless sleep, and in the morning I dressed carefully all over again, made up the bed, and left that motel room neater than I'd found it. Parts arrived from Shelby and the bus was repaired. We left Bessemer City in the afternoon.

I keep thinking of my two years gone and it doesn't seem that long, just a breath of busy time. Harris tells me as we get older, each year seems shorter, because it's a smaller part of our lives, and once we reach sixty it really is all over in a heartbeat. He says time is relative, and I know he's right. But I want to come home with my time away marked on my face and my body, my expressions and my carriage changed for their distance from Edisto, as if I know a secret or two that I'm not telling. It's in the way that I've dressed myself up, in the care I've taken with my hair and my makeup. It's a simple change I feel the need to show, and I want it to be simply obvious.

My freshman year I came home for my holidays, for a few weeks at Christmas and around Eastertime. But in the summer, I got a job at the Mast General Store on King Street because I liked Boone, its mountains and its coolness, and staying up there made sense. Everybody thought so. I was glad to take my free days and spend them how I liked, especially after I met Harris. There were long lazy weekends in his apartment, whole hours watching TV or reading magazines and knowing we had nothing more important to do. Harris and I found the trails back along the ridge, the quarries that had flooded up to be swimming holes, the banks of meadow grass that held the sun best. I taught myself how to bake in his kitchen, and Harris would eat my sweet things until his stomach ached and then he'd drink a glass of milk and lie on his sofa and pull me down on top of him.

Before we knew it evening would come, and then the night, cool and starry, and Harris would lead me out of doors and we'd wind down the streets of Boone for coffee and a newspaper. It would be like we were the only two people in the world and our waking and our sleeping was enough event to set time by. I know it was not always this way. I know we both had jobs and work to do, and sometimes I didn't bake for weeks, but when I think back, those summers were sweet like cake and fine naps and there was always night coming on and on and on.

Those summers with Harris were magic, and I loved them.

Even so, something could sweep across me like cool shade and I'd want to see my mama, want more than her voice on the phone or her words in a card, and plans would get made, tickets purchased, and I'd be packed for Edisto. It could happen all that fast.

It seemed always something would come up. Last Christmas I got the stomach flu and stayed in bed until New Year's. There were exams and papers that took longer than I thought they would, and in the spring, I was walking out the door to meet the bus, and I just sat down. I found a chair and sat down and was still for a while. It was important to me that I could do that, that I could change my mind and not go and be still. It was important that the plans were mine to change.

Then there were the times too that I'd be walking out the door and Punk would call, ask me instead to run up to New York State and look in on an old friend at Taylor Winery, get an answer to this or that delicate question, pose this or that proposition. These were in-person errands, things he'd want to do himself, but I was closer or packed already, and it was an honor to be trusted this way. Plans are Punk's to change as well and I've been to the winery in Fredonia for him and to Texas where they grow grapes in the dirt, to Minnesota where they develop stock, and up and down, across and over the state of North Carolina. I'd always go alone and I've come to love the travel.

I'd call Punk when I got back to Boone, tell him what I'd learned, and he'd thank me. He'd always ask if I'd gotten myself a souvenir for my trouble.

Of the twenty passengers who spent the night in Bessemer City, there are only a spare few left on the bus. Most got off in Columbia, here and there along the way, with their trails of bags, armfuls of things. I have the feeling the bus is lighter and faster now, feel as though I'm all alone, but I know I'm not.

Across the aisle from me there's a woman huddled into herself as if she's cold, as if she's trying to keep something inside her blouse from escaping. She is Asian and slight of form, her face thin-edged like a piece of porcelain, her clothes crisp as if fresh unwrapped from plastic. She has creases to her, the posture of paper. She looks as though she's been dressed and set in place and told to stay put.

I think how this woman is still, like me, but not like me at all. She rests in two dimensions, still without the want of motion in the near or distant future, like a fallen feather or a stone, and me, I am swelled full and at rest, all things stored up. It's then I see a bead of water skein from her hair to her lap, her skirt blue and bluer yet in places, her face wet with tears.

She makes no sound. No sound at all.

The tears roll down her face, some falling from her nose, her chin, her lips, and some catching in the wisps of hair about her face and glistening there in the warming light, like late ice in treetops.

I reach into the canvas bag on my lap, sift through the contents for a tissue or a handkerchief to give this woman, but I have nothing like that. In fact, I know I have forgotten something, something left in the motel room for the chambermaids to find, like a silver earring, or a cake of powder, a photograph I might miss later. Last night in my pacing, I emptied this bag across the bureau, spilling pots and jars and tubes over the veneer. Something could have slipped away from me then. Something I won't know how much to care about if I can't remember now.

I prop my elbow on the window ledge, train my eyes out

the window. If I can't give this woman anything for soothing, anything to dry her tears, I don't want to stare her down and make her uncomfortable or feel the need to stop. I feel so for her my tongue's gone salty. I've been on this bus so long, it's a taste in my mouth.

I watch the roadside quicken, the bus picking up speed to make the rise to town. Punk's farm fades behind us, giving way to other pastures, other land full of burdock and ragweed breaking to bloom, dry grasses, horse nettle forcing up through the crackish clay. The land at school is so different from here, verdant and wet. In springtime it rains up there for weeks at a time and I like the rain. I used to sit in the library, waiting for Harris to finish researching this or that. I'd just sit and listen to the rain on the skylights, listen to the rain on the thin roof, a spread sheet across my lap.

Edisto is a simple ratio of water to dust, water like the river that moves and tangles, water that glasses in the heat and pales under white dust. My mama got this idea that she's allergic to dust, and when she tells me about it, she holds her hand over the phone's mouthpiece as if to make sure her words sift clean through the jammed-up air.

She'll say, "All this dust comes from someplace. It comes from ash, little bits of things far away. I swear as we sit here, we're probably still breathing in parts of Pearl Harbor and forest fires in the Northwest, that great quake of 1910."

That's Elsbeth. She's my mama. She thinks about the things that make up dust and send it way up into the atmosphere, like fires in distant places, fires in Oregon, Sweden, and Tasmania, volcanic eruptions in Hawaii, fires at the center of the earth, strip mining in Utah, coal mining in West Virginia, land mines left over from World War II, the A-bomb, the H-bomb. All those women all over the world, beating out rugs they've hung on clotheslines.

I turn in my seat to watch the Edisto dust billow out behind us.

And when I turn back around, my eyes sweep over the woman sitting across the aisle. She's not moved, her tears coming and coming, and all this dust and land passing by her window unseen. I wonder where she's going, who sent her on this bus and where she will get off. She has no luggage with her on the seat, no bags above her head. I get the idea that she might just ride this bus forever, for something to do or be or seem to be doing. If this were a vacation or a homecoming, she would have luggage.

I carry two suitcases with me underneath the bus, and the rest of my things I sent on ahead. Over the weeks I'll receive the boxes I shipped. They'll come from New York and Arizona, Jackson, Mississippi, and Jackson Hole, Wyoming. One will come from Thailand and one will come from my next-door neighbor. But I don't know that yet. What all I do know is I graduated a week ago with a degree in business, and I come home now, a few days before my Aunt Hazel's wedding.

Hazel is my aunt, Aunt Hazel. She's thirty-three, too old to be a bride. I'm twenty-two, old enough to know when a woman is clutching at straws. I know this because I know how to audit assets and liabilities, to prove they're properly valued, incurred, recorded. I know there are fifty-two busts on display in the Accounting Hall of Fame in Cincinnati. I know how to draw up books and balance the balance sheet. I know loss is inevitable. I know clutter is a sign of despair and I know the furniture in Harris's apartment is arranged according to the forces of entropy, that red wine should be stored on its side, that the heart travels the body, and that blood is thicker than water. I know that men like to have love in the morning and lunch in the afternoon. I have a liberal arts education, but a degree in business. I think, therefore I am.

I got that degree only a week ago, but I didn't go to the ceremony. Nobody came up from Edisto either and I didn't send down invitations as there was no reason, no circumstance in which I would have needed them. This degree was only what was set before me. What all I took went beyond paper and lawn chairs and champagne, and such learning doesn't hold audience.

But I can tell how it came about. I saw all these things at college I'd never see in Edisto. I saw a very famous Irish poet read his poetry, but now I can't remember his name. I do remember leaving the reading room and hearing two girls talking. One girl said, he is the most handsome man I've ever seen. The other said, yeah, except for my father. Then they twined their arms about each other and kissed on the lips, and I must admit I could not look away. They were pretty, holding each other like that, or at least I like to think of them that way now.

I've developed my own tastes too, things I appreciate and things I don't. I like good coffee and long skirts. I like the smell of old books, old papers, manuscripts in the library that haven't been opened in thirty years. I like things you have to go places to get, apples from a roadside market, fish from a lake, beer from a bottle in a bar, and men too, men with long ropy backs and sweet shoulders, men who are smarter than I am, and you might find such men in the library, or smelling old books, or wherever you least expect it. I like the unexpected. I like thinking those two women were pretty, even as I wouldn't trade my place for theirs.

Owen is to meet me at the station in town. He was to meet me yesterday, and he will be there again today, I'm sure of it. Two weeks ago he told Punk he was headed for Saudi or South Africa or someplace else; he was heading out at the end of the summer to do it on his own. He'd had enough of the small town, the small time, and he'd been learning Arabic from tapes he'd ordered through the mail. This was it; this was his life that was coming around. He was going to have a big time.

Owen is my uncle. He's six years older than me and we'd play together when we were kids. He had these plastic hand-cuffs and he used to cuff my hands behind my back and see how long it took me to turn a doorknob. Then I'd cuff his ankles together and see how far he could walk.

We talked on the phone days back, but you don't talk much to Owen. You mostly listen and you don't make much effort to understand.

He kept saying, "Let's see how long this one lasts. See how long this one lasts."

Owen used to meet me after school when I was too little and too scared to ride the bus home. We'd walk down Main, by the Rexall Drugstore, crowded with older kids, kids Owen's age, but he'd want to be with me. We'd go by Boyd's Tire and Tool, by the Edisto Bank and Trust. At the Dixie Home Store he'd give me two quarters for a Coca-Cola.

He'd say, "Here, getcha that Co-Cola."

Then he'd move on ahead, knowing I'd catch up, find him at Miss Pauline's Boutique, sticking his face in double-D bra cups. In Edisto, it'd still be hot in the fall in the schooltime, and the ashen dust from the road settled in our throats.

Up at Appalachian in the fall, it was cool, and I was older. The leaves turned a thousand colors, and the ground frosted as early as October. It was October when that Irish poet came. It was like he had a word for every color.

And when those colors were bright, Harris used to take me over to Blowing Rock to see how the mountains turned like fire. We'd toss maple leaves off the edge of the outcropping and catch them as they rose back up, sometimes for hours on end. There's a Cherokee legend about Blowing Rock, something about a brave and his woman being in love, and him jumping over the edge of this rock to avoid her father's anger, to kill himself for her love. She, this Cherokee woman, wept at the edge of the rock and the winds bore him back up to her. If you love something, set it free and all that. And maybe it's true.

But Harris says the velocity underneath the outcropping is of the magnitude, and the direction is of the angle, to create an undercurrent spiral, allowing something like a leaf to fall to the basin of the wind and be swept back up toward its point of release in the undercurrent. He says it would never work with a whole body, says it all at once like that, and it is the way he's now come to speak in the falltimes when he is serious and working on his papers and his manuscripts.

So, I will admit I am more in love with the way Harris is in the summer, the way we would eat 'til we were full and sleep when we were tired and not ask much else about why or how. It's easier to love a person that way, simply, plainly, and with belief. How you love is how you love, and you can't help that.

Outside Edisto we pass by the carnival grounds. They're all grown over now, green and viny with kudzu that bodies the Ferris wheel like a hide, like fleece, a few cars short of full. Its frame is rust-old, like the carousel that still turns and chimes in the wind, and looming over all is the roller coaster, Thunder Road, a trestle of plank and rail, the sun settling in behind it every night.

I was too young to remember this carnival as ever working. But Owen knew about it, the reason it up and left its pieces here, on a dry lot at the outskirts of Edisto.

You know why they shut this sucker down, don't ya, Mavis? That boy lost his leg on Thunder Road. I saw it happen. Nothin' between his ankle and kneecap but gristle and blood. You never seen blood flowing like his, not in your life.

He'd pause, draw off his cigarette, and I'd sit on his lap in a Ferris wheel car, the great bleached remains of the coaster highing up in front of us. The cars were stuck at the top of the highest track, just thousands of feet in the air, like floaty black tubs filled with rusty rainwater.

His thick fingers tracing the veins in my wrist.

The only girl I've ever loved, her name began with the letter M.

He'd whistle low in his throat, make that M on my wrist, his palms smoothing down my skirt, over my bare calves, fingertips tapping at my shins.

Yep, tried to get him down from the tracks, that boy, but his bones hung up underneath and each pull cracked 'em and splintered 'em; you could hear his bone snappin' like twig in an empty forest. They say he died up there, long before any doctor ever saw him.

He'd turn his face to mine, make that low whistle.

He'd say, *You wonder about things like that? Like dying on top of a roller coaster, or underneath a combine, or in a car. Maybe in a airplane or chock full of buckshot. To be twisted up in metal. To have metal twisted up in you.*

I'd shake my head, no, never. Maybe other ways, other ways to die I might have wondered about, like in water, or in fire, or coming out of the air, getting sucked up by the earth. I wondered what it would be like to die in my own bed. I was six years old. What did I know?

I'd whisper to him and we'd whisper even as there was no one else around, no one else to see and sit and listen. I'd ask if he'd ever climbed up on that thing, looked for any pieces or parts of that boy.

He'd say, *And fall through all that rotten wood? I'd rather kiss my own ass.*

And then he'd cup my knee and sigh, run his hand under

the arch of my foot. He'd look me flat in the eye, make me hold his stare.

He'd say, *I saw the thing that happened here, I saw what happened.*

And with a jerk, he'd open his legs and I'd fall through in the direction of down, toward the floor of the Ferris wheel car, before he'd catch me. I'd know all along it was coming and I'd wait for the scare.

He'd tell me to get on home now, and he'd start off the lot, his steps heavy and loud on the gravel path, the kudzu licking at his ankles. He'd go off 'til dinner, sometimes even into the night, and he'd do things I'd never know about.

I'd sit back up in the Ferris wheel car and watch him go down the gravel path, into the trees, slowly Owen, then the sound of Owen going away. Even at twelve, he could disappear like that.

2

The bus is a racket, a great wheeze and pitch as it reels into Edisto proper. After it passes the old carnival grounds, Highway 321 bleeds right into Main Street. From the same land as the riverbanks and farms and pastures, the town builds itself from the sidewalk up, rises into being like any other formation on the earth, and of a sudden there are bricks and blocks and big barrels of flowers in the middle of the road. Main Street is town, and there are lanes off it where town people live, the houses pretty and painted and kept, and the kudzu burned back every springtime.

The last time I was here was for my mama's birthday Aprils ago, the spring of my sophomore year. It was a weekend visit and after I returned I was working in the library when I first met Harris. He walked past me, trailing his fingers over the back of my chair, and I'll confess I shivered. I'll confess, too, I stood and went after him and stared just a little bit and when he asked me where to find the maps I said, "Follow me."

He had been back from Rome only a few months and he looked different from the other boys I'd seen, foreign and smooth, and he was older than me, closer to Owen's age. He asked me out the very next night to an old-fashioned resort over in Linnville. It was the kind of place where the dinners were courses and the band played songs that were dances, not just music, and we talked and danced and talked some more until the maitre d' finally asked us to leave. It was a date, not him meeting me somewhere and us going somewhere else, and I liked the just-so way it went along. We held hands as we left the dining room and all the way to my dorm in his car, and I didn't think about coming home again for a long while.

I have changed since I left Edisto that last spring; I have grown older and smoother and more certain in myself. It's not been a transformation, but an ascension. I've taken numbers and facts and people and places into myself, grown big and brimful with these new things, and I like to think such a difference is a matter of ripeness, a change of shade and flavor and volume, of density, consistency. It's a small thing, a small matter of bigness.

This bus barrels down Main Street and I find myself collecting up my things, sitting to the edge of my vinyl seat. I think of all the other places I've been these two years and how I came into those places, how I could watch the land go to dry on a bus in Texas, how the lights of Saint Paul came up to meet my plane and how that was a glorious and perfect sight. There was a Christmas I went up to New York City to see the tree at Rockefeller Center, to look in the windows at Saks. I met a girlfriend of mine at Grand Central Station, where the ceiling was painted like the heavens, and we had hot chocolate at the Plaza Hotel. I've never in my life seen a bigger hotel than that one. I've seen all these grand things, I've seen all this countryside and skyline, and I'm still beside myself to see the Rexall Drugstore coming up ahead of this tin can bus. It's like taking a swim in ninety-eight-degree water; it's not that it feels so good, but it's wonderful because I know it and I've known it for as long as I can remember.

I know Punk's house will feel this way too. It's big and white, on the edge of town, and that's where we all live. There's me and my mama Elsbeth. There's my mama's sister Hazel, and Owen lives with us too. All Punk's children live with him and Miss Pauline, and he likes it that way. I like it too. When I was at school or traveling I could call Punk's house and talk to anybody and everybody I wanted, and I never worried I'd made someone all alone with my being gone. Lonesome, maybe; I think my mama missed me in a lonesome way, and Owen missed me listening to his stories and Hazel missed me the way you miss a summer day in wintertime, but no one was all alone.

It's more than that, though, more than my presence or absence and how that worked in Punk's house. It's like this: Punk is like gravity. Gravity pulls all objects down to its center and holds them fast and close to its heart and that's a great force. But it's like this too: I was away, and my awayness had an effect of its own. I had pull and force and consequence, too, in ways I wouldn't have if I'd been in Punk's house all this time. It's simple physics, bodies in orbit, the moon and the earth, me and my home. I was away, but I was still in touch.

The bus stops first at the Rexall's, up a bit from where Owen will meet me. The woman across the aisle stands now, stands just as the bus comes to a complete stop, and her hair marks her face where it's dried in her tears like so much brand or scoring. She has stopped her crying. From beneath her seat she pulls a pillowcase full of things soft and lumpy and a brown paper grocery sack. As she passes down the aisle, I see a note pinned to her blouse, written in a tiny hand.

She's the only passenger to get off here and she stands beneath the Rexall sign, her pose just as papery, just as closed up, and she sets her things at her feet, watches the doors hinge closed and the bus move on. I can't imagine what has brought her here. I think how this small town holds no secret long, and I turn to get just one more look at her, but she is gone.

Disappeared from the sidewalk, from where there is not too far to go.

And then we're too far to see her anyway, passing the Dixie Home Store, Miss Pauline's Boutique right next door. I used to work there in the summers during high school. She has everything, Polly Flinders church dresses, chiffon scarves and white gloves, T-strap shoes from 1952, and those double-D bras that Owen thinks were invented for him to fit over his face. He used to tell me he wanted to have a woman who could fill one of those, a woman stacked like a Mack truck with a waist that fit the span of his hand.

Miss Pauline's got a drawer in that store where she keeps the Frederick of Hollywood things, merry widows and teddies, silk stockings, seamed stockings, garters, crinolines and satin slips, peek-a-boo bras and thong underwear. These are what she calls love undies, things for a bride's trousseau. Owen can never seem to find the key to get in this drawer, as Miss Pauline keeps it tucked inside her own brassiere.

That's all on the ladies' side, and through a curtain to the men's side Miss Pauline sells overalls and work boots, thick rawhide belts and dungarees. She's got every weight flannel known to Adam and pure cotton long johns for the wintertime. Man's clothes. Work clothes. Plus dry goods, threads, yarns, and basting tape. Patterns made of filmy paper, needles of all sizes and shapes, enough material to sail a ship.

Up at Boone, the Mast General Store reminded me of Miss Pauline's Boutique. It fit Boone the way Miss Pauline's fits Edisto, and I think that's why I liked to work there. There was a time Mast sold everything under the sun: coffins, tallow, lanterns, bag balm when the town was full of hill folks and that's what they needed. But I sold things for college students: camping equipment, tents and sleeping bags, blue jeans and thick wool sweaters, pottery, candles, and tortoise shell combs, the color of my own eyes. I do have eyes the color of tortoise shell. They are my father's eyes, the most different eyes in my family, flecked with bits of gold and black and mossy green. They are the only thing I hold of his, the only thing left on this earth of his, I'm told.

At the corner of Main and Trade, Owen sits on the hood of his Ford convertible, the very same car he's had since high school. His hair is shorn for the Saudi heat, the collar of his denim jacket flipped up in the breeze that rises when the sun goes down. He stubs out his cigarette as the bus shudders to a halt. He's got a grin as if he's just told himself a joke.

"Mavis girl," he says, making his low whistle, losing it in his breath. That's what I wanted. I didn't want him to say *you haven't changed a bit, sweet Mavis*, or *Mavis, you're still my girl*. This morning in the motel I thought about this as I teased my hair up big and full, as I shaded my eyes for the gold and brown inside them. I am still Mavis girl, but there's something else, something that overspills those old words for me. I'm glad to know Owen sees it too.

He reaches out his arms, hugs me as though I'm lightness. He holds me a long time, holds me to his chest, and my arms move around him too. His breath is warm on my shoulder. He has that great smell, that smell like saffron or chlorine, that great smell like a man. I close my eyes. I have come a long way to be here. I have come through time and space to rest in these arms, to take in these things about Owen and this town, and it feels good, like a warm towel, a blanket 'cross my shoulders. I have the wish that the small papery woman on the bus could have this feeling, that she could've been met by a man or a woman with open arms and a familiar face, something small in their pocket they'd bought for her and only her, a gift. And then Owen hooks his thumb in my bra strap and snaps it, snaps me back from where I've gone.

"College done right by you," he says. "Yes, ma'am, God bless higher education." He bows and I curtsy and we both laugh.

"Oh, Owen. It's been a while."

"Sweet thing you are, all grown up and no place to go."

"I'm here, aren't I?"

"Yep. Here you are."

He takes my bags from beside me and tosses them in the back seat, opens my door. The sun is almost down and the breeze has sharpness to it. I tie a scarf around my hair.

I'm tired of a sudden in the lap of this motionless car. I've come a long way to here, and now I'm still and I'm tired and I don't feel like moving. It's snuck up on me, as if my bones have been pulled out of my skin without my knowing it.

"Can we just sit for a while?" I say.

"Don't know if I've ever been able to do that."

He laughs and props his foot up on the dash, shakes out a smoke. He snaps a match off his front teeth and lets out a big-ass grin.

The seats are hot 'neath me, and the backs of my legs stick to them, seem almost to melt into the leather. I can feel sweat run inside my arms, down underneath my dress, and I rest my arm on the side of the door to catch the breeze. In the lap of this car, I've made it home. I've heard it should be like riding a bike or dreaming in color, something you never forget how to do, but I look around me now and things seem a different size and hue and cast than they really are. It's as though I'm still coming upon this town, still moving forward and everything else is standing straight and tall and exactly where it should be. I close my eyes and lay my head back on the seat as if it's a problem of vision or light, something like vertigo or a bad headache.

"It's real fine, Aunt Hazel getting married," I say, and that starts him off.

"Yep." Owen sighs. "Sal. Salvador Arceldi, the man with a new bag of tricks. You know what he does for a living."

"No."

"Owns a winery."

"A winery." I shake my head, my eyes still closed.

"Sal owns a winery in Adams County, Pennsylvania. Punk

and me and Hazel drove up there in the spring to check out one of those mechanical pickers, those Chisholm Ryders, on a farm neighboring Sal's. Ever been to P.A.?"

I shrug my shoulders, not bothering to answer. I don't know if passing through constitutes been to. It wouldn't make a difference to Owen anyhow.

"Makin' a long story short, we were standing in this barn checking over this monster of a machine and all of a sudden, BLAM!, this guy drives his Sedan DeVille through the broadside wall. Big ruckus, shit falling all over the place."

Owen laughs and I can hear him draw long on his cigarette and laugh out the smoke.

"You know Punk, he never batted an eye, not even when a beam near to clocked him on the back of the head. Sal was real shame-faced about the whole thing, started throwing around blank checks and asking us over to his cellar for a glass of grape. Well, after an hour of tastes, Hazel jumped right in the front seat of that Caddy and they took off through his vineyard, plowing that thing right down the rows."

"Good God."

"Yeah, well, his place was fine. I mean, he had thoroughbreds and a big ole swimming pool off the back of his house, shaped like a goddamn kidney bean. And this wine cellar full of good wine from California, France, expensive stuff mixed in with his own yield from vines right there. After we had a few bottles between us, he put us up for the night in his guest house."

Owen starts the engine. "The rest, that's Punk's doing."

"Are they in love?" I say, opening my eyes, turning toward him.

"Well, you know Hazel, she always wanted to have a nice wedding. When it came time for us to get on back, she stayed with Sal. Just stayed up there, came down a month later to plan the festivities."

I watch Owen's face as he tells me this and I think how glad I am that he is here and now and telling, how these are the stories I've missed, but not missed because he's saved them for me, like so many newspapers. I smile at him.

I say, "And she's going to marry this guy."

"Hell, Sal is fantastic," Owen says. "Has two daughters, one's married, the other's real cute, but his wife ran off years ago. He needs a woman, and Hazel needs a man. Punk needs a winery for his grape, so Hazel gets a wedding. Just like that."

He snaps his fingers and it seems the only sound in that instant, the only thing to be heard for miles around. This makes sense to Owen, a wedding like this that suits a need. I imagine it's the only way he could see clear to taking on a wife for himself one day.

He shifts the car into gear and gives the engine some gas. My head feels heavy and I let it loll back, closing my eyes again. Such an orchestration, a wedding. A large order of music and food and color and flowers and presents, men and women, boys and girls. Punk must be having quite a time, he himself being one for fine parties and planning. And I know that he loves Hazel, and Hazel, down in herself, loves the idea of her big day in fineness, regardless of what else may come of such an arrangement.

Harris and I have never really talked about marriage, but somewhere down the line I've thought we might fall into it. Sometimes I wonder if we have what it would ask, if we could tend something up between us that would grow older and older still between us, if we could cultivate a thing like that. But Hazel just hopped in this guy's front seat, a guy she hardly knew, and she stayed with him. This seems more romantic to me right now than it probably is or was or could ever be.

I'm happy for her, though. I'm happy for me, too, as this wedding is a way to find my place again, the stir that will pick me right up and blend me back into this house without awkwardness or surprise. I will just be where I should be, moving as I should, just a bit more myself, and that's what I wanted.

～✍

On Main, Owen and I drive the three blocks to the house on Sorghum Lane. As we pull up the driveway, I realize I'd forgotten just how full of laze and sprawl Punk's house is, how it lopes over twice the yard of any other house on Sorghum, how it is taller and wider and crisper in its paint. In my mind's remembering, it was a smaller place, and I'd wonder on this, but I see Miss Pauline waiting in the kitchen doorway, a shadow in the screen.

"Oh baby Mavis, we missed you!" she trills.

I see her there. She's lost weight and her skin hangs in swags about her bones. And then I'm in her arms and I can feel the curve of her spine through her cotton house dress, solid and deceptive like a tree that's grown parallel to the ground. Her hair smells of lavender and her skin of roses.

"Miss Pauline, you smell like a flower garden," I tell her.

She laughs and pats my hand. I'd forgotten the way she smells like a flower garden, the way the kitchen light is no brighter than a candle. I look down at our hands. I'd forgotten the way the first joints on her fingers turned in, the way she paints her fingernails cherry red.

"I've missed you too, Miss Pauline."

I pull her to me again, looking at my own hands on her back, smoothing 'cross her shoulders. Beside us, Owen trips in from the car loaded down with my bags.

Miss Pauline whispers, "She's in her room. She's been waiting since yesterday."

Then Punk has us both in his arms and her voice disappears into Punk's huge shirt sleeve, reaching across her to give me a hug. He smells of wintergreen tobacco and motor oil, faint as moth wings.

"Sugar pie, my Lord. You're gettin' a bit fleshy, ain't you?" He snaps the back of my bra. "At least you're not one of those goddamn hippie girls, burnin' good underwear."

I laugh and he rocks me back and forth. Hippie girls are still his idea of what's what, current events. What a young lady would do to break her grandpappy's heart.

Owen flops down at the kitchen table, peels himself some Hershey's Kisses. There's a wastepaper basket full of silver wrappers, and a pile of chocolate on the table top.

"Check this out, Mavis. Sal brought down a whole case of Hershey's Kisses. A whole fucking case."

"Watch your mouth, Owen," Miss Pauline says.

"Nah, Mavis, you should've seen it," Owen says. "A whole fucking case."

"Go on back and chat with your mama," Punk says. "She's been waitin' on you."

He holds my elbow in the cup of his hand, his eyes lagging over me, telling me I'm not the child in this house anymore. He gets his hands about my face, then squeezes my ears, says again, she's been waitin' on you.

I pass by the table and Owen gooses me, even as he hands Hershey's Kisses into his mouth. I slap him away, untying my scarf with one hand as I go, my heels clicking on the parquet floor down the long hallway.

I stop at her door and wait, take a moment to breathe. I have not seen her in two years; one last moment wouldn't mean one thing or another.

"Mama . . . it's Mavis, now."

I push lightly on the door to find her asleep. She's fully dressed in her best suit, white gloves folded across her rib cage, high heels still on. They are clothes I recognize. There's a corsage on her wrist, gardenias and baby's breath. She's laid herself out like a dead woman so as not to wrinkle. I walk quietly to the edge of her bed, kneeling down. Her hair has grayed, streaks of silver at her temples, sifting back to black. My mama is forty years old and I am twenty-two, the difference between us but a girl's age, a girl that would be younger than me.

I pass my hand over her face, her skin creased and soft, the cords of her neck strung tight like a cello or a small bird.

All this time, all this past week since school ended, I've fancied myself standing somewhere really crucial, somewhere on the edge of being grand and occasional and completely new. I imagined myself thick with what I know and coming back to this place to find the space I'd left grown thicker too. I came a long ways home to feel this thing out, to fit myself to what I am, and in this house my mama sleeps in the same bed she has slept in her entire life. It's a grave thought, me the swell and span I've come to be, and her exactly the same she's been since she was a girl.

In a very small way, I curl my legs beneath myself, sit back, and wait my piece. This is what it is to come into this house, where news keeps on and anticipation takes to bed and my part in it is to do exactly what I'm doing, to wait. This is my mama sleeping here, and I know I could wait on her all night long if need be.

3

I was born when my mother was eighteen, down in Charleston, tucked away at the Florence Crittenden home so she wouldn't cause a stir. Not married, nowhere close, and five months knocked up before she even knew such a thing, but that's not so strange. I've seen women tell themselves anything to get through the night, tell themselves it's stress, it's the flu, it will go away. I knew a girl at Appalachian who told herself she had a tumor for nine months, something small and hard and parasitic in her belly. Actually I didn't know her but knew of her, and in the end she went through a home like my mama did and put her baby up for adoption.

Miss Pauline collects baby clothes, wrappers, and blankets to send down to Charleston, every year at Christmastime.

"All those girls in trouble," she says. "Broken up, that's what they are. Like shards of glass."

And I imagine they are broken up, pieces of themselves falling away too early in their lives, bringing something into the world to take care of before they can take care of themselves. I wouldn't want to be in such a state. But, then, my mama took care of me. All alone.

My daddy's daddy was the famous Nub Jackson, come up from Florida. Back in the early war years he drove up every summer in his stakebed, sold cantaloupes in the square on Main and Trade, right where Owen met my bus. And when the cantaloupes sold out, he'd run back down to Florida and bring up watermelons.

In 1941, just days after Pearl Harbor, a notice in the *Edisto Observer* called for trucking companies to haul gunpowder. Loose powder from Du Pont in Wilmington, Delaware, to a shell plant outside Edisto. The famous Nub Jackson totaled up his end of gas, oil, and labor and multiplied the whole thing out by six and put in a bid for the contract. He was low man, and in May 1942 he went down to Edisto Bank and Trust and got a loan against the contract for six trailers. He ran gunpowder four solid years from Delaware to Edisto, considered himself lucky, because the truth of the matter was he'd skipped out on liability insurance to make low bid.

A truckload of gunpowder packs quite a wallop. He never hit a pothole without fear and loathing, and he never ignited a truck. He drove without insurance, and sometimes that's the way you make it in this world.

And he made it. He hired on black men, men he called coloreds, men from town who'd welcome work that wasn't picking or day-to-day, men who wanted some regular place to go every morning and weren't choosy about things like insurance or sleep. He made these men well off for their risk, well off for their entire lives.

Sometimes I think about the famous Nub Jackson and his men, piloting trailer truck loads of gunpowder through the South, coming down through Baltimore and D.C. along the Potomac, through counties like Sussex and Southampton and Halifax into the Carolinas, across Lake Gaston, down through Rocky Mount and Fayetteville, passing the Carolina sandhills and the future Darlington International Raceway. I think it was different then; I-95 wasn't even a gravel path.

The famous Nub Jackson eventually died of a heart attack down in Florida, an old man, famous and lucky and lived-out rich, but he'd had a son, born in '43. Wyman Jackson sat in the first grade with Elsbeth Black and from day one impressed the hell out of her. He wasn't so lucky as his father.

Years ago, on a brittle August evening, Wyman Jackson pulled over to the shoulder of 321 to get a rest, falling asleep in the cab of one of his daddy's trucks, a photograph of Elsbeth Black taped to the sun visor, and a load of misrepresented and highly volatile chlorine gas in his tanker. A palsy in the earth, a bolt of lightning, or a spontaneous forest fire struck him down, dissolving Wyman, the son of the famous Nub Jackson, into a frost of ash and flame. As Owen says, by then they had insurance, but what the fuck good does that do.

My mama was secretly pregnant, and her true love, my true father, Wyman, was dead. Nobody would ever understand the circumstances, the weight and carriage of her courtship, its untimely demise, so she gave herself over to the space that separated her and her lover. She became the woman she is now.

I've heard this story again and again, from my mama, from Owen, and even once from Miss Pauline, and this is how it begins, this is how it ends. But I know my mama never dated another boy, another man after my father died, never had a drink on her front porch on some summer night waiting on a gentleman to call around. Not that I could ever remember. She loved Wyman Jackson and that was all the love she wanted in this world. She weathered the happening of him, the presence, the absence, the here, the gone away, their love pure and hot and always moving, evaporating to the touch like steam off skin. This is quite a thing to have come from, and I've always felt blessed for it.

I sit with my sleeping mother for a long time. This room hasn't changed since I was a child. In the corner, the same black electric fan trembles on, smooths across my face and back across again, and the particular smell of her comes with it, a low smell like earth. Her things are all about, her scarves heaped up in baskets she makes herself, her flowers and herbs hung drying on the wall. There are postcards I've sent her, pictures of me in New York City and one of an adobe church in Texas, all slipped in the edges of her bureau mirror. There's a silver hat pin I sent her from Boone for Christmas on her dressing table and she's wrapped it up with a red ribbon to keep it from tarnish. I know what it is, though, even from across the room.

The light from the nightstand is warm, like sepia.

My mama doesn't have a driver's license, which is fine for Edisto, because no one cares much about such things here and there's no place to go that she couldn't walk to anyways. But she could never drive up to see me at school. She wouldn't take a bus or a train because of the dust they kick up, and she doesn't fly. Once Punk wanted me to go out to Washington State, all the way across the country, to see the vineyards they keep there. He bought Elsbeth a plane ticket too and we were going to meet in Walla Walla, rent a car, and drive to the Pacific together. She got all the way to the airport in Columbia before she backed down.

Miss Pauline told me later something just came over her. She got quiet watching those planes take off, watching them land, and then she just asked to turn the car around and why didn't they just go on back home. The smallest smile came over her face like she'd found something long lost, and then she said she couldn't bear to be up in the air that way, so very high, and not be able to tell for herself how pure it might could be.

And so I never went to Washington either. I talked to my mama on the phone, my plans all rearranged, and she got upset with me about it.

She said, "I so wanted *you* to go, Mavis. I wanted you to see something amazing and then, later, I wanted to ask you about it. I wanted you to tell me how it was."

I've made it my business to tell her all manner of amazing things since then.

I sit on the floor beside her bed. I could wake her, but I don't. From the kitchen, I hear Punk's big voice, the screen door slapping, slapping again. I hear champagne corks and high bright laughter. Further out, beyond my mama's window, the cicadas come up, full night sound, and the cars off Main. The whole town seems filled up with celebration, and I like that I can just sit here in the quiet and be out of the way.

A tap at the door brings me to myself, and I scramble to my feet. I see the time, and it's been hours I've been dozing in and out here on the floor, and now someone's come to check on me. I open the door and it's Owen, his eyes trained past my neck, to the bed behind me. He loves his sister, and standing here at her door, he is hushed. They are almost twelve years apart and by the time she got done changing his diapers, she was changing mine. She's more a relation to him than sister. Quietly in the doorway, he watches her sleeping.

With the door open I can hear more people in the house, a lot of people. I can hear high heels and glass against glass, Aunt Hazel's laughter. I can hear Punk. I can hear Punk say, ". . . a whole fucking case of Hershey's Kisses."

Owen snaps his fingers. "Mavis needs a drink," he says, the way you'd say I forgot my hat, or the horse needs water, or I think I shot myself.

He takes my hand and leads me out the parlor door, avoiding the commotion in the kitchen, avoiding the bride and her groom, avoiding Punk in all his glory. He's sneaking me 'cross the threshold. We climb over the car doors so as not to slam them. Owen pushes the clutch, letting the car roll soundlessly down the driveway, hitting the engine only when it'd be too late to stop us.

Owen fishes for beer in the back seat cooler, finds one, and opens it with his teeth. He hands it to me and I take a long pull, the bottle still wet from the ice. He guns the engine, screeching out onto Main, and he is so smooth, like something cool in your chest. He wears his blue jeans low and his white T-shirt clean against his tan, tall and blond and handsome. I don't think he's dated a girl since high school. Not just one girl, at least, and no one I'd call a girl anyhow.

The night is thick and cool; small goose bumps crawl 'cross my arms and chest. There are parts of this moment I want to never end, like the blackness, the wind, the bareness of my shoulders, the stops and starts, the small anticipation in my stomach like a bird, the being in Owen's car. The being in Owen's car with Owen, heading out of town.

He drives fast over the blacktop, catching air, turning up the radio as we pass the kids on the street corners, on the benches in the square; and the neon signs on Main stream together as we slip by. Owen's car is a '70 Mustang convertible with a 351 Cleveland V-8, the block said to be rebuilt for Richard Petty according to his own specifications. I've heard more than I care to tell about this engine. There are rings and pistons inside, harmonic balance and canted valves, metal that's bored, channeled, sprung up, and waiting to cut loose. It hauls ass, and I've seen it do it.

Elvis Presley comes on the radio, "Blue Hawaii."

Owen says, "Oh, man, now this is music that stirs, music for the back seat of a car."

His hands flex on the rim of the steering wheel. He starts to swell his chest and opens a beer for himself and drinks until tears come to his eyes. He reaches into his pocket, throws a handful of Hershey's Kisses into the air.

I think, oh, Owen. Oh, Owen.

I think about the last back seat I was in, back at school, the night before I left. Harris drove me out on the overlook on Linnville Ridge, brought a bottle of wine and a glass, a very old bottle from Bordeaux, a wine that is so red it's black.

He said, "This wine has been in this bottle for twenty-two years. This wine is as old as you are."

He said, "Taste it."

He poured the wine into the glass, taking a slim sip. Holding it in his mouth, he drew me toward him, his mouth opening over mine and the wine rushing in, the kiss underneath it all, the thick heavy slip of his tongue across my teeth, and the wine, full and red like heat.

His hands were soft, his fingers long like vines barely resting on my chest, my stomach, the hollow of my hip, and the thick silver band he wore on his index finger was cold inside me.

It's a ring he got in Italy, handmade from a Roman cast with gargoyles and raised acanthus leaves. Harris is in graduate school, getting his master's as a Renaissance scholar. He's a Renaissance man, really; wants to be a professor, practices archery, runs a Renaissance Faire down the mountain in Lenoir during the summers. He bought the ring when he was in Rome on a fellowship, just after he finished his undergrad. It's a ring he bought too big for his ring finger.

"Where are we going?" I ask.

Owen steers with one hand, fishing again in the cooler. He grins.

"Where have you been?" he says.

We have passed through the lanes of town now, and along the highway are trailers and simple houses, garden patches of land. Owen pulls the car up a dirt drive, coasting onto the lawn in front of a double-wide. Another trailer is set back in the woods and a third is kitty-corner to this one. Owen cuts the engine and fiddles with the key to make the music keep on. He raises himself out from under the steering wheel, perches on the top of the seat. He whistles through his fingers, taps the horn with his knee. He opens his beer with the edge of his cigarette lighter.

There's a picnic table up close to the double-wide, a barbecue grill still glowing hot. They must have just eaten, these people. Children might live here, because there are toys left over the lawn for the hound dogs to gnaw on. Across the porch, rows and rows of Chinese lanterns, across the yard, citronella torches spit wax. This double-wide is lit up for the dark and its lanterns thread over to the others, lighting a trace of path between each. There's a sign at the edge of the light. It reads EVELYN'S HOUSE OF BEAUTY.

Inside the double-wide, the lights go off and two brothers I remember from high school filter out, Evelyn Metz in tow. She was a trombone player, two years older than me, and now she runs Edisto's only beauty parlor. Long blond hair falling from its pins, a half-empty bottle of Thunderbird almost carrying itself in her hand. She's wearing a short flippy skirt, and mostly no underwear.

"Hey there, Owen honey."

Evelyn Metz doesn't walk so much as she sashays. She floats our way, catching the heel of her pump in a tangle of weeds, turning it into a sway of her hip, a turn of her ankle. Owen reaches out to steady her, grabs her elbow, and her arm snakes over his neck, pulling him to her, her hand brushing the fly of his jeans. When they kiss, she pulls his bottom lip through her teeth. I watch her do it, then look away.

"Hey, Hale. Hey, Stanley," I say.

"Get in," Owen says, and they all do, climbing in from both sides, and it's then I see that Evelyn Metz has on less than mostly no underwear.

She settles in the back seat, between Hale and Stanley McClain, two brothers who had to be cut apart at birth. They were connected at the elbow and again at the edge of the knee. When they were separated at the medical center in Columbia, Hale got the elbow and Stanley got the knee, but you'd never know it to look at them, just small slips of bone they shared. I know this because they used to bring in baby pictures for show-and-tell in grade school, pictures before the operations, and they'd make us feel around their joints for the missing pieces. I guess that makes them more than twins, connected by more than blood and looks, and what with Evelyn between them now, they even seem connected by her.

Evelyn's head sinks over onto Hale's shoulder, his hand slipping up her thigh. She is something else, like a doll with weighted eyes, long almond eyes that look just as striking closed as open. I wonder what she does with herself, what her head fills up with when she's alone, or when she's in her beauty shop, when she's not talking, not thinking. I trust it's not all boys and men and hair. She's got a layer of something wrapped about her, something she brings with her into the car that charges everything with heat, makes the boys sit up straight and lean in close to her, touch her skin, take her head on their shoulders.

We knew of each other when I was in high school, the way everybody in Edisto knows of everybody else. I knew Evelyn played the trombone. At the homecoming game when I was in tenth grade and Evelyn was a senior, she was the homecoming queen and she wore a red dress with a slit halfway up her thigh that sparkled under those field lights like nothing I'd ever seen before, and every single breath caught and every single head turned as she marched right in with the rest of the band as if she was born to play trombone in a red dress. No one knew where she learned it, but it was always clear that she was good.

I take a long drink of my beer, and Owen floors the engine, knocking the bottle against my teeth. It hurts so my eyes water, but he didn't do it on purpose. He didn't do it to me. I could say, goddamn you, Owen, but he'd say he already has. I go ahead and have the conversation for both of us and let it be, rub my teeth with my tongue.

Hale dips his spare hand into the cooler at his feet. I hear the ice rolling against the bottles.

"Owen, man, I love goin' out in your car. You always buy good beer, you buy bottle opener beer."

"What's bottle opener beer?" I say.

"That's the kind of beer you need a bottle opener for." Hale pushes his feet off the cooler top and digs his keys out of his pocket. "I should remember, man. I should bring the damn bottle opener when I hear your car in the drive."

Stanley leans up from the back seat, licking his lips, lighting his cigarette out of the wind. He taps Owen on the shoulder with a cassette tape.

"What the shit is this," he says.

Owen reaches back and takes the tape, pops it in the player, and it's not music but words, thick sonorous words that seem to have no beginning or end. I've always thought of the way Arabic looks, but this is the way it sounds, and I can't make heads or tails of a single phrase, Owen's mail order language coming through the speakers in the night as we drive.

"Arabic," Owen says.

"Arabic," Hale tells Stanley, and Stanley says, "Yeah, what they speak in Arabikia."

And then Stanley pops Owen on the shoulder again.

"Know what'd be good?" he says. "Watermelons. Pink ripe watermelons as big as your mama's ass."

Owen swerves off the road, jounces down in the drainage ditch and back out, his front and rear tires making the straddle.

"Watermelons you want, boy, it's melons you got. Get out there and pick us a couple," Owen says.

"Melons," everyone says, and Hale and Stanley are over the doors.

"Ooooh . . . melons." Evelyn leans her head up and smiles. She slips off her heels, climbs over the boot, and stands on the trunk of the car. Owen watches her in the rearview mirror, watches for a flash of skin, a taste from underneath that skirt.

"I'm gonna break a couple open," she says, "just to smell 'em. Sweet Jesus, they do smell good."

She leaps from the car, her bare feet sinking in the field clay. She laughs like it's the best feeling she's had all day, her feet in the earth and this Arabic coming through the night, and she takes a moment to swirl her hips, lifts up the edge of her sweater, and watches her belly button.

"Just like fucking Mata Hari," she says, laughs, and takes out after Hale and Stanley.

I roll my eyes at Owen, make a face, but he isn't looking my way. He's watching Evelyn's legs stitch across the black-green fields, enchanted by how they speak in Arabia. He reaches back, rummages through the cooler for another beer, pops the cap off with the flat of his hand edged against the steering wheel.

"So, you really going to Saudi?" I say.

"Yeah." He pulls absently at the neck of the bottle. "Yep . . . head out this fall."

"But Punk . . ." I say, and can't finish.

"Fuck Punk. I'm going, I know I'm going. I leave this fall. He can plan and propose all he wants. He's just jerking off."

And then Owen gets riled up. He turns himself toward me and his eyes flash hot. He goes on.

"You know, he's had time to bring me in on this farm and he's taken it. I ain't nothing but a hired man out there; get my check like everybody else at the end of the week and work like a dog. Fuck him. Fuck him and I'm gone."

The night goes quiet. Far away, in the big desert, there's oil underground, pools and pockets of it wrapped in shale. I think about a guy I knew my first year of school, Larry Boyer from West Virginia, a guy who just died in Saudi with my postcard in his pocket. I saw his picture on the eleven o'clock news, found in the sand somewhere. They think he had a heat stroke.

I swear, it's people's livelihoods kill them, kill them piece by piece like black lung or radiation, kill them all at once like a ton of glass on a glass cutter's back. I know Owen's going to die, die young, and I know I can't stop it. But if he goes to Saudi Arabia, I won't be there when he dies, won't be anywhere close. I would want my postcard in his pocket, my hand in his pocket, or laid 'cross his heart, his last breath beneath my palm.

Evelyn throws a watermelon at the windshield and it splays across the glass, all moist and pink inside.

"Cute, sugar," Owen says. "C'mon now, y'all, let's get a move on."

Hale and Stanley lope over, Hale clearing melon guts from his face, Stanley nursing a pop in the eye. Two brothers romping in the mud, awkward like bull calves, tripping over lengths of irrigation pipe.

Owen drains off his beer, throws the bottle over the side of the car. I think about the house on Sorghum, Punk draining off a beer at his kitchen table, Miss Pauline and my mama watching him do it.

Hale scoops Evelyn off her feet, the thin film of her skirt falling away from her ass, small and bare and white and heart-shaped. He arranges her over the side next to Stanley, gets in himself, and Owen slides the car to reverse. I can't help but wonder what he thinks of Evelyn and the McClain boys, if it bothers him to see their arms about her, if he even notices. We jostle once over the lip of the drainage ditch back onto the road, heading toward the carnival lot.

Hale's hand brushes my neck, his fingers lifting the hair off my shoulders. He pulls, tugs a little, and I turn around.

"What are you doing, Hale?" I say.

"Nothing," he says. "Nothing a'tall, Mavis Black." His fingers stray up over my ears, smoothing back, twisting my hair into a thick coil at the base of my neck. "Your hair's all one length, ain't it, sugar?"

I nod. "One length, Hale."

"Don't you ever cut it," he says. He lets loose the coil and winks at me. Maybe they're just hands-on sort of boys, these McClain brothers, wanting to touch what they like no matter who it belongs to, no matter if it's my hair or Owen's beer or Evelyn's thigh.

Evelyn slides one clay-covered foot up the center console, her toes rubbing Owen's side, leaving tracks on his T-shirt. The toes of her other foot brush my arm. I wonder if she thinks it's his arm. I wonder if it'd make a difference.

"Evelyn," I say, turning toward the back seat, "it's me."

"It don't matter, honey, it's all skin."

Owen pulls the car over a corner of the carnival lot, cuts the lights and it gets dark, kills the engine and it gets darker. He reaches down for my hand, I think, but runs his fingers over the flat of Evelyn's sole.

"Evelyn, honey," he says, "get me a beer out of that cooler."

He opens the door and gets out, sits back on the hood to light a cigarette. The rest of us follow, perching, sitting next to him. I'm on his right, Evelyn on his left, Hale on the windshield, and Stanley sprawls in the grass at my feet. We watch Owen, watch the things he watches. He throws his arms languidly around Evelyn and me, and his palm slips inside the sleeve of my dress.

"I was here the day they closed this place down. Yessir, I saw what happened."

His fingers flex and release, pulsing against my shoulder.

"It was a few days after I was five years old, but we were celebrating my birthday, hangin' out at the carnival, ridin' all the rides. We were standing in line for the roller coaster and I was watchin' the folks on it already and a boy stood up at the top of the coaster, stood up at its highest part, threw his hands up in the air, and sat back down."

His fingers roam down my arm, smooth over my elbow, coming to rest on the hood next to my hip.

"This was way before they thought to put those signs around, keep all hands and feet inside the cart at all times. So the boy came around again, did the same thing. He laughed like a wild man, sat back down. Well, the owner of the carnival, worried about safety and all 'cause these things aren't built for shit and a few days earlier they had a big woman almost lose her tit in a Whirling Dervish. Anyhow, the owner came out of his ticket hut to yell at that boy."

I hear Evelyn moan quietly, her legs spanning under Owen's hand, her body cocking toward him. I hear Hale spitting slips of watermelon seeds, a melon in the crook of his arm. I hear Stanley rummaging through the trunk, looking for a knife to split his open in a clean way.

"And the coaster came around again, and the boy stood up again, and the manager started to yell. He was a short little guy, looked sort of insane anyway like Hitler or one of those munchkins with the evil eye. So the boy's girl, sitting next to him in the seat, reached up to tug him down."

Owen's little finger brushes my hip, almost a stroke, almost a caress, almost reaching underneath me. Evelyn leans back on her elbows, her heels up on the bumper, her chin to the sky, her eyes closing. She holds Owen's beer to her neck, to her temples, to her lips. Her tongue wets the corners of her mouth, and Owen goes on.

"Well, when this boy's girl tugged on him, he lost his balance. He fell forward. He almost stepped forward right over the nose of the front car, like off a street corner. His leg got all mangled and crushed to hell when the coaster caught over him, nothing but blood between the ankle and the kneecap."

Owen puts his fingers to his mouth, the fingers that have

been touching Evelyn. He licks them slowly, as if he's tasting something subtle and sweet and known, like a wafer. He turns his face full to me, his tongue running over his fingertips.

"Mavis, you know this story," he says, smiling, taking my hand in his that had been touching Evelyn. "You know this one. You know the boy's name was Wyman Jackson, and the girl, the girl that bawled when they pulled him off the tracks, that girl was Elsbeth Black."

And then everything is quiet.

I turn my eyes away from him, pull my hand from his. I feel like I've been slapped, like I've charged to the end of my tether and been snapped back on the ground, flat on my back, like a fool. But I smile just a touch.

"You know that's not true," I say.

And then Owen's laughing and shrugging his shoulders, roughing his hand through his hair. He slides off the bumper and around the side of the car for another beer, his voice already kicking up again, telling some new thing he's thought to say. He could go on and on. He doesn't have to talk about me or himself or anybody here, and he could go all night long.

I slip away. I say something about needing to pee and I can feel my back unfurl, my bones standing up beneath me, my feet moving me away from the edges of Owen's car, and the air turns on my face and the darkness comes on ahead, but it's as though I'm nowhere, as though I'm floating or falling or yielding under the touch of a single fingertip. My skin stings. It was a mean thing for him to do, tell something like that on me as if it was a secret, and I must admit I'm flustered.

The twine of kudzu is thick and trapping on the outskirts of this lot, but I keep walking as if it were no more than water at my ankles, no more than weed to move through. There are stories about people getting swallowed up by kudzu, stories about high school kids gone parking and lost forever, about traveling salesmen running off the road in a thunderstorm and their cars not found until the frost. It's said this vine feeds at night, and it'd as soon eat what's handy than creep up another telephone pole, but this is all story, just tale and telling. Hell, I probably heard half of it from Owen.

He knows the real story of my father. Everybody knows, all this town knows how he died before I was ever born and how I never knew him, and it's not something that begs talk anymore. It's not even a story anymore, but an event, a happening, a sentence in the past: *He's dead.* Owen was teasing me, and he's always been one for that, but it's the way he did it, the long slow touching way he did it that makes my face hot now.

And then I can't help the tears, the feverish pang in my eyes, and I press the butt of my hand against my lips and sink down into the shadows. I think how this is not such a sad or awful thing, how this is not such a big deal, but the tears just come, and I take deep breaths, rest my head on my knees, and let the tears wet my stockings. I'm tired. I am so very tired now.

I think of the woman from the bus today, the woman who ran tears from her eyes without any sound to guide them and how those tears clung in her hair, wet her lap. I think how they might've kept coming if she'd gone farther on that bus, how her tears might've made a river underneath the seats in front of her, might've poured out the door when it swung open near the coast and coursed right into the ocean. I think she cried as if to send the water that makes up her body out into the world, as if to send it to a more comfortable place, and that was heartbreaking.

I don't cry that way. I cry because I'm tired and finally home, because I've had myself embarrassed and I'm too spent to let what Owen said hang out and away in the air and not get beneath my skin.

I dry my face. I stand and brush myself off. I walk back to the carnival.

When I get back, Evelyn Metz is still on the hood of the car. She presses herself up on the crown of her head, bridging her neck to meet my eyes. She smiles like a cat.

4

Owen drops Hale and Stanley and Evelyn off at the trailer where he found them, takes me to the house on Sorghum. I shake like a leaf in the wind, cold, even on a June night like this.

"That was mean, Owen, that story you told."

I've been quiet for the longest time, but Owen's never made me feel embarrassed before, and now I feel he should have a reason for this and I feel I should know what it is. I want him to say why; I want him to say he was only teasing, or he didn't mean it, or he's sorry, but I know he won't. He doesn't have it in him, the small thing that rises to a conflict, takes interest in fear and anger and pain.

He says, "Tell Miss Pauline I'll be home for the wedding."

He leans across me to open my door, but I beat him to the handle and get out, almost slamming it on his fingers.

He rolls down the driveway, silently, popping the clutch at the bottom, and I stand there just a moment longer than I have to, watching him go.

Inside Punk's house, my mama waits for me. It's late, midnight, and I go to the kitchen door which's always unlocked. Through the open windows I can hear voices, my mama telling a story.

". . . so I'm sitting at the counter and it's noon, the place is quite busy. Full up, I'd say. There is this couple sitting behind me, a sort of pear-shaped couple, you know. Large around the seat."

Glass clatters against porcelain. She must be washing

dishes. Her voice is the same and I can see her doing what she's doing, just as if she's in front of me. Just as if she's telling me this story.

"Well, I'm eating along, and they're eating, and the place has a sort of roar to it, everybody talking really low. All of the sudden, out of nowhere, the woman member of this couple lets out a squeal, a strange pig-squeal, completely inhuman. Everyone in the entire restaurant falls to quiet."

I hear Miss Pauline laughing softly, asking what happened next, and I stop my hand on the screen door to listen. To not interrupt, to not walk in before my mama gets her due.

"I just go on eating. Anyhow, the couple soon pay their check, get up, and leave. These two old women sitting at the counter, women you'd know, but that's not important, these two old women turn to me and say, 'Can you believe that?' and 'Have you ever heard anything so awful?'"

Miss Pauline sighs. She says, "There's sad things in this world, Elsbeth," and I think how she's a mother talking to her daughter, and me, another daughter, I'm listening.

My mama says, "Well, I just told them. I said, 'You know that can happen to a person. It's happened to me.'"

She turns off the spigot and the pipe's clatter sounds out to where I am. That can happen to a person. That can happen to my mama.

I open the screen door and it slaps shut behind me.

My mama turns from the sink, wiping her hands on the apron at her waist. Her face sets open like a fruit, like something soft inside her coming out, like something coming alive.

"Mavis. Where have you been, child? Your bus was supposed to get here yesterday."

Coming over to me, she reaches her arms around my neck and hugs me close, and I feel awful for waiting so long to see her. Awful for not coming home, for not staying home when I got here. I should have stayed right by her bed, waited for her to wake and me to be the first thing in her eyes. She waited up for me. Even in her sleep she waited up.

"Mama, I called and told Miss Pauline that the bus broke down. I know she told you. She wouldn't have not told you."

"Oh, yes. Yes, she said something to that end, but I was expecting you yesterday. Two of your boxes arrived in the mail, and I guess I just thought you'd be right behind."

She leans back, her arms slipping around my waist.

"My, my, my. Don't you look grown up!" she says.

She turns to Miss Pauline, who's putting the dishes away.

"Doesn't my baby look grown up?" She hugs me again and I close my eyes. I'm in my mama's arms. I pull back to see her face, holding her hands in mine.

"So, how are you?" I say.

"Fine. Is this new?" She fingers my dress, rolling the fabric in her hands.

"Yes. Well, sort of new, I guess."

"And are you still tied to that boy up there, the one with the bow and arrows?"

"Mama, we're not tied."

"You know who I mean. That boy, man, rather. The one who's been in school forever."

"I don't know, Mama. I really don't know. How are you?"

"I am fine, baby. Just fine."

The three of us stand there in the kitchen light, my mama and I holding hands and Miss Pauline smiling on us from paces back, as though we have air to share amongst ourselves and she would not want to interfere. She sighs. "It's so good to see my girls," she says.

She comes and pats her hands on our shoulders, says her good nights, and goes up the back stairs for bed. My mama and I link our arms and stroll into the parlor, turn on a lamp, and settle ourselves into the curvy purple settee. It's so good to be close to her. We rest our heads on the high back of the settee and hold hands still and I can hear the refrigerator in the kitchen humming on, the grandfather clock in the hallway, the sound of Miss Pauline running her bath upstairs. I can hear my mama smiling at me, the sound of her eyelashes on her cheeks.

"It's so good you're home," she says, "I can hardly believe myself."

I say, "I missed you."

It's so true how I missed her. She would be the one I'd call and talk to for hours on end, the one in this house I wanted to be with me at this moment or that; she was the one I sent postcards to and took pictures for, and I saved up my best stories for her. Sometimes I'd even make lists by the telephone of things not to forget to tell my mama when we talked and they would be long lists on two sides of legal paper. Now I hold her hand and I listen to her voice, and I feel I could cry all over again.

"Mama, you never rode on any roller coaster with Wyman Jackson, did you?"

"No. No, I can't say we ever did that. We used to ride his truck and we used to swim in the river, but we never once rode a roller coaster. How'd you get such an idea?"

"Owen told."

"Well, Mr. Owen there better watch what he's telling people. That's not a true story. Not a true story at all."

My mama sits herself up and cradles her hands together. She has something to say and I can see her spine go all straight with it, her fingers ticking off points like so many varieties of kind.

"Firstly, Punk says a man can't be just muscle and sweat anymore. He's got to have a head about him. Punk says Owen's had the same years you've had to get smart. The same years, and all he's come up with is Saudi Arabia."

My mama shakes her head at this as if it's a sad and crazy thing, her eyes wide and serious. I can tell Owen's caused a stir of late and there are things afoot here I don't know about, ways Owen's been getting beneath everybody's skin. Punk seems to have had quite a bit to say about him, and it's not like Punk to bring business to the house or to the dinner table, places where my mama would come across it.

"Owen's been gallivanting all over the place. He's not been around for suppertime. He didn't get to the farm 'til Tuesday noon this past, Punk says, and he's always laughing and joking with the hired men and acting like he's not got half a care in the world. Punk says it's not fitting. Not fitting at all."

She's run out of her own fingers and she reaches across our laps and takes my hand in hers, strikes off my fingertips as if it's the numbers that are important, the sheer amount of complaining Punk's done about Owen recently, and she doesn't want to miss a one.

"And then Punk says there's business and there's big business, and by God Owen should care about the difference. Punk says he's got to step into the traces if he's gonna pull. He says things are gonna change around here, and I think he means it."

She stops pulling at my fingers and squeezes my hand between her own. Just as quickly as she sat up, she curls herself back down on the settee and shuts her eyes. In her quiet, the sounds of this house come back, the whir of fans and the clang of pipes. Nothing is ever completely silent.

"Things are gonna be different with you home," she says.

She smiles at me and tugs me closer. Our foreheads touch, resting on the back of that settee, and my mama tucks my hand beneath her cheek. Her face is so warm and soft, her skin like suede, as if some of it might just rub off. I shut my eyes too and breathe her in.

"Things are gonna be different, Mavis," she whispers. "I can feel it."

We drift toward sleep like that, head to head, close together on the settee in the parlor, and my mind goes off and comes back, goes off and comes back, and then I can hear my mama softly singing beside me, a languid song about moonlight and sycamores and lovers in Vermont I can remember hearing from her before. Every few bars she just hums the tune, her eyes still closed. My mind is awash with sleep and still tiredness and the nearness of my mama. Her singing is so soft, so old. I whisper, "But Wyman," and there's nothing else to say.

"Oh, honey," she says, and her eyes come full open. "Mavis, that man is everywhere."

She runs her hands along my arms and tells me how she thinks about Wyman Jackson blown to morsels of a man, just spoonfuls and mouthfuls and thimblefuls of him up there in the coolest parts of the air, in the night sky with the stars and comets and all the other heavenly dusts and going higher and higher and higher.

She says, "That's how he's going to God, you know. He's floating there, bit by tiny bit, and collecting himself up at the gate."

She tells me how she wouldn't ever want to breathe him in, by accident, a sliver of him not making it back together whole someplace else. She tells me she would do it, too, that she wanted him so when he was alive and with her that she could have eaten him up, taken him into her body, and kept him there. She tells me she's careful now around the dusty things in this world, she's careful, and it's self-control.

She says, "It's not far from the farm, you know, where it happened."

"Where he exploded?"

"Yes. I've never taken you there?"

"No. No, Mama, you haven't."

"Oh, we'll go then. There's a big crater of a hole and some burned ground. That's about all there ever was. The rest of him made it away."

I like that there's land to this story of my father, a place to go to and see, a thing to picture there. It doesn't matter what Owen tells, what he thinks of as true or not true, what parts of his carnival story could have happened, or might have happened, or really did happen. The details, they are as changeable and migrant as he can make them, because that's the way life really is to him. Owen looks into the world and sees the so many things that seem true and aren't, like solid ground and blue skies, centrifugal force and light and dark, and these are things we see every day, things we touch and feel moving beneath us. This is the truth to him, whatever he can make up and get somebody to picture, what he can say that somebody will believe again and again and again. My father's story is different. It has a time and a place and a woman to hold it close to her heart and remember it often.

My head goes heavy again. I listen and the clock ticks on, the floorboards creak and groan, the lamp in the corner buzzes and cracks. The sounds of this house come back up, and sleep comes over me again.

And later, it's my mama's whisper in my ear, her voice low as she can make it and her fingers stroking at my hair.

She says, ". . . and this dream, it was like Oz. Punk was there and Owen was the scarecrow or one of those flying monkeys . . ."

She says, "And you were like Dorothy. How funny, but I thought about that dream like you were Dorothy and you were coming home in a big balloon or a spinning house . . ."

She says, "Or in a dream yourself. You were coming home in a dream yourself. I knew it wasn't true, but what a dream. What a dream to have."

And my mama kisses my cheek and strokes my hair and I'm not even certain I've come out of sleep but for her hands about my face, her breath so close on my ear. My mama and her thoughts. My mama and the things she remembers, the things she dreams, and with these I finally come home.

5

It's morning and I have slept in late, way past noon. Sometime in the night, my mama and I made our ways to our own beds and I feel all swept up in this house again, feel as though I've been spun 'round and 'round in some soft familiar arms. Slivers of my mama's talkings drift in and out of my mind like the remnants of dreams, and I realize they are of dreams, hers and Punk's and Owen's, however scattered and frightening and simple they may seem.

As I walk into the kitchen, I expect it to be all abustle, but everyone is gone. Tonight, I'll rehearse being a bridesmaid for Hazel, and afterward we'll all go up the river for dinner at a fancy French place, but for now I am alone. This is my chance to call back to this house the things I know about it, the things that make it comfortable, the things that make it mine, too. Miss Pauline left a note by the coffeepot. It says: *Punk and Sal to pick up girls in Columbia. Your mama and me to get hair done up at Evelyn's. Leave your dress out to press — Love, Miss P.*

I pour myself a cup of coffee and take a chair at Punk's kitchen table. The day before I went away to school for the first time, Miss Pauline sat me down right here, at this table, for some things she had to tell me.

She said, now when I went to Appalachian, it was still a teachers' college, not near as big and fancy as it is now. That first year, it snowed and snowed and snowed.

She pulled a white paper bag out from under her chair and from inside shook out three mohair sweaters, one cream-colored, one pearly gray, and one black with silver buttons up the front. There were four pairs of woolen tights, a flannel nightgown with a high-buttoned neck, handknit mittens and mufflers, and a pair of kidskin gloves the color of buttermilk. I stared at it all laid out on the table.

She said, Mavis baby, that first year I was there it snowed so much they wouldn't open the roads and let us come home for the Thanksgiving holidays, and I was so homesick I cried and cried about it 'til I'd like to have broke my heart. I wasted so much time, child. Now I'll not have that for you.

She patted my hand.

She said, we'll miss you too, you know. Especially Elsbeth. But you just stay put, find out all about being on your own. Then you come on home and we'll be waiting right here.

I suppose that's just what happened, just what I did. I think how I've come home to this table, to rest my arms across its edges, rest my chin in my hands. My spine sags against itself and it feels so good, my bare feet on the floor so cool, and this coffee like I could never make for myself at college. I think this is what it is to be still, to be home in myself, and I could sit here all day. The soon-to-be wedding has made it easy for me, made it easy for me to slip back into this house quietly, and I like that.

I sweep my hand across the table. I usher into a pile flecks and shards of silver paper and tiny white streamers that say *kisses, kisses, kisses, kisses* in blue letters.

This kitchen table Punk made with his own hands. It's blond and broad, solid pine. I remember he took me out in the woods around the edges of his pastures, told me, "Mavis girl, I'm gonna hew myself a table, a table for my kitchen with wood from my land. Now go on, pick us out a tree."

I was just a little thing. I cocked my head back on its stem and pointed first to a spring dogwood, then to a scrub cedar, then to a Chickasaw plum, beautiful flowering trees, trees I did not know. Punk shook his head and laughed, loaded me back in his truck, and we went on down to H & H Lumber in Bethel. He told me to try again and set me loose in the weaves of wood, and I pressed my nose against slabs of oak: white, water, and live. I ran splinters under my fingernails. I smoothed my palms to the grain of teak and cypress up from Florida, linden and sugar maple from North Carolina, pecan and black walnut from the Gulf Coast. I chose pine, clear, sweet long-leaf pine.

Punk said to me, "Mavis girl, this is wood enough to do me proud."

And what he did was right, it was smart. A kitchen table is more than boards and nails. It's something hewn, something to gather 'round, something to eat from, all that it spreads before you. This is a kitchen table, and I helped to make it by picking out its boards and touching each one before they were finished.

I trace its surface now, the knots, rings, and colorations. I count the lines to the grain and remember something about trees and lines and age. But this is a table, and I know how old it is. I saw it built.

I sit at the table's head, facing out the bay window to the side yard. There are some Hershey's Kisses left in a basket and I make a breakfast of them, drop a couple in my coffee cup to melt. This kitchen is where Punk's house ends, where the screen door opens out to the yard, and I can feel how there is so much house behind me, so much underneath me, so much above me.

When Punk got his first contract with Taylor Winery, he gave Miss Pauline a bundle of money to redecorate, told her, "Miss Pauline, I want a house that sports my trade."

It was always a big house, and Punk felt that was fitting enough. Hazel and Owen and I all have our bedrooms upstairs, and there is a guest room too, and Miss Pauline and Punk's master suite. Downstairs, there is a grand parquet entranceway with a parlor and a dining room to each side, and my mama's room, and the kitchen. This is a big family, and we all have our places here.

But when Punk got his contract, Miss Pauline got new carpets, gold like his Scuppernongs, and in the parlor, heavy velvet drapes of Concord purple. In the entrance over the parquet floor, there is a Persian rug, pale and tan, then going blood red like the clay under Punk's vines. Over their bed in the master bedroom, she had an artist friend paint a mural of Punk's land, his vineyards set to roll across his head at night.

There are things that never change, though, the things that sound themselves only in this house, things akin to chatterings and voices, all the sounds I listened to last night with my mama on the settee, and more. There is the floorboard in the dining room that whines like a baby, and there is the wallpaper in Miss Pauline's parlor that sweats off the walls in August heat. There are squirrels in the attic, swifts in the chimney, bats in the belfry. I know these things the way I know a sigh in my own voice, the taste of my blood. It's a wonder to be this close inside a place, like being inside a skin.

The birds drive Owen crazy. The chimney shaft runs up the side of his bedroom wall and the swift babies squawk loud in the early morning. When I was in high school he tried to smoke them out, climbed to the rooftop and bricked the chimney over. He set a charcoal fire in the grate, parked himself on the settee with a bucket of water, and fell asleep. The swifts winged through the heat into the house and the whole parlor filled with smoke before Owen came awake.

I caught the birds in baskets and set them loose on the back porch, Owen too confounded and Miss Pauline too scared to touch them.

She said, "Brown birds are omens, Mavis, signs of a death in the family."

She had to get her velvet drapes dry-cleaned in Columbia after that.

Last night, Owen never came home. I didn't hear noise of him, no footfalls on the back stairs, between waking and sleeping, and there's no sign he's been here this morning. I don't know what I'd say to him anyhow if he were sitting here across from me, if I'd tell him not to worry, tell him I still loved him like a wide-eyed girl, or if I'd scold him like his mama, if I'd tell him not to be so untruthful and smack his hand.

Harris made me feel that way once, half between shaking my head and slapping his face. It was Mother's Day, the summer before my junior year. He was calling his parents out in Sun City, Arizona, calling to tell them to take care, to take their Cardizem and B$_{12}$, to take Harris's mother out to dinner. He spoke to them as if they were children, as if they needed him to restock their thoughts, give them something to do.

When he hung up, I called my own mother and it was different. She talked on and on, Punk this and Punk that, about the postcard I'd sent from Minnesota, about dust collecting in her hatboxes, about Mexican field hands coming in for the peach harvest, begging change on the street corners, and her voice coming clear, then lidded, then clear again like music in an elevator. I didn't answer much, just listened on the edge of Harris's bed. He watched me, wrote a note on a file folder asking what she was talking about.

I shook my head, rolled my eyes at the ceiling. If I could have recounted her conversations in a sentence, I wouldn't still be on the phone.

When I hung up, he said, "Mavis, has your mother ever been checked out? You know, talked to someone about what she thinks?"

I asked him what he meant. A professional? A shrink?

Such an idea from him startled me. Harris had never met her, but they'd talked on the phone and I thought they'd gotten on well. I couldn't believe him, as if he could speak about her sanity or strangeness of thought. I asked him if he was serious.

"No," he said. And then, "Well, yes, I am."

I let him have it. My mama is a lonesome woman some-times, I told him, and I am her only daughter. She's allowed to talk however she wants to me, say whatever comes to her mind. I folded my arms across my chest, turned away from him on the bed, but he stood up, moved around in front of me.

He said, "Mavis, I've just noticed her mind tends to ramble on. I mean, she's been through a lot in life and there could be aftereffects, depression or whatever. She could be ticking like a bomb."

I wouldn't look at him, kept my eyes to the floor. Harris is from Arizona. He doesn't understand A-1 about my mother, about what it is to get excited on the phone, to save up things to tell me.

He said, "Maybe she should see someone. Talk to someone before she gets worse."

He looked out the window as he said this, looked away as if it were an easy thing to say.

I lay down on the bed and shut my eyes. He didn't under-stand that was my mama he was talking about, not an old formaldehyde frog or the widow woman down the road. I closed my eyes and thought of things to say that would shut him up, things that would make him feel like a dog for speak-ing that way about her, but I know he just didn't understand. He didn't know any better. Shortly, he slammed the door behind him.

Maybe it wasn't a big thing then, maybe I've made it big. But I don't trust him always now, and there are things I don't tell him. Because of this, there is something loose in our relationship, something that hangs open and weeps like an old cat scratch.

My coffee is long cold and the afternoon is getting late. Out the bay window, I see rabbits in my mama's garden, chomping parsley, peppers, okra. I see her watermelon vine and her tomato stakes. I see her garden hose curled like a turban, resting in the corner plot beside the woodshed. The sprinklers are out to keep the lawn from browning without rain.

I don't know what Hazel will do if it rains on her wedding day. I've heard happy is the bride and all that, but she'll be madder than a house afire with anything less than blue skies. Back in the spring, she wrote me to tell she was getting married, asking me to be a bridesmaid, and she had big plans for an outdoor wedding. She called it a garden wedding, even though she was talking about Punk's vineyards.

Everyone was involved. Hazel told me about the arbor Punk was training with roses down by the river, and the imported lilies he was shipping in to float on the water. Anything she asked for, he would get her. And Miss Pauline ordered her an elaborate dress specially through the Boutique, a long lace veil and bolts of silk shantung she was going to furl down the plow rows for Hazel to step in her satin shoes. Evelyn Metz would fix her hair, and they'd had a ball going through stacks of magazine pictures to find the perfect this, the perfect that. Hazel's planned so much, I wonder if she's ready for it to all be over.

Harris got such a kick out of all her notions and I wonder if I should call him. Would I call him up at home, or get him paged out at the Faire? I wonder what I would say first, what I would say to let him know it was me.

Maybe I'd say, hi, Harris. I'm home.

Upstairs in my room, I unpack two pasteboard boxes I sent ahead, the only two that have arrived. All in all, I mailed a dozen boxes, books and clothes, things that were too much to carry on the bus. I think how strange to get a package I sent myself and I'm even a little excited to see what's inside. This one is from Harris's apartment, things I collected and kept there, things he brought me back from Arizona when he'd visit his parents. There's a goldfish bowl full of wine corks, wines from all over the world, and a poster of Blowing Rock with a couple of brochures. There are tapes, a toothbrush, a pack of condoms I hide away in my jewelry box. There's a heavy silver urn from Florence that Harris gave me for my birthday.

He'd said, "It's the kind of urn to keep ashes in. You could keep my ashes in it when I die, you know, put it next to your bed, in your underwear drawer or something."

I think now, what a birthday thing to say. There are times when he and I move in separate circles in ourselves, times when I'm fast and he's slow, when I'm close and he's far, times when our words fall apart, one after the other. Sometimes I think this is what our love is, meeting and gapping like plates in the earth, and I think there will be times when I'll love Harris so my heart will spill open, and times I'll love him not at all.

I clear the floor, stack the full box in my closet. It's time for me to move, to shower and change and be clean. Tonight will be busy, and I've taken all the time I can.

The pipes clatter when I turn the faucet in my bathroom, just as they do all over this house. The water is slick and soft and seems to be full of soap and slightly brown with river tinge, like rust that won't sieve out. I remember my mama and I once collected rain water in the springtime to wash our hair, water that was clear and clean and spilling over our glass pitchers and terra cotta pots. It was chilly in that rain and we were outside with our wet heads and wet feet, and Miss Pauline scolded us to beat the band, saying we would catch our death of pneumonia. My mama just laughed and laughed and washed my hair, washed her hair and rolled it up in pincurls, and she looked so pretty the next day she took herself to the movies up in Bethel. But I was scared for her catching some awful cold and I stayed up late that night, waiting for her to get home, and I listened for her to cough, the sound of her sniffling, instead of sleeping for myself. The night was long and quiet. I think I used to worry for my mama more than I needed to.

I step out of the shower and towel off, sweep my hair back, and wrap a towel around it too. I feel stretched and snug in my joints, clean and fitting rightly, and I head back down the hall to dress up for dinner.

There are people in my room already. Women sitting, lying on my bed, women in recline. They are long, lean women with pretty faces, pretty clothes, and expensive luggage at their feet. One brushes a young girl's hair, silk auburn hair that curls down her small back, curls over the brush in the woman's hand. This woman speaks softly to the girl, and the girl dallies with the ruffles on her panties. The other woman lies on the bed beside them, her skirt hiked up her thighs, arms thrown overhead, one slender-heeled shoe hinged from her toes. She's still wearing black sunglasses, as if she's a movie star or has a headache.

"Y'all must be Sal's girls," I say, and I hear my voice come from a long way off.

6

Merrilee Banks is Sal's older daughter and she has a daughter of her own. Her family lives near Sal's winery in Pennsylvania and her husband teaches at the college next town over. He is not here. He's a professor of psychology, teaching summer school. Merrilee is a housewife. She likes being a housewife. She tells me all this, says she likes the way it sounds when she says it, and I think what a grand idea, married to a house. The place where she lives must be warm and red, it must smell like her. I think her house must love her back.

Merrilee's daughter's name is Anna and she's six. She sits very quietly on her mother's lap and watches me dress as if it's the most normal thing. I pull a sundress from my closet that I bought up in Boone, shake my hair loose from its towel. I will wear sandals tonight and I wish that I'd thought to paint my toenails.

Kat is Sal's other daughter, just out of high school and headed up to Wellesley in the fall. She is excited about college and college boys and fraternity parties and getting the hell out of her father's house. She thinks romantically of New England and Massachusetts. She thinks of becoming a debutante and she asks me if I know any.

"Hazel always wanted to do that," I tell her, stroking lotion over my elbows, down the flats of my arms.

Hazel wanted to be a debutante up in Columbia when I was nine or ten. She told Punk all about the high society thing and how she would be a member of the Columbia Guild, be invited to lavish parties for the rest of her life. She would wear white and he would walk her down the aisle of some big country club, present her to the audience. She would have five stags waiting in the wings, marshals to attend her like a princess. She would be married. She would be famous.

Punk wouldn't hear of it. He'd said, "Parading around like a goddamn herd of cattle. All high-and-mighty missy, I ain't puttin' no girl up for auction."

That was the end of it. But I don't tell Kat this part, tell her instead the other things I know.

I tell her how I once went to a deb party up at school. It was wild, a casino party, and it was before I'd met Harris. The girl's parents gave away a trip to Bermuda to the person with the most chips at the end of the night. There was a champagne fountain, a chef making crêpes and bananas Foster for anyone who wanted it, a fifty-nine-piece orchestra. There were swans in the swimming pond when we all got drunk and went skinny dipping. When we left the next morning, the hostess gave us boxes of chocolate cake, soaked in rum and sprinkled with gold flakes. That cake tasted like heaven.

Kat smiles, turns the arm of her sunglasses in her teeth. She thinks that party would be something to behold, something to tell your children about, like going to the White House or to meet the Queen of England, but it wasn't so important really. It was just a party, a party with very good cake. I face my back to her and she zips my dress, fluffs out the skirt for me, and I thank her.

Merrilee asks where the rehearsal is, and I tell her Punk's vineyards. I tell her about Hazel and her garden wedding, about Punk and how he decided this was a marriage of lands and earth and how he wanted the ceremony in his grapes. I tell her about Miss Pauline's parlor house out there, a little bunga-low she fixed up for her bridge friends and garden club meetings, and how she keeps fine crystal and club chairs and gaming tables even in the midst of Punk's vines and tractors. I go on and on and watch her face. The part about lands and earth seems to pass by her understanding, and I think maybe it's not talked about in these terms where she lives.

"It will be beautiful," I say. "Like something antebellum and fantastic."

"Dad will be so pleased," she says, shakes her head, and laughs.

Then I remember they are to be bridesmaids too, so I go to the wardrobe, show them the dresses they will wear with me, all pink lace and tulle. Kat rubs the lace between her fingers.

"Chantilly," she says, and she is right.

There's a flower girl dress for Anna, ivory satin with little ballet slippers trimmed in lace. She loves the ballet slippers, takes off her shoes and puts them on then and there. Anna takes ballet classes up in Pennsylvania and she knows how to plié and arabesque, to carry herself and to leap.

Merrilee sweeps her daughter into her arms, and it's time for her bath. I go to get fresh towels from the linen closet in the hall and when I come back she is running water for Anna, her blouse laid across the toilet seat. She has an all-over tan, and with her dark hair she looks as if she's from someplace rare and exotic.

"You have beautiful skin," I say, and hold my own hand against her shoulder, just to set it off.

She looks down at my fingers, pale on her shoulder, and laughs. "We look like different races," she says. We smile at each other and this is something nice.

I step back into my room and sit at the vanity, flip my head over to dry my hair. From upside down, I watch Kat spray her French twist with a can of Aqua Net at the bureau mirror. She pulls on a pair of long white gloves, pulls each finger one at a time. Her dress is short and sleeveless, a pale yellow. I don't know anybody who wears long gloves anymore. She looks like Grace Kelly.

"Where'd you get that blond hair?" I ask, flipping my head back up, turning off the dryer.

"My mother is blond," she says. "I got her coloring, and Merrilee looks like Dad."

I had forgotten these women have a mother, a woman who'd been with Sal before Hazel. I don't know how to ask the questions in my mind, but Kat is ahead of me. She tells me her parents got married because her mother was pregnant, pregnant with Merrilee. They were both Mormon, living in Salt Lake City, and this was what was expected. They got married in the temple. Their wedding was blessed. But before long they were at each other's throats.

"They did awful things to each other, just awful things. Mean things. Both of them. Merrilee remembers," she says.

Her parents were separated when Kat came along, and their mother took the girls to Mexico, tried to disappear, but Sal hunted them down, got sole custody in court.

"Dad says I almost died from dysentery down there. He says I could have died," she tells me, her eyes wide and pooling.

I think this is sudden, think this is personal, and I have just met this girl. My head goes simple and I want to change the subject, talk about something easier. There are times people reveal themselves to me and I'm just sad. It makes me sad to hear parts of their lives I'd keep close to myself if they were mine. I would never think of telling how Wyman Jackson turned to ash on that brittle August night, pulled to the shoulder of 321, not out loud and to a perfect stranger.

"So, are y'all Mormon?" I ask, not even knowing what this means.

"No, no. You can't have a divorce in the Mormon church."

Kat collects herself, turns back to the bureau mirror. "You can have two wives, but not a divorce." She laughs.

I laugh too, and this is all it takes. Everything seems better now. There's something in the way she snapped back from where she'd been that makes me think it's common for her to make or break a scene, and I can feel the distance closing up a little between us. I feel as though I know something on Kat even in such a short while, and now we aren't quite perfect strangers.

Merrilee and Anna come out of the bathroom and Anna looks like a doll, little satin ribbons in her hair, naked but for her ballet slippers. She steps into the middle of the room, turns like a ballerina, her fingertips on top of her head. Kat claps for her, coos, and tells her how pretty she is.

Anna is pretty, but pretty in an old way, with an old face and old-colored hair like washed silk. I wonder if she will be pretty still even when she's my age. I sit at the vanity behind her, out of the way. I think she doesn't notice me, or doesn't remember meeting me at all. I just watch.

"Mavis," Anna says.

She says it very quietly and I am surprised to hear her speak my name. I stand from the vanity bench and go to her, crouch down so she can see my face.

"Where are you sleeping tonight?" she asks.

"I'm not sure." I hadn't thought about it, but with so many people in the house, probably not this room. "I'm not sure, Anna. Where are you sleeping?"

"In the dark." She smiles at me. It's a joke.

We leave my bedroom, three women and a child straying downstairs to the kitchen and the others who are waiting. Punk makes a big production out of losing his breath.

He says, "Take me, Lord. I'm ready for the boneyard."

Everyone else is outside, getting into cars to leave for the rehearsal. Hazel lingers at the screen door, hugging and kissing, waiting to load us up, ship us out, get us to the church on time. She looks gossamer, very beautiful, and just the way she should on such a day.

She says, "Mavis honey, come and meet my groom."

I take her hand as she leads me past a row of cars full up with family and friends. We pass Miss Pauline and Punk, pass my mother fretting over something or other, her eyebrows tight and high. Sal's friends are here. They flew in from places like New York and San Francisco, and drove up from Columbia in three rented Mercedes. They're handsome and dignified people, the men folded up at the wheels of the cars, men Sal's age with sharp suits and graying hair, men with younger women who check their lipstick in compact mirrors.

We pass a car full of Owen's friends, Hale and Stanley McClain. I wonder if Owen rides with them, wonder if he made it home in time. I doubt he thought to try, not out of any meanness, just his being someplace else and doing other things. Maybe in another town with a woman he picked up or knew. She'd be just now eighteen and trailing her fingers along his shoulders like he was a thing to be stroked and telling him how he was like the river currents and thinking he was her ticket out. That's what Owen does, lets you go on thinking all manner of things, but then the next thought comes and he's miles gone, just a breath of dust on the road.

Sal stands at the passenger door to a long Cadillac parked front and center. He's tall, with shock-white hair, and he's wearing a seersucker suit. He is browner than Merrilee and seems large and vital standing next to this car, seems like an artery or a vein, an organ you can't live without. I am impressed; he spills over. He reaches his arm around Hazel as she introduces us and they look happy, I think, as I kiss Sal on the cheek.

He says, "I promise to make your sister very happy."

I don't correct him by telling him Hazel is my aunt. She

looks so full of being a bride, so young and flushed and pretty, that I let it pass. We stand there smiling for a moment, Sal and Hazel wrapped together at the shoulder, my arms wrapped together at the elbows, and a car honks behind us.

Sal opens the passenger door of the Cadillac, bows slightly at the waist, and neither Hazel nor I move. This bow, this gesture, could be meant for either of us. Easily, Sal slips his arm around Hazel's waist and pulls, his lips at her neck, her head thrown back and laughing. They fall into the car, Hazel falls into his lap, and she chirps and titters; they are lovers in love.

The car honks again behind us as I step into the fine belly of this Cadillac, the bride and her groom arranging themselves on the seat, all of us ready to go.

$\int$

At night I sleep on the settee in the parlor, rich French food thick in my stomach. Now the house is full up with people: Merrilee and Anna asleep in my bed, Kat on a hideaway, and Sal in the guest room. Owen's bed is empty. He never showed, never came to his own sister's wedding party, and I wonder where he's shacked up for the night.

He missed quite a meal. We drove from the rehearsal on Punk's land up the river to a little French place called L'auberge Hank. The owner and chef, Hank du Talion, has family from wine country in Bordeaux, and he and Punk have been thick as thieves since Punk started up his vineyards.

The restaurant is in Hank's boat house outside a little town called North. It's a place with slender walnut tables, fresh flowers, and lead crystal, Hank's great-grandmother's Chippendale chairs. Miss Pauline fancies her parlor house to have the same kind of charm and grace as L'auberge Hank, and it sets her aflutter every time she steps inside.

She says, "Imagine, Persian carpets over water and such fine linens — my word, what a swanky place."

Tonight was clear and starry, so Hank spooled up the awning he uses to cover the old water entry for boats, and we ate with the sky on the river waves. We ate to the hushed wheeze of Hank's youngest girl on the flute, which she was learning to play for the marching band. Most of the songs she knew were Sousa.

Hank delivered everything to the table himself from the

outdoor kitchen, starting with fresh steamed shrimp and a lobster salad full of pale mushrooms, spinach, and morello cherries. There was pheasant en brioche, soufflé, cheeses — Brie, bleu, Emmenthal. There was fresh fruit and Hank's wife's pear Charlotte for dessert, weightless on your tongue. Hank and Sal got along instantly, played their wine minds against each other, Sal taking the first bite from all of us, choosing the perfect wine, the exact vintage. With the salad, it was a '77 Pinot Chardonnay, sweet and lemony, and with the pheasant, a '67 Bordeaux from Hank's family at Château Margaux. Claret, champagne, late-harvest Riesling with dessert, and we were stuffed like hogs for the roasting.

I watched Sal's friends, three couples he's known since he started his winery in '72, maybe even before, from California. The men were beautiful and groomed, their hands wine-men's hands, fingernails buffed to a high gloss. Their women cooed over the food, clapped when Sal chose an expensive bottle of wine. They knew each other well enough to talk in half stories, half sentences, and still be understood. They knew Sal well enough, dropped words between them about Paris and Napa Valley, about country houses and French featherbeds. Every time one of them got up to go to the bathroom, the other two went with her.

We all ate with the water close, the river running and pouring beneath us and before us, and it was as if the river was land and we were standing on it. It hasn't rained in Edisto for almost a month, the land and water very separate, but L'auberge Hank swelled and tolled with the river, it was cool and moist like the river, and when we stepped on land to go home it was as if we had to get our legs back.

But Owen never showed up, missed the whole nouvelle cuisine scene, missed the water and the wine, and he's not here now. Miss Pauline, Punk, they never said anything about his absence, and I know he does this all the time. All the time, like when we were kids, but different because he's twenty-eight now and should know better.

Driving home, my mama said, "Well, Mavis, you'll see there's little that's new in this world, and there's even less that's new with Owen."

When we got back to the house on Sorghum, the whole lot of us collapsed around Punk's kitchen table, too full to move, too full to breathe even. Merrilee carried Anna in from the car and took her straight upstairs to bed, Miss Pauline set to fixing us strong coffee which she said would aid our digestion, and Hazel held Sal's hand in her lap as if to make sure he didn't go someplace without her.

She still sparkled. When I was little and Hazel was a teenager, I can remember following her around for an entire summer because I thought she was mysterious and knowing of great secrets. I would skulk in corners, eavesdrop on her telephone conversations, slip out of the house when I knew she was going somewhere, and follow her down the lane 'til there were no suitable places left to cover me. Sometimes she would go to the Rexall's with her girlfriends for a glass of tea and cigarettes, and I would make like I had something important to fetch for Miss Pauline or my mama just so I could see her all arranged and pretty and laughing behind her hands. I suppose I still think of her as endlessly more sly than me, because in all my spying I never saw her do something wild or silly, and yet she seems to have a reserve of adventures stored up within her. She seems to have a past that somehow escaped all of us.

Miss Pauline served the coffee and she tapped at her watch. It was almost midnight.

"You best drink that coffee fast, Mr. Sal," she said. "I am a superstitious woman."

Sal laughed, but she was serious, and we all knew she was serious, so Sal kissed Hazel on the cheek and took his coffee up the back stairs to the guest room. Hazel watched the staircase long after he was gone, watched the ceiling at his footfalls overhead. Of course, we were all watching her watch the sounds of him. It was as if we expected her to suddenly run around the kitchen with her skirt over her head or go to sobbing or white as a ghost. She didn't. She got this look about her face someplace between pale and euphoric and then she sat up straight. She turned to Punk and set him to talking, to filling her head, to biding her time.

"Punk," she said, "what's gonna happen down at the vineyards without all those Mexicans?"

"Goddamn barn will probably stay in one piece."

We all laughed. Up until this year, the migrants would come up from Mexico, through Florida and Georgia, all kinds and colors of people camped out in Punk's barn for six weeks of the summer, and they would bring their babies and their fortune-telling cards, fresh fruit from wherever they'd last been. Punk would have a big picnic for July the Fourth and there'd be food and fireworks, and then those people worked their hands into knots of bone and gristle the rest of the summer through. They picked for fifty cents a bushel basket. It was cheap labor, but hardly cheap enough when Punk lost his barn.

I was in high school when the hired man W. G. Marvelle came to tell Punk his barn burned slap to the ground with three hundred Mexicans as audience. They didn't know how it started and they sure didn't know how to stop it, and when W.G. came to break the news in the morning, he kept saying how thankful he was nobody was hurt.

Punk said, "Hell being hurt. Did they get my truck out or not?"

But at that kitchen table and years later, it was a funny thing to have happened, especially since Punk himself laughed about it. This year would be different because Punk had ordered one of the mechanical pickers out of California, a Chisholm Ryder, and he wouldn't need the migrants. It would mean a noticeable change in the mood of the summer, in the harvest itself, and we were all hoping for the best. Hazel seemed nostalgic tonight, though, and she seemed almost to grow wistful over her cup of coffee.

"I'll miss that," she said. "Remember the eggs? We used to go down to the barn and there'd be messes of chickens in wire cages and some old Mexican woman always gave us fresh eggs."

Punk looked to me with a wily grin.

"Salmonella," he said.

"But the chilis, and the pots of food. They made these beans that tasted like smoke and coal and fire for days. That was good food."

"Heartburn," Punk said. "And flatulence."

He grinned to me again, and I could not help but laugh.

So Hazel turned to Kat, as if to explain to her how the olden days were here on Punk's farm, because we were not cooperating. She told about the leather-skinned women with their shawls and spooky eyes and their ways with the palm of your hand. She told about the cages of snakes and turtles and rabbits they raised for their suppers, the pickled chilis and dried herbs they carried with them everywhere, and the lottery game they played on Saturday nights, like bingo only prettier. But Punk had got me giggling, and then my mama and even Miss Pauline, so that finally Hazel just got frustrated.

"Fine," she said. "I'll see you fools in the morning."

And she raised her chin just a little bit and waltzed up the back stairs.

"Oh, Hazel," my mama called, "don't be that way."

But all we heard was her good night from upstairs, and then the sound of the pipes gone to clattering with the faucet in her bathroom. My mama got concerned. She stood to go after Hazel, and Punk laid his hand on her arm.

"Leave her be, Elsbeth. She's got her reasons for going to bed," he said.

And then he grinned again like the devil himself. Punk can be quite a tease, and it was fun to be his accomplice like that. He was in a fine mood and being light with Hazel. She knew it. Like he said, she had her own reasons for going upstairs.

We were not up much longer ourselves and I managed to doze off here on the settee, but now I'm awake and fitful and I've had enough. I get up, drag my covers up the back stairs to Owen's room. He's not going to use it tonight, and I'm not going to get any sleep otherwise.

In the hallway, there's a crescent of light from beneath the guest room door and I can hear soft laughter coming from inside. Sal and Hazel are up late, and I guess her scene was just that, a reason to get to bed. I think if I were getting married, I would want to see my groom the night before, maybe get some good-night loving or at least a few kisses in the darkness. I think it would make me feel better about the next day, all bold and fearless, sort of like tempting fate or breaking a mirror. I step quietly past the room, staying in the shadows of the hall and trying not to be heard, but then there's Hazel closing the door behind her, herself trying to be quiet about switching beds in the night.

"Lord, Mavis, you startled me," she whispers, and puts her hand over her heart.

"That's bad luck, Hazel." I smile at her. "Miss Pauline would have a fit."

"Oh, you, hush. We aren't children, and Sal's done this whole thing before. He says superstition can't ever fix what's broke anyhow."

She motions me down the hall and we step into her own bedroom, dark but for the moonlight. She flips on the bedside lamp, smooths a place on the covers for me to sit down. In the corner hangs her wedding dress from a hook in the ceiling and even being so high up its train still puddles on the floor. I tell her she will be so beautiful and Sal just might be brought to tears and she gets a look on her face that is miles away. I wonder how she feels about this being Sal's second marriage, if she feels strange because it's fresh and new for her but old for him.

"Y'all got something between you that's broke?" I ask, and she laughs as if it's a silly thing to ask.

I imagine it is, but you always hear about cold feet, second thoughts. I can tell she's in the mood for talking, all wound up in her face and waving her hands about. I would want to reassure Hazel if she was worried, tell her how everything will smooth out after tomorrow and all the excitement passes, but she doesn't seem to call for that, and I wouldn't really know about such a thing anyway.

She reaches into the top drawer of her nightstand and pulls out a crumpled pack of Chesterfields, but she has no lighter, so she just runs her fingers along a cigarette, rolls it in her palms. She seems to pick words out of the air, tells the first story that comes to mind as a way to occupy her lips, bind up her mind for a moment. She tells me about when Sal was growing up in Utah. He was twenty-one and a Mormon; he was waiting on his call.

"His call?" I say.

"From God," she says.

She tells me how all Mormon boys are supposed to get a call and sometimes it comes in a dream and sometimes in a voice and sometimes from the telephone itself, but it's the call that tells them where their two years of mission work will be most needed. All Sal's friends were getting called to Cincinnati, to Omaha or Elkhart, Indiana, some even getting called to the Arctic Circle or the jungles of Indochina. Nowhere places, and Sal didn't have a mind for something like that. He got the idea he'd be called to Florida, and he'd have to leave Salt Lake directly by way of Miami Beach and a few rum drinks served in coconuts.

Without a second thought, his father bought him a train ticket and a brand-new suitcase, and Sal took the girl who would be his wife parking one more time before he left town. His train pulled into the first station out of Utah and Sal traded in the rest of his ticket for a down payment on a '51 Ford coupé as slick and black as the day it was made, excepting a fender dent the owner couldn't account for.

"He ambled that car halfway across the country before he thought to head down Florida's way," Hazel says.

She laughs and there's a sparkle to her face as if this was wild and reckless and half of what she loves about Sal, such a story of a boy and his car and the plain land speeding past. All I can think is that it sounds like something Owen would do, given the chance.

Sal's father had expected his train trip to take two weeks, and he'd called ahead to the Mormons in Miami Beach and let them know to expect a new missionary on their doorstep shortly. It was just days later he walked into his office and found Sal's girlfriend's father perched on his desk with a shotgun and a story about how his little girl was pregnant and should Sal come back home for the wedding or should the wedding come to him.

"Well, the missionaries hadn't seen him and the train had no record of his passage outside of Utah, so Sal's father called the cops," Hazel tells me.

There were missing-person reports and questioning, and the man who sold Sal his Ford got pulled off the train somewhere near Fort Myers and treated like a criminal. He gave the cops a hard time and the car's license plate number, and Sal was taken into custody somewhere south of Key Biscayne, his trunk full up with fifths of rum and green coconuts.

"He had his heart set on disappearing into the sunset,"

Hazel says, "but instead he got a police escort back to Salt Lake City, and he was married and a father before he could say lickety-split."

That's when Sal took his new family to California and got his job working at Martini. The wine was good and the marriage was bad, both changing from year to year with the warm seasons and the ones with too much rain. Hazel tells me he loved his wife at first the way a boy loves his girl from home, but then he was just too much for her, too busy, too absorbed, too far away. I think how he and Hazel are different, how she's no normal girl from home and a little faraway herself, but their marriage plans are still crazy and reckless and spurred on by split decisions and the want to seal things up and set things right.

She talks so easily of Sal's old marriage and how it happened, without a trace of jealousy or anger. She honestly feels it's a good story about him, and one to be told. I wonder how Hazel sees her part in Punk and Sal's business affairs, if it bothers her at all, but I get the feeling the thought hasn't crossed her mind. She has her own reasons for wanting this wedding. She's thirty-three, and she's lived in her father's house all her life.

"Hazel, how come you never went to school?" I ask her.

"There wasn't much there for me to learn, dollbabe. Not much that had to do with me," she says. "Nope, I figure this was just what I was waiting on, getting married."

I know her to mean that different than it sounds, different than her wanting to be a wife and have babies and keep a house. Hazel wants her big day. She wants laughter and champagne and presents and her at the center of it all, her hand warm and soft in the hand of the man by her side. It's what she's always waited on, and I'm glad to see it coming around to her.

"I figure you're about right," I say.

We smile at each other in the dim light of her bedroom, both of us happy for her, and she's got a flush to her face like she might never need to sleep again. I find myself wanting to tell her a story, to stroke her hair and listen to her prayers, tuck her under her covers. But I don't. I sit by her side still and she rolls her unlit cigarette in her palms like a smooth stick or a dowel meant for just that purpose, and we think our separate thoughts, mine as simple and hopeful as they are, and hers, the depth and twist of which I will never know.

8

～～～～～～～ Owen's room is small, smaller than mine and neat as a pin. The single bed fills most of the floorboards even though it's pushed against the wall, attic ceiling sloping down over it. There's a rag rug next to the bed and a cleaned and oiled Winchester laid across the dresser. He has no books, never reads them, and the only decoration on the wall is an NRA poster with Heather Locklear in a bikini. It's signed. It says: *Dear Owen, Don't just keep it in your jeans. Love, Heather.* I think that's quite a thing to say about a gun.

I lie beneath this poster, shut my eyes. I lie still a long time in Owen's bed and fall to dreaming while I'm awake, my mind hemming over and hemming over again. I dream of Owen's room, see it with my eyes closed, myself in his bed, my hair fanned 'cross his pillow, see my own eyes closed, see myself sleeping. The phone rings, and for a moment I can't tell if I've dreamed it ringing or if the sound is here.

"Oh," I say. "Oh, my."

"Mavis girl," and it's Owen.

I swing my feet to the floor, rest the receiver in the cradle of my neck. It's as if I've conjured him up, as if he knew where I'd be and sought me out, as if I've been waiting for him here in his room, and I think of Hazel's story about Sal and the call from God. Not that Owen is God, but there I am, at just the right time and just the right place for him. Since I've been home, I've been thinking myself to be different in what I know and where I keep that knowing, thinking myself to be wrapped with knowing like so much shell or fur or scale. But with

Owen, I am stripped clean. I will always be by the phone for him, and he will call me before no other.

"So if you could get the shovels and come down here and bail me out," he says, all sweet and innocent, "it would save me some time and pain. Bertel is busting my nuts on this thing."

"Shovels?"

"Yeah, shovels. To dig the hole, sweetheart."

"Jesus Christ, Owen, you've shot somebody," I say, and for a moment this is true.

He laughs, long and hard. "Just come on down here, Mavis. Get me out."

"Five minutes," I say, and the line goes dead.

I think, this is the way with Owen. He leans in close before he steps away and he counts on you to be there, he counts on you even though you do not count on him. I move to his bidding even as I'm out of our practice and this is so soothing somehow. I feel the blanket of the past come 'round me, and grasping its corners I'm not really twenty-two, but still only sixteen, still a child, and Owen's put me up to digging a hole to China.

I pull a pair of Owen's jeans over my hips, tuck in my nightshirt. The only shoes I could get to are my sandals, left beside the settee in the parlor, so I go barefoot down the stairs and out the screen door. I get shovels from the woodshed. The lights on Main are still burning, even though it's way past midnight, and I walk the dry grass in the medians so I don't cut my feet.

It's wee in the morning and I'm sleepy and barefoot, and I'm walking the streets of a town I've been gone from to help a man I've been gone from and it strikes me that I wouldn't have it any other way. I do move to Owen's bidding, but I also summon it upon myself, wait and expect and cherish the way he counts on me and not Punk or Miss Pauline, or Hazel or my mama. I don't think he'd've called if I'd not been home. I walk down to the police station in the middle of the night carrying these shovels because he's asked me to, because I still think of him as cool and wise and restless, and I want to be close to that in him before he disappears again.

And someday Owen'll see real trouble and I know this too, but he wouldn't shoot somebody. Rough them up, maybe, bruise and bump them, but I've heard it takes a certain coldness around the eyes to kill a man, and if he had killed a man, Deputy Cy Bertel would just drag him out behind the jailhouse and kill him back, wouldn't even give him a phone call. That's the sort of justice Cy Bertel believes in, and he's half the law around here, and the other half just some politician who carries a gun. They come and go and big Cy just sits tight.

Cy Bertel gives me the willies. He's a sweaty man, a big beefy man with a grin that's not right, makes me think he inflicts unnecessary pain on the small things of this world. He's deputy and he also runs the cab stand, the Texaco station, and a shine still down by the river. It's the cab stand I pass walking down Main. He has a sign posted, free one-way tickets to New York City for any black man who will sign an oath never to set foot in Edisto again, not even to visit for a weekend.

He says, "Yankees and niggers, they's about suited to one another."

But Owen likes to mess with him. Back when he was in high school, Owen used to drive by the police station on a Saturday night, car loaded down with people, and lay on his horn. He'd wait for Cy to get to the glass front office before he'd let his Mustang loose, squealing the tires on the station drive. Cy would chase him all night, his cop car engine too small to take Owen over. I imagine it's still the same, Owen in this same sort of trouble again. Probably got busted and has to dig something out, trench an outhouse somewhere. Community service.

I drop the shovels. I open the doors to the station, a small brick building just down from Miss Pauline's Boutique, and Owen sits handcuffed to a chair. He whistles low in his throat for me.

"Why, Miss Mavis, you sure cut a figure in those jeans."

"Save it, Owen," I say.

And there's more I want to say, more that wells up, like being bothered in my sleep, like being tired and hurt from last night when he embarrassed me, like being surprised and glad right now that I still know my way around him. I hold my hands open in front of me like I'm holding the air in my palms, the air that's hot and dry and full of dust, and my body leans toward this air, toward my palms, but does not touch them. This is a small thing, as I have no motion for the call between Owen and me, and the words have just slipped away.

Owen looks into my face, travels my body and returns to my face, and here I am, his Mavis girl and close to him for just the night as if we were both busted and both handcuffed and both in jail.

From the desk in the corner, Cy Bertel laughs and slaps his knee.

"How you doing, Mavis Black," he says. "Come home from college to box this boy's ears?" He laughs again, and he spooks me. He could do anything he wanted to Owen and me, and that fact is loose in this jailhouse, charging up the air, and of a sudden I'm nervous.

"Hey, Deputy," I say, sugar-sweet. That's the only way I know to get out of here before sunrise, to get out of here at all. "There's some papers I need to sign or something before you open up the kennel?"

"No, ma'am," he says, looking me straight in the eye. "But there's a dog y'all got to bury."

"A dog?"

"My dog."

He stands and unclasps Owen's handcuffs.

"Your uncle here done run over my old bluetick with that hot little car, and now y'all git to dig her up a gravesite."

He laughs, rubs his belly with both hands. I look at Owen and he's flexing his muscles, squaring his T-shirt on his shoulders. He takes my hand, we get the shovels and follow Cy Bertel to the police car.

The ground is hot, hard like asphalt, and the lawns must be watered, fields irrigated. It could take all night to dig a hole in land like this to bury a dog into. As we drive, I look out at the sky and pray for a sudden storm.

I've never ridden in the back of a police car before. It looks the way it does in the movies, vinyl and chicken wire, radio static, sort of like a taxicab in New York City. Maybe Cy Bertel sets his police car up like this because it's how they are in the movies and that's about all he knows about being a policeman, what he can get off the big screen. Or maybe he always dreamed of being a cab driver but got to be a cop instead; this is just Cy Bertel's police car looking like a taxicab because he runs the cab stand too.

I glance over at Owen, his head resting on the seat back, and he is asleep. He's so comfortable, he's asleep. I think Owen was born in trouble and this, this ain't nothing new to him.

Cy Bertel hums a low tune under his breath, checks the rearview mirror for my face.

"Just up a little piece," he says.

We pass Evelyn Metz's trailer drive and pull over to the side of the road behind Owen's Mustang. I slap his arm to wake him up.

"So you were fucking around and ran over a dog," I say.

"No, honey. I wasn't fucking around. I was tomcatting."

I think, what's the difference? Cat's a cat, a fuck's a fuck, and this dog is dead. But I'm not really mad, not really surprised either. Owen's sort of scrapes always involve a car and a woman and the deep of night.

"Hey, now," Owen says, stretching his arms overhead. "Evelyn wanted to come to the festivities, but when I explained that it was just family, well, she got shy."

"I'll bet she did."

"You know, Mavis, she's a real shy girl."

He grins and hands me the shovels and I open the car door. I follow Cy Bertel into the sere thistle, brown and sharp at my foot soles.

He stops ahead of me and there's the dog, flat black in the moonlight, on the berm of the road. I expect so many things. Harris hit a deer with his car last winter and I expect those things, the hind leg turned and splintered with bone, the dark patches of flesh, pools of burst vessels, the glassed eyes, the cold, the heat, the heaviness. But this dog is whole, sleeping. I swear I can see her chest rising and falling, the swell of her belly under the moon.

"This dog's not dead," I say.

Cy Bertel flares a match on the heel of his boot, lingers it over the dog's grayed muzzle, down her body.

"Those are dead eyes, missy," he says. "And that's a dead heart."

He toes the chest of his dog with his lizard-skin cowboy boot. I think about movies where the great dog goes lame and the boy has to take care of her himself, think about Sounder and Old Yeller. I want to feel sad for Cy Bertel's big barbed heart, but instead I say, "Those are some fine boots you got there, Deputy."

Owen kneels down and cradles the dog in his arms, lifts her up, and she is stiff like a husk, like a cicada shell. He follows Cy Bertel through a stand of red tips on up to his house, a double-wide on a cement foundation like Evelyn's next door.

There's a pen out front, chain link full of sleeping dogs and kid toys, old barrels rusted pale with dust. A little girl in Cy's undershirt sits atop one of these, tolling her heels against the metal.

"Git on to bed, Sissy," he tells her, and she doesn't budge.

She's got big blue eyes and a runny nose she swipes at with the back of her hand. She watches Owen carry the dog to the side of the house. She watches as if it's a parade, as if it's something she's been waiting on all day. Cy Bertel's wife peels up the window shade, says for the girl to get on, and she slips down from the barrel, sleeping dogs nipping at her heels.

"You've done broke her heart," Cy Bertel says to Owen, but I can tell that isn't true.

Cy Bertel marks off a plot a few paces from the double-wide, a yard square. The grass flattens under the toe of his boot, even the wild onion and the cornflower gone to rust in this dry.

"Six feet deep," he tells us. "A proper gravesite. But I'll settle for four." We watch him go inside the trailer, and through the window watch him pull off his boots by the television, sit down beside his wife for a cold beer.

I hand Owen a shovel and we dig. There is the coppery smell of the dog around him, about his arms and chest. It is a smell I've never smelled, but I know it anyhow and this surprises me.

Through the trees, I see the faint light of Chinese lanterns, the broad white edge of Evelyn Metz's trailer. There's a silhouette in the window closest to us, the form of a woman, and I think it to be Evelyn herself. I see her lift her hair off her neck and shake it back out. I see her unbutton a shirt and slip into the sheets of her bed, leaf through the pages of a magazine or a book. I imagine that Cy Bertel watches her every night, sees her through his own bedroom window, and thanks the Lord he lives in the spot he does.

Suddenly, I feel protective of Evelyn. This dog, this isn't her fault, she's just swept up and I feel as though she needs someone to help her take care. It is now she gets back up and pulls her shade, her skin catching in the lantern light.

I glance at Owen, stay his eyes. I wonder if he has seen what I have seen, but he's been digging all along.

I punch the steel neck of the shovel with my bare foot and it goes nowhere, hardly moves. The ground has seized up, stone tight for water.

So much passes for what I feel since I've been home, passes through me and before me, and so much of what I feel right now is the want to hide out, the want to stay here in the dark night and not talk to anyone, to be alone with Owen, which is almost truly alone. The quiet of this yard comes 'round me and the past which I've taken on myself, and I think I've come to this place from being versed and unfolding, from being up at college, and now I'm so nearly the girl I was when I left four years ago. It's as if I stand beside myself, here in the moon-light, in the dust, in the hot earth opening at my feet.

I've come this way by choice, and I've been happy to do it.

It seems a short time, and I have blisters and cuts, splinters from the wood of the handle. My hands are a wreck and my feet are worse, split and torn, the dust giving way to earth, skin giving way to blood. The deeper I get I expect to find a body, some bones left here in Cy Bertel's yard. I expect to get somewhere, get to something, but there is only Owen, knee-deep, then waist-deep in this grave, hollow after hollowful of dry earth chuffing up into a pile.

"That'll do," Cy Bertel hollers from the foot of his steps, tired with his watching.

I look over, more startled by his voice than if he'd cocked a pistol. I'd gone to thinking Owen and I were all alone, but Cy is right there, and children stand around him and his wife looks on from behind the curtains. I look over to Evelyn's trailer and she has come out on her front stoop as well, the shine of some slippish robe about her that takes light when she moves, and she's been there for I don't know how long.

"Git that dog over here, woman," Owen hisses at me, the center of too much attention for too long and it's made him testy.

My hands are stiff and hot and when I walk across the lawn they throb with each step or heartbeat, either one. I bend down and cuddle up the front end of that big dog and try to lift her, half drag her over to the hole we've got going. She is heavy like a sack of quicksand, and the harder I pull her from where she's lying, the closer I get to her body, and finally I'm all in there with the dog, face to face, nose to nose.

It's now something happens where her jaws open up wide like a great bird of paradise and her tongue lolls out and laves over my face with a big wet kiss.

She moans long and low and I've heard of such things, things too old and hard and heavy to die the first time around. I lay her down and back away, still crouched over.

I say, "Come on, big dog."

I say it again and she gets up on all four legs, shakes her skin all over like she's shaking off water or dust or death itself. She looks at me all wide-eyed like I've caught her with the Thanksgiving turkey, and then she tucks her tail between her legs, bears herself away into the bushes, resurrected for all to see. Me and Owen and Cy Bertel and Evelyn over at her trailer, we stand with our arms at our sides, our mouths open. And the four of us, we've not seen a greater thing yet than that dead dog on her feet, not standing up or crouching down, in an empty grave nor clothed in cloth as incandescent as scales of rare, night-moving fish.

I can't imagine that we will.

9

I am without sleep, in a daze. I watch my eyes sag in the bar mirror at Miss Pauline's parlor house while Owen takes care of my hands, washes them out with peroxide and salve at the sink. We got back to the house on Sorghum just as the sun was coming and neither of us went to bed. We showered, changed into our wedding clothes, sat at Punk's kitchen table, and drank black coffee. We finally drove the miles out here to the vineyards to stay awake, to clear our heads, but I can't make sense of anything. My hands ache. My hands ache and I need to sit down.

From the front windows of the parlor house I can see the blunt edge of the barn, and from there the vineyards peel away in skins of green, vine rash and florid, leafy in this morning's heat. I know the fruit's not even ripe enough to eat, but Punk's crop is lush, so different from the ground it grows from. And that ground stretches before me for miles and miles, and behind me it runs right down into the river, all his. All Punk's. For the first time, I think it's a good idea to have a wedding on this land, in this place. There is life blood here, enough to spare and spare.

I get dreamy and I think it's my own life blood, this land teemed and coursed with the same that teems and courses in me. I learned to swim in this river. I learned to bait a hook, scale a fish, shoot a squirrel. I suntanned bare as can be until I was seven right outside this house, and it was here I first drove a car, Owen's car, through these leafy rows gone brittle in

February frost. These things I've learned, things I've held, done, or wanted; they're part of this place, this place in this earth.

It's now I get a fleeting wonder at why I stayed away so long, why I didn't try harder to get home, why I spent my summers and my holidays up at school, so far from this place. I've missed it more than I realized. But I know there was always a reason, and it was circumstances, or what I wanted at the time, or what I could do for Punk, which is what I could do for this farm. And then I get the idea again that I have in fact been two places at once, that I've managed to touch this spot from hundreds of miles away, and that makes me smile.

Owen pats kisses on each of my palms, tight and throbbing. Last night he didn't go to Evelyn, but he came with me and I didn't have to wait on him. That's the first time something like that has ever happened, me going, him following behind.

He whispers, "I owe you one," and his lips brush my ear. I think he does, he does owe me one that comes when he least wants or expects it, some favor that will require him alone, and this satisfies. I have a small thing held above him, and I might be the only woman in the world who can say that.

Something catches his attention beyond my shoulder.

"Mimes," he says. "Fucking mimes."

Behind me at the French doors there are men in skullcaps, their faces harlequined and white with paint. They make gestures, motions, as if they're inside a box and can't get out, as if they have keys and are opening doors, as if they're falling off high places.

Owen seethes beside me. "Fucking mimes," he says. "My ass if they want in here."

He goes to the windows, yells for them to go away, and they jump back, huddle together, and bite their imaginary fingernails. They quake in their floppy shoes. Punk hired mimes to direct the guests, to park their cars, and it would probably be a safe bet that these are the ones.

Mimes really freak Owen out. Some people don't like marionettes, stuff from a taxidermist; some people don't like scarecrows or mannequins or clowns. With Owen, it's mimes. I back away from the bar, back into a wall by accident and bump my head on a picture shelf. Owen gets wild on occasion, occasions like now.

He says, "Move away from the window. Move away from me, you fucks."

The mimes raise their eyebrows, shrug their shoulders. They act as if they don't know what he's talking about, and this is not smart. You have to be smart with Owen when he's this way, when he's tired and worn down. I know this. They don't. I think maybe I should write to the country of Saudi Arabia and warn them too.

Owen throws his arms out, jukes around, and mutters things under his breath. It's like watching something feral, something slipping from its own control, and the toe of his shoe catches a leg of Miss Pauline's mahogany end table, sends the whole thing toppling over. Picture frames, a decanter of brandy, glass busting and broken 'cross the floor, and Owen sets upon the wreckage, lets out a sound from low in his throat, and wings a shatter of something at the French doors, throws another, another and another to splinters on the jamb.

He gets right up against the window, his breath clouding the glass, nose to nose with a mime.

He says, "Get away from me," and the whole troupe flees the back deck.

I close my eyes and my head butts against the wall again. Just when I think all this has come down, I can rest, I can smile, just when I settle and breathe deep, that's when all hell breaks out. That's when I break out, rattle loose of myself as if my bones are lined with tinfoil and ready to crumple. I have no bottom; it just keeps going through me like an echo of an echo of an echo.

Owen cut his own hands and he bends over the bar sink, picks glass from his palms. I watch him from the wall, pulling bright slivers from the bed of his fingers with tweezers. He winces and sucks the blood.

I think of something else. I think of Harris. Hands are the sole reason Harris believes in God. Hands, red cabbage, and blooming things like cactus. But hands are his big reason; he says no coincidental force could have aligned so many bones, so much cartilage, then polished up a working thing with as many functions as a hand. Harris thinks about how often he uses his own.

He says, "Man is the measure of all things."

He hasn't called. I haven't called him either, but I expected him to wonder how I am, to make sure I made it home all right. I think about our words at the bus station, waiting in his car. Maybe they're emblematic of our relationship, the last things we thought to say to each other before a long separation.

He wanted to know what happens next and it's a question he's had since spring. He wanted to know when we'd be together again, and why and where and how, but I didn't want to give him an answer. It's become caught up in my pride, a matter of who backs down first. I think I spoke about decisions and choices and the differences between the two. I think I spoke about distance.

Harris said, "You'll find that you miss me, that distance stains the heart," and maybe he's right.

At the bus station in Boone three days ago, I thought about how our arguments are like puzzles and I wish I could remember the pieces I put in this spot, the way this whole thing fit together last time.

The caterers arrive and Owen is still at the sink. He curses to himself. He drops the tweezers down the drain. They pretend we're not there, cart in trays and trays of food, the waiters in tuxedos and white gloves. They fuss over cleaning up the brandy and glass, but no one asks what happened and I lead Owen to a seat out of the way. He sucks his fingers, pinches his cuts to force the blood.

"Owen, honey, I almost think you made them talk," I say.

"Mimes," he says. "Fucking mimes."

I lean over and rest my head in his lap. I feel so lumbering and numb, I could doze off even now, stretched across these chairs. I think about sleep the way I thought about it as a child, like jumping sheep, or rows and rows of trucks with their beds full of sand. I realize I'm counting to myself. I realize I'm clenching my teeth.

But it's not long and Owen stands and shifts my head onto a pillow and walks away. I hear Hazel and the other women, hear my mama, and I don't want her to ask what I'm doing, so I sit up and put my feet on the floor.

Hazel bustles at the bar mirror, still in her long-line corset that came from Miss Pauline's secret drawer. Evelyn Metz puts the final touches on her hair, teasing and spraying, and Hazel looks a vision. Piles of curls and ringlets spill out of her satin bow, and her face, Evelyn's created a woman ten years younger. Hazel looks a girl, looks a blushing schoolgirl here at thirty-three.

Miss Pauline says, "Honey, we're all sixteen when the veil comes off," and Hazel smiles into the mirror.

I sink back into my chair and watch Evelyn and Sal's girls lift Hazel's dress over her head, lift the train, and let it buoy on the draft from the air conditioner. The silk settles like spume, like whitecap. Hazel is a water of white in this dress, ordered special from Atlanta for its cathedral train, its Viennese lace, the hourglass shape of the bodice that makes Hazel's waist look but a trace.

Evelyn reaches out and skims a sleeve with her fingertips, tells Hazel how perfect she looks. She says, "My mama always told me a wedding dress should make your waist look tiny and your titties huge."

I'm dizzy with these women of mine. I remember a class I had up at Appalachian, a literature class, and we read books by women, watched movies about women, talked a lot about men too, but not the same way we talked about women. I watch Hazel getting ready for her wedding, and I think this is what she's always wanted. I think about the exception to the rules, the rules for the exceptions. There's a difference between selfhood and how a body thinks of herself when no one's taking notes, a difference between how we sound on paper and how we really are. Men do the things they do because of us, because we call them to it; we dress in white and take them into our hearts and they have no other choice. Men lie in the hands of women. It just comes out seeming the other way 'round.

Hazel smiles into the mirror, pleased with herself and her day. She's been like my sister, the closest thing I know to a sister, and now I want to have something to say, but my mind is all aflutter. I want to make a declaration, like Evelyn, like Miss Pauline. I want to have a saying in this place, something that ties us all down and says this is how we are right now, and maybe later we'll want to remember back. We'll think, that was true, what Mavis said. I'll think, that was me, right then.

And in the next moment I want my eyes on my mama. I want to feel her hand at the small of my back and see her the way she was when I was small, when I was a girl and she was but a little more than that, and we would do silly things in Punk's house, when she would hold my hand while I said my prayers at night like she taught me to. I want to be six years old again and sitting on an irrigation pipe and being told to stay put and see the sight of her coming across the fields with the sun at her back, coming for me as she said she would.

I stand and move behind Hazel, my steps heavy in my soft-soled shoes, the pink tulle of my dress catching on the ointment at my fingers. I touch her shoulder with the back of my hand.

"Good luck," I say. "Break a leg."

She laughs, and her eyes grace over mine in the mirror.

Merrilee goes to the bar refrigerator and brings out Hazel's bouquet, bliss roses and lily of the valley, some ivy mixed in. Hazel pulls a rose for each of us.

She says, "For love," and my mama has to get a handkerchief.

The ceremony is short, doesn't take long for the joining of lands and earth. It's a song and a vow and back down the aisle, the crowd clapping and teary and smiling. I feel a few steps behind even now, a glass of champagne in my hands and the orchestra playing the Sonata in D. So many faces, people I cannot remember, will never remember in a million years, people from town, people I used to help in Miss Pauline's Boutique, people who used to live next door when I was small. They brush my arm, smile, and kiss my cheeks. I feel like royalty; I feel I should be tossing flowers or candy or money.

I think a bite to eat will set me right. Maybe I think that because I'm hungry, or maybe I just know that inside the parlor house, the table is set. There are sirloins, spitfired chickens, stewed veal, leg of lamb, roast suckling pig, sausages cooked in sorrel. I fill my plate with some of everything. I take salads, aspics, molded fruits, and pâtés. I take collards with vinegar, fresh corn, stewed tomatoes and okra, scalloped summer squash, and mashed potatoes. I take bread, a glass of wine.

I pull a tapestry chair to Miss Pauline's bridge table and lay my spread before me. I eat slowly, at first delicately, then with little regard for anything else. The food is good, and when it's over, I feel unclouded for the first time all day. There's dessert too, and I still have room for that.

The wedding cake rises up from the buffet, mountainous, white-iced and chocolate-filled, covered with tiny spun-sugar roses. The roses look so real they should be soft like petals, sugar petals, and I could eat them right off the cake. No one would miss a rose, one rose from all these.

I steal around to the back and I realize how enormous this cake is, how really enormous. It must have two dozen tiers, enough to feed a thousand people. I start at the bottom and count six when someone touches my shoulder.

"Mavis." It's Sal, caught me counting the tiers of his cake.

I try not to look suspicious, open my mouth in congratulations, but he is already laughing.

"Looks like I caught you with your hand in the cookie jar, Mavis. I caught you red-handed," he says.

I look down and my hands are red, peeled raw. I draw them behind my back and smile.

"It was a beautiful ceremony, Sal," I say. "Really beautiful."

He nods, rolls his lower lip between his thumb and forefinger. He looks very handsome in his tuxedo, silver and Mediterranean, and I wonder if he looked this way at his first wedding, years ago in Utah, fresh from a cross-country police escort. I doubt he was so relaxed, so smiling. I have a hard time picturing him as he must have been so many years ago, a boy then much like Owen now, a boy on the run with a car full of coconuts. He is so solid standing here before me, as if he might never move with speed, but rather only aim and sure intention.

There's a piece of confetti stuck to his cheekbone, tissue thin. I reach my fingers out and brush his cheek and hold the confetti for him to see.

"Stuck to you," I say, but he is looking at my hands.

It's now when the caterers throw open the front door and the room fills with people lining up to eat and heap their plates high like mine. I slip my hand from Sal's and tuck it into the folds of my skirt. I don't want to explain myself, not my hands, my eating, why I feel bad, why I feel good. I take a few steps backward and Sal is swallowed up in the crowd.

Guests throng around the food. There are so many people, too many people, and I need fresh air now, some room to rub my stomach. I head for the door, slipping a few clusters of grape garnish off the end of the buffet to sweeten my mouth instead of cake roses. The grapes are Scuppernongs, too ripe to be Punk's own. The caterers must've gotten them out of Mexico or Napa Valley, where grape grows faster and is more plentiful than here. I roll a few in my palms, gold as goose eggs. Owen used to call these God's eyes when I was younger. He'd tell me eyeballs had skins too.

He'd say, "I could pop yours out, sweet Mavis, and they'd taste like honey, those honey-colored eyes."

But that was Owen's way when I was younger, teasing me, and I believed every word out of his mouth. I imagine that's what he was getting at the other night, out at the carnival lot with his roller coaster story. I imagine he was only teasing, but I'm too old for that anymore. Since I've been home, Owen and I have been back and forth, up and down, he pulls me so hard and then lets me snap like a rubber band. It takes a lot to make me angry with him, not much to forgive him, and I wonder if this means I am weak. I wonder if Owen makes me weak, but he has that effect on everyone. I realize Owen being Owen has nothing to do with me. I make what lies between us; I call and he has no choice but to answer.

Outside, my mama sits at one of the linened tables talking to a man I don't remember anymore. She motions for me to come over, say hello, but I can't think of this man's name or what he used to do around my family. He sits next to my mama, and he smiles and laughs with her, touches her hand from time to time.

"Mavis, you remember Fuller Foley, don't you?"

Fuller stands and kisses my cheek. He is a round man, a rosy man, and his eyes are bright and brown.

He says, "My God, missy, last I saw you, you were knee-high to a titmouse."

My mama says, "Mavis just graduated from Appalachian and she's come home to work for Punk. She's going to be his bookkeeper."

She looks at me all proud, and Fuller laughs and pats his belly. I laugh too. His name is familiar to my ears, even as I don't recognize his face. A friend of my mama's, I suppose.

"Fuller and I went to high school together," my mama says.

"Yes, ma'am. And your Elsbeth here was sweet on me, I reckon. She sure was the sweet part."

My mama blushes and she tells Fuller Foley to go on. I think she's flirting with him, and it's a nice thing to watch. I make some excuse, I tell them I see someone I meant to say hello to, and get out of their way.

The crowd is thick, so much cram and jam spilling out of the parlor house, glasses filled, plates piled. Guests eat, talk, eat some more. Watching, I feel a little sick, woozy, and too full. I decide I should nap a while, stretch my stomach out and digest it all, maybe wander down to the river and soak my poor pretty feet. I have intentions of being the life of this party and dancing to every song. I just have to get myself on balance again.

On the edge of the river there's a weeping willow tree, its switches long-hanging like a drape. Inside that tree the air is sweet and green, and I can lie down. I can take a few minutes to collect myself. I sneak around the edge of the party and slip between the limbs and no one notices.

No one's noticed Owen either, flush against the willow trunk, Owen with Kat against him. No one notices at all. I do not move but stay between those limbs and I can see them and it's as though they become all I can see. If I'd not paid attention I could have walked right into them.

His hands chase up her thighs and smooth her ass, cupping her fast to him, with him, her skirt around her waist. His tongue slys against her ear, along the tendons in her neck like cord, and she tosses her head and then she has her tongue on his skin, her teeth at his neck, pulling him into the grass at their feet.

And then I see them again and this time it's a man and a woman, two people making love under a willow tree, out of the June sun, out of the press of the party. It's a man and a woman and it's dark and wild like a painting, or a picture in a magazine performing before my eyes. I cannot look away. They hold me fast, like a natural disaster, like a gale or hurricane. I feel as if I've just walked into a hurricane, as if I'm churning in the air above the ground, spinning and tossing.

She's just a kid, and he should know better. I don't know what to hold on to, whether to cough or to call out. I don't even know if she's really just a kid.

I feel all that was full in me sink away, back through the branches the way I came, and find another path to the river. I don't know what I've seen. I don't know what it means. I think of something else. I think, oh Owen. I think how easy it would be to damn you, if it weren't already done.

Alongside the river, there's a boy in white, dressed for the wedding. His pants are rolled up around his knees and he wades in the water's edge, cooling off. A girl sits on the bank and she leans back on her elbows, she turns her face toward the sun. The boy splashes her, light mist across her bare arms, her legs, her white tights skinned off in her hand. She doesn't move. She lets the sun dry the river off her cheeks, she lets the boy tease in the water, she lets the afternoon pass into dusk, and she is still, and cool, and quiet in the sand.

〰〰〰〰〰〰〰〰 I carry my shoes in my hands. I've lost a heel in the kudzu by the water, the tendrils there knotted to a mat of creeps and latches, holding tight like something limbed and human. My stocking feet are picked full of holes and soaked through, cool and wet and brown. In this time by the river I've gotten away from something. I feel better; I feel as though I've been gone for a long time. The boy and the girl, they follow me back toward the music. I don't know who they are, just the children of people come to the wedding.

Music drifts across the lawn to me, something old and brassy, and talk of things old and brassy, the sound of ice against glass and perfume in the air like ripe fruit. The boy and girl disappear into the crowd as if they never happened. I hang upon the fringes of the party, pause myself outside for just a moment longer, and then there's Evelyn Metz coming out of the crowd and she's coming toward me like steam, soft low rolling like fog off the river.

"Mavis, honey," she says. "You look like you've romped in the briar patch."

"Oh, Evelyn," I say, and there's more to say but then she's touching my face.

She brushes my hair into place with her fingernails, whisks my cheek with her thumb. She pulls burs from the hem of my dress. She takes my shoes and heaves them into the stands of brush I've wandered from and gives off trickles of laughter. It's her perfume I smell, heady and warm and all around us.

"There," she says. "Pretty as a picture."

Protectiveness wells up in me, a motherish feeling, and I hug her to me, my arms pinning close. I don't want Evelyn to be hurt. That's all I can think, I don't want Evelyn to be hurt. She's like a tightrope walker, like one of those women who spin by the skin of their teeth.

I say her name and she rests her cheek against mine.

"Owen's going away from me," she whispers. "I can feel him going."

This is the story I expect to hear, the sadness and the heavy wet cloak of being left behind. These things settle in her voice, these things settle around us in the air like nimbus, like shadow and thunderhead. There are a million words I could say that would make her turn from me and not go on, but I don't call them up. I pull her tighter and I stroke down her back, one direction, as if Evelyn has a grain to her, a way her skin lies best.

"Sometimes late at night he speaks that Arabian and he whispers low to himself. He thinks I'm asleep. He speaks another language."

I hold her. "I know he does," I say.

And we stand here, close by on the edges of highness and brightness, the edges of music and people, and my arms around her arms so close together I can feel her heart in her chest beating so to bruise, beating like a blunt instrument, an organ gone to self-destruction.

Evelyn pulls back and passes her hands over her face, the fear and heartbreak passing the way they came, her face an apron of sand, a place of deposit and erosion. She clears and washes clean. She gathers herself and holds tight, and I think, this is a force, this is a talent she possesses; something in her wanes and another thing waxes full.

It's now something happens between us like need, like admiration. We are still close together, she in her shoes and me in my stockings, and we listen to the music. Evelyn's doll eyes drop closed and she wavers, gently rocks in the air like something half full of helium. We are so close now I can feel the hem of her skirt brushing mine and I can feel the fabric as if it's my skin, as if it's part of me and touches Evelyn. We are so close now I feel we could dance, we could hold hands and kiss like friends or sisters or lovers long in each other's company.

When she speaks her eyes peel open and chime; they split the dark wide open and break this spell between us.

She says, "When Owen thinks I'm not paying him mind, his eyes wander all over the place. I swear, I know every move he's got, ain't one I haven't seen, and there's something to that, isn't there."

I tell her there surely is something to that.

I tell her I need a drink. I need a few drinks and I'm betting she does too.

She says, "Vodka stinger, honey. On the rocks."

I wander to the parlor house, and inside the caterers scurry 'round the cake, ferry its platter to a bier. They stand two on either side, one hunched beneath for balance, but the tiers weave like a bridge in the breeze, like one of those bridges that's been mal-aligned, mis-engineered to buckle up and swallow a car. This cake is big enough to swallow a car, layer upon layer upon layer, and I count ten before my turn in line.

I ask the bartender for a stinger and a glass of champagne, watch the wedding cake teeter over his head. I think how cakes are flour, eggs, milk, soda, and sweet, that's all, and I remember taking a bath when I was small, watching my mother take a bath with baking soda, watching Miss Pauline bathe with milk. I remember right now the time I went to draw my own bath and sprinkled flour in the water, my mama coming in to wash me.

She'd said, "My God, Mavis. All you've done is make glue."

I take the drinks outside to the table with Evelyn, but she's gone, up and dancing to the orchestra. She does a two-step with Hale McClain, waltzes with Stanley. She looks as if she's having so much fun, her head thrown back and laughing, her skirt twirling 'round her hips like a ring of water from a hose, something amazing to see suspended in the air. She's in the arms of other men, their hands at the small of her back, their eyes on her, and I know how that can be a good feeling.

The guests are thick and swaying and I see my mama dance, too, in Fuller Foley's arms.

When she found out she was pregnant and my daddy was dead, I've heard, Fuller Foley wanted to marry my mama. He wanted to give her an honest life, a house of her own with a man in it. He went all the way to Charleston when I was born and he saw my mama hold me to her heart, he saw her coo and sing to me, saw her rock me close to her. He got down on one knee next to her hospital bed and asked her to be his wife, but she turned him down. He was eighteen.

She said he'd see things differently one day. She told him she could make it fine on her own, told him she could make me a fine life, but he was sweet to ask.

I think Fuller Foley left the hospital that day and left South Carolina all together, went up to Charlotte, and made his way. He could never get my mama out of his mind. He's come back after all these years to touch her hand at a table, to make her blush and waltz to a slow song.

The orchestra strikes up beach music and Miss Pauline tries to teach Sal to shag. He gets the basic steps, but she near about breaks his arm with one spin too many. Somehow Evelyn and Hazel have come to be dancing together, and there's Punk with Anna on his shoes. She holds tight to his legs as they step around the floor, her face turned up to him as if he's come full blown out of Sesame Street.

I think how nice to watch people dancing. They look so happy. I can't seem to wrap my mind around anything other than that, that these people look happy, and right now, that's good enough. These guests will leave this party, the friends, the family, and all this happiness will stay here. They will discover things, they will return to things, but for right now all is well.

There's a tap at my shoulder and a tall mime with a bowler hat and black tails. My Lord, I think, he wants to dance. He bows at the waist, flourishes with his arm. I hope he's not one of the guys Owen scared the piss out of this morning. I don't want to feel beholden.

"I'm sitting this one out," I say.

But the mime draws his face out long, makes as if to wipe a tear away. He drops down to his knees in front of me and holds his hands pleading. He kisses the hem of my dress.

"No, thank you," I say.

I know I sound chilly, but I feel foolish talking to a mime, as if I'm talking down a long echo hall or into a cave. But then I think, what the hell, if a man can't say the right things he might as well not speak at all, and on that account, a mime's as good as anybody.

He gets up off the ground and pulls a rose out of the table centerpiece, places it between his teeth. The orchestra plays the opening to a tango and the mime reaches for my hand once more.

"Oh, why not," I say.

Why not, I think, and I slip my hand in his.

I love to tango. It's a wild canyon of a dance, sexy, and I'm good at it. Harris and I took tango lessons back last summer. We'd put this crazy mariachi music on his turntable and follow each other around the room, his thighs with mine, his hand at the small of my back. I had this pair of ankle-strap heels and I'd put them on with a short skirt, pull my hair back tight at my nape. I'd slip a rose between my teeth and he'd lag it out with his own, brush along my neck with the petals.

I miss that. I miss Harris too on a night like this, full of music and warm breezes and good food. I think that's why I tango with this mime I will never see again, this man I would never recognize on the street, in plain clothes.

But now the band is on, no records, and my mime comes behind me, his hand at my waist, our arms stretched out together. We just go. We are flashy with this dance; we do the steps as if we've planned them out, as if we're being filmed and we've rehearsed. Every movement is smooth and full of tension. He's lost his mimeness, his exaggeration, and we dance, my body responding to the pressure of his hands.

He spins me 'round and 'round.

I weave my legs with his.

Times like now I go someplace within myself. I dance a dance that tastes of sex with a man who hasn't even asked my name. We don't talk, we don't laugh or try to know each other, and I don't even look into his face. It's like a grope in a dark corner, like hands and thighs, like brush and graze. I feel shameless. I feel his eyes cross my collarbones like pitch, thick and cleaving.

I think, I should grow my hair longer, to my hips.

I should wear perfume, sweet, like Evelyn's.

I should read the collected works of some long-dead writer, naked in the bath, learn to smoke cigars, learn to do the dangerous things in this world like sit still for long whiles and listen to myself roll over in tides of crazy thoughts. I should tick like a bomb.

I should slide my stocking foot along this man's calf, right now.

I look into his eyes and they are pale blue like arteries or veins, like the insides of my wrists, and they hold me to the spot. I imagine what could pass between us, what we've played up to and what would happen if we played it out in some darkened corner, some darkened bed. I imagine I'd ask him to wash his face. I imagine I wouldn't, and his vein-blue eyes would track my body and we would kiss as if we were eating grapes from a cluster, eating something crisp and sweet and held aloft, and his face would come off in my hands, white and black and red across my skin like newsprint. I would be all these things, long and sweet and naked and dangerous, and he would be mysterious to the quick like something beating in my own body.

Then with a flourish and a dip, the song is over.

People rush around me, touch my shoulders in congratulations. "How pretty," they say, and, "How graceful you are," but these were not my thoughts while we were dancing. I was thinking things I shouldn't have, letting loose that part of me that's easily convinced, the part of me that's indulgent and stupid, and I know if I'd been alone with that mime I'd have done things to him to make these people's eyes curl.

He disappears in the press of crowd around us, slips away like heat, and that's how I feel him to be gone, the warm parts of our bodies no longer touching, a chill at the small of my back. I didn't even get his name. I think how there are other ways to recognize people, the codes of skin, the puzzle of my hips and his, my arms and his, my belly and his pressed upon each other. And then his eyes. I find myself wondering if I could find him, if I could seek him out among the other mimes, and I have half a mind to do just that.

How strange on a day such as this, a day when all the bustle is around me but not on me, a day when I can disappear, and I can't seem to stay out of trouble. I think the wrong things, open the wrong door, choose the wrong card. I see the things that happen when nobody else is looking.

Across the parlor, the caterers make to roll the cake outside for the big event of the reception, dessert. Out of the corner of my eye, I watch a caterer lick a smear of icing from his finger, tasting before it's time.

The cake goes out the front door and I head out the back and around the deck. I confess I would not mind running into that mime just now, and then I hear the French doors slam behind me.

It's Punk. And Owen. And they're angry. I hear Punk rumble and I duck behind the caterer's van, pulled up close to the house.

"Look, boy. You keep your prick in your pants or this whole deal is fucked to hell. That there is Sal's little girl, you hear?"

Owen doesn't say anything and I hear a crack, the slap of a backhand on a face.

"You hear me, boy?" Punk says, low in his throat.

Punk's throat is different from Owen's; an anger lies in wait there that is ruthless and centerless, beyond this world and loosely reined. When we were children, Owen and I did something, hurt something close to Punk, and I can't remember what we did, only the sound of Punk's voice in the walls of the house, something purely chilling taking over in my chest, my lungs, my heart. And another time, Hazel came home from a date and she was crying and Punk boiled up out of his chair and caught that boy before he could back out the drive, near to ripped him out his open window.

But now, in the face of him, Owen is silent.

"I got the whole ball of wax on this one, twenty fucking years. Twenty fucking years and if this shit don't fly, it's all over, Napa Valley's gonna eat us up. Not gonna be a thing left, and what about when I'm gone, you kids won't have shit."

Owen's voice thin like reed: "I don't have shit now, old man. Not a goddamn thing and it don't matter if this pot with Sal makes millions, I ain't gonna see a drop and you know it."

"We talked about this, son."

"We talked about dick."

Punk's voice knots and snaps. It sends things along my spine that are too large for my skin.

He says, "This is big time, Owen. You don't have the balls."

I hear Owen take it down the deck stairs.

"Get back here, boy."

Punk raises his voice and Owen just keeps walking. I come into the light in time to see Punk rage after him, in time to see Punk take him to the ground.

"You show me something, boy, you show me some balls. You stick me out."

Owen shoves against his chest. He shoves again and Punk slams the flat of his hand against his ear.

"Show me," he yells. "You show me."

Owen shoves him once more and Punk belts his stomach.

I cry out. I've never seen a punch thrown close, a real punch like this, never heard the heavy slab of sound it makes, and I feel my stomach burn, something in my chest spit and gall. I press between them and their fists lash 'round me so fast, so fast my hands open and are cool and stinging 'cross the front of Owen's shirt.

I yell again and they separate. Punk's face is wet and there are tears in his eyes, but his features are hot and liquid like melting rock. He does not weep, but seems to break open and seep out of himself.

"Fucking show me, Owen," he yells.

But Owen is walking away, down the drive to his car,

passing Cy Bertel leaned up in the shadows, there all the time and never opening his mouth or lifting a finger in aid or obstacle.

Punk sweeps the air where Owen had been, closes his fingers as if he held something by the scruff of its neck.

"Owen," he yells after him.

"Owen," I yell, but he just fades away.

22

~~~~~~~~~~ Edisto River comes light now, sunset in the middle of summer, comes red and orange and flamed out of the tangles to the west, and I think to swim it, think how it would be warm and temperatured like my blood, but that's not so. I know the deeps are always chill and cold and moving.

I sit at the water's edge, Miss Pauline's parlor house and the vineyards behind me, and trail my toes in the warm surface of the currents. It's as if the warmest water is what's colored, like the Gulf Stream down in Florida running pale blue along the coast. I think what it would be to wander out into this river, to feel its skin of sunset necklace at my ankle, then my knee, my waist, everything beneath gone to cold.

It's July's heat around me, the air so still and heavy to make me crave that cold of the riverbed, the air enough to make me sweat even if there was no sun at all. In this heat, I have visions of Owen like mirages, not knowing where he's gone, how long he'll be.

He's been gone a month and I imagine him at first light in Saudi, in the hot hot desert with his feet sinking to sand. That heat would be different from Edisto's heat. It would be dryness and lightness. I imagine him at night in a tent against the wind, stretched out on Persian rugs, a long thin Arab woman feeding him red grapes. I imagine him far away, but he could be next door, up the highway. He could be lying low in Punk's attic and the house would never know it.

He's been gone thirty-one days now, and each new day comes easier to think of him as gone. Miss Pauline and my mama, they seem as if it's no big deal, it's just Owen being Owen, but I know something snapped in him. I know this is different, this is the big time, and I can't say he's done right. Not by Punk, or me, or even Kat, for that matter.

Punk's been different since the wedding, something moving in him slow like molasses. He's been reflective, pondering, and sometimes I can see his lips work and no sound comes out.

Kat's still here, stayed on with us to fill the house. She told Miss Pauline she'd like to visit, she'd like to help out. Sal and Hazel were on their honeymoon and she was to stay with Merrilee, but Merrilee said it would be okay for a little while. A little while's not what Kat has in mind, though, and she has been here thirty-one days too. She never went back to Pennsylvania, stayed right on after the wedding, and Merrilee sent down a box of clothes, most items black and fit for a widow. She took up in Owen's room, wears his old shirts to the breakfast table, and moons around. She tells everybody who'll listen she's in love with Owen. She says the funniest things about love at first sight, fate and faith, about the heart and all its rooms swept clean. She wears her moods like so much costume: sullen, moping, petulant, somber. I think she's got herself a part in the play as Owen's long-lost lover. I think she wants to move in with us; she's got it bad and she plans to pine away.

My mama and I talked about it this morning when we did the breakfast dishes.

She said, "I know what it is to want something like that, to miss someone when they're away. I missed you, Mavis."

She said this to me and I think how I missed her, too, and how she was lonesome here without me. Miss Pauline and Hazel and Punk were here. Owen was here then but I wasn't, and that makes it different. I'm her daughter and she's my mother, and in a way, my being here even makes her a different person. I'm sure she missed that.

"This is not the same," I told her.

"But it might be the same to Kat. She's made herself heartsick over Owen; like a baby bird she doesn't know any better. She knows to want, and that's all."

"But she's got college," I said. "She's going up to Wellesley and there'll be lots of guys to date and such. Guys that aren't like Owen."

"Like your Harris," she said.

"Sure. Like Harris."

My mama shut off the water and turned to face me.

"Sometimes a woman just wants a man like Owen. Sometimes she can't help herself and she can't do anything more than wait for him. Love is not a playpretty, and it's not a solid rock either."

She dried her hands on a dish towel and let her motherness hang in the air about herself and me. This is true, what she said, but it's true in the way you never want to hear. It's true because it's not what you're taught or what you dream about or what gets talked about when people are happy and in love, but it's what happens. It happened to my mama. She lost my daddy this way, Wyman Jackson, a solid man hazed away to ash when his truck exploded, and there was nothing she could do but wring her hands and wait. For me. I was coming, but in the cost, her man fell out from under her and this makes me sad sometimes in a very small corner of myself. It also makes me reverent, as if she's been through something and back that I couldn't conjure up in my darkest parts, something sweet and black and tearing that few are offered in this world.

These days I work in the parlor house, a back room now an office for me, filled with Punk's receipts and calculators and things that are automatic. In the long afternoon I can hear the hired men, Punk in the fields. I can hear the hum of tractors, mixing in the barn, low voices, calls. But no one comes to see me and I work all day inside the air conditioning. Air conditioning is enough to make anyone lonesome.

I was so caught up in coming home, worn down and tired once I got here, and the wedding surging on. But all that's finished. Now it seems strange to get a full night's sleep, to be in bed by nine with nothing to do but think. These are times when all I want is to be in another's company, to listen to someone's voice I don't know well, sit still while someone moves around me. I'm a little lonesome now for sure, so much of everything blown over like a thunderstorm.

I watch the mail for my things from school, five boxes still out there in the world. I take long showers before and after work. I tumble into chairs, into my bed, to the ground when I'm out of doors. I do things without much control over my limbs. I think of Harris at night, but I don't pine for him. I don't mope or wear his shirts around or feel like someone who doesn't know better.

He called a couple days ago. It was very relaxed, and neither one of us mentioned the bus station argument. He said the Renaissance Faire is in full swing, and I said work is still slow, will be until Sal gets back from Jamaica.

I said, "I've been thinking of making a visit, coming up some weekend soon and us heading to the Outer Banks or something."

He said, "I'd like that."

And that was all.

I think tonight will be enough. Tonight's the fireworks; and the picnic for the Fourth held here at the parlor house for all the relatives, employees, and hangers-on is already in full form. Miss Pauline, Kat, my mama, and Punk, pulled pork barbeque and corn on the cob, more peach cobbler than you can shake a stick at. Some of the hired men stayed on for supper, some went home to their families, and some will bring their families back here for the fireworks. Punk's a man who loves his fireworks, and his show runs from just dark to the wee wee hours.

This year's picnic is much smaller than the ones I went to as a child, on account of the fact that Punk doesn't use migrant pickers anymore. I will confess the other day I had a pang for the way things used to get done. I walked out in the rows to get Punk's word on something or other, and the Niagara grapes were ripening and sweet-smelling enough to cling in the air. I took a bunch in my hand and popped their skins and the smell was syrupy, the juice darkening on my jeans where I wiped my fingers. But the fields lay so quiet. I could hear birds, some clatter way off at the barn, a tractor in the far distance like the sounds of storms.

Last year this time, I know these same rows were filled with half-ton carts and bright colored backs and the smooth clip of Spanish. Punk harvested a bit earlier to compensate for the extra picking time. The grapes keep sugaring, on the vine and off. They don't stop ripening because you want them to, and too much or too little sugar, Taylor Winery turns the whole harvest away. Timing and action are everything.

Back then the barn was depot to trailers and eighteen-wheelers brimmed to take Punk's harvest on the highway to New York in twenty-four hours or less. In the rush and scramble some fruit gets crushed, and its heavy blue scent gums its way into the wood and paint of the barn, so that even now, even without a grape harvested this year, I can walk inside those walls and smell the sugar of Punk's fruit, dense like perfume, like sweat itself.

There's just five hired men to work this season, most all to crew the Chisholm Ryders when they get here, Punk's and Sal's. This cuts the cost of labor near to the ground and each Ryder will pick four tons an hour, every hour, 'til there's no more grape to be picked. They have lights, and only need one man to run each one, day or night. They'll stay in the barn without burning it to the ground, that's for sure, and when I do payroll, they're not something I have to cut a check for.

W. G. Marvelle still works for us even after the barn-burning incident, and Cash, called Cash because that's what you make his check out for at the end of the week. There's Roger and Samuel, and they'll be here tonight with their wives and kids, but W.G. won't bring his family around. When I was small, the authorities came out to get him at the farm because there was a baby in his house to which he was both father and grandfather. After all was said and done, nobody could remember much of what actually happened. There was no record of the baby's birth, as he was born at home and W.G.'s girl kept saying the fathering party was some man gone like Bosephus. W.G. was back with us the next year, singing, "I'm My Own Grandpa," and maybe his house is not so different from my own, all full up with relatives and families on top of families, but there are lines I'd cross and lines I wouldn't, and the one between families and authorities is one better left to stand.

Miss Pauline and Kat made fresh ice cream this afternoon and I sit here by the river with a bowl in my lap. I can hear my mama on the lawn beneath the back porch, dragging a chaise longue through the grass, coming away from the noise of children and men and people having a good time.

"Over here," I call.

She pulls the chair up behind me and settles herself into it, rests her bare foot on my shoulder.

"Oh." She sighs, and her toes wrap around my skin.

We sit quiet for a while watching the sun swamp into the river, watching the red and orange and gold pane across the running water. It is so simple out here, away from the picnic, so quiet I can hear the crickets and the grass, I can hear the sound of her skin on mine.

"How's things at work?" she asks.

I look to her over my shoulder and she holds a glass of wine in two hands.

"Slow for me 'til Sal gets back. Punk's been going through the paces with the hired crew, the last sprays, working on the irrigation system and such. The Niagaras start at the end of the month."

"Really? Well, then."

And she looks to the river, looks back at me, and seems to be in want of something to do with her fingers, knotting and unknotting them around the glass. It's as if holding something is not enough; she wants to shape, to mold. I reach to my shoulder and take her foot in my hand, knead the bed of her toes, and she slackens, lets her head loll back against the chair.

"Which ones are the Niagaras?" she asks.

It's now I realize how little she knows about the farm, how she's been around Punk and Owen working out there every day and still she knows little about what they do, what develops, and what it might take to see that thing develop. The Niagaras are white grapes, harvested in late July, then the Concords first of August, the Catawbas last of August, Scuppernongs from Labor Day until first frost, their seasons layered like this so that Punk could achieve maximum acreage for hand-picking without losing any yield.

My mama sees the cast, the form and physicality of the vineyards, but she's not concerned much beyond that. It exists, and in that existence wondrous things seem to occur. It is where people in her house go when they're not there. She hadn't even thought about who'd take Owen's place for the harvest.

Punk promoted one of the hired men to that position, Eldridge Tapon, Jr., a man everybody calls Tee. Tee has worked fruit this part of the South for most all his life, strawberries, blueberries, peaches, and he's worked for Punk the better part of ten years. Tee's wife died last December hanging out of the back of his car. She was drunk and out the window of his Chevy, trying to get some air, and Tee ran too close to a telephone pole. It took her head off, clean as can be. Punk had been over to their mobile home the week before, Thanksgiving, bringing Tee some coveralls and a bottle of bourbon.

Tee's wife said, "Ah, Mr. Punk, come on and stay for supper."

And Punk thought for sure something had died in that kitchen and they were cooking it up and he said, no, I must decline as Miss Pauline's cooking for us back at the house and I got to be getting on, but I'll have a sip of that bourbon with you all. But finally he could not help himself, and he asked Mrs. Tee just what the hell was in the oven, and she opened the door to a coon's face, roasting in the pan. They'd skinned the coon but left the head on for its flavorfulness.

Punk said, "Tee hadn't even treed the damn thing. He'd run over it with his car two days earlier and had been driving around with it in his trunk."

Tee knows tractors like the back of his hand, but Punk's real hesitant to let him behind the wheel of anything that travels an open road, what with Tee's wife losing her head and all. These are the risks you take, the exchanges that must be weighed. Tee will run the Ryder Sal's sending down, and paired with the one Punk's got on order, all 625 acres will be in Pennsylvania in less than three weeks.

Punk says, "That'll be a bitch of three weeks, you can count on it. Even if Tee don't kill nothing."

I know time is what this is all about, getting the grapes to Sal in time for him to use them while they're still fresh and whole and smelling clean. Fester sets in quickly, and Sal won't want that. He'll get other things he won't want, though, things the Ryders pull out of the vines because they weigh like grapes, things like baby birds, parts and the whole of snakes, mice, chips of cedar posting. I've even heard of a man's hand getting labored through one of those machines out in Fresno when the idea was brand-new, but I don't think that happens much anymore.

I tell my mama these things at the edge of the Edisto River, press the sole of her foot in my hands and tell her what all I know about the vineyards, and I like being able to do this. It strikes me I know quite a bit beyond accounting. I'll hear something and I'll remember it.

My mama smiles, says, "I never did have a head for those sorts of things, Mavis, never did. You're so smart. And pretty too."

She sets her feet on the lawn and trails her fingers 'cross my forehead.

"My baby Mavis, all grown up and so smart. You've traveled all over this country. Did you ever find any place as pretty as here, any place you'd be more to home?"

"Not one," I say.

"I'd not imagine so."

She looks tired and sweet, tired like a human being should be and looser since I've come home. I think back to the day I sat beside her bed and she slept, all dressed up and taut and waiting for me. Today, instead, she's swept her curls off her neck for the heat and she wears a long calico sundress, a thin chain of silver catching on the skin of her neck. She smiles. She looks quickened now, more living than not, and I wonder if the change has been me.

My mama stretches back in her chair, crosses her ankles, and sips her wine.

"I haven't been out here since the wedding," she says. "And before that, well, probably last Fourth of July."

"Really?"

"Yes, it was last Fourth of July. You were gone to school and Owen was here. Last summer."

The last time I was truly with Owen was in the parlor house, mimes on the back porch, and the glass, all the glass, and his kiss on my ear, a promise, but I haven't seen him since that day. He frightened me then, with the mimes. I remember being frightened then, and I remember all the things he's done that frightened me before then, in one way or another, frightened me myself, or in his stead. He used to have a bowie knife when we were in school and he would trim skin from the soles of his feet, from the beds of his fingernails. He used to drive fast and slam the brakes. He used to play dead. He used to say he'd go away and not come back, and I guess it's only now I believe this to be true.

I am so foolish to have thought of him the way I have, to have loved him the way I have, to send that feeling out there in the wild open spaces Owen travels, always moving, always in and out. He'd be here and I'd see him someplace else, Owen, the shadow of Owen, or his whistle, or his clean smell, all of them Owen to me, but in truth just reflections, pieces of him in two mirrors, a trick of light or heart. I thought there was some tie between us, but it was all me all along, and that stings now that he's gone again in ways it didn't when he was here. I almost feel jilted.

There are times I think I'm no more free of him than Kat.

She's here, up to the parlor house at the picnic. Miss Pauline tried to get her interested in other boys, even called Hale and Stanley McClain to come out to the farm, show her a good time, and they jumped at the chance. They probably thought Kat to be young and impressed with older boys, easily convinced to have a date with one or the other. But I saw all three earlier in the evening and Kat was just grilling them hard about Owen, wanting to know this and that, things they've done with him, things they haven't. I have to admit I felt sorry for Hale and Stanley, lag-eyed at a pretty young thing with only words of Owen on her tongue.

My mama reaches down to me and puts her hand on my shoulder.

"Come with me a minute," she says.

And she pushes herself out of her chair with my shoulder, takes my hand, and pulls me from the ground. We walk along the riverbank, not talking, my mama leading, and we walk in that fashion almost up to the highway. My mama still has no shoes, and she picks her path delicately through the kudzu and the pebbles and the coarse white sand as if she is a mountain lion or a pack horse, as if she is an animal used to finding its own way. She walks on the balls of her feet, the tips of her toes. She carries her arms outstretched, for balance.

We come upon a gravel drive, a service shoulder that dips below the highway and onto Punk's land, connecting back up with the highway a hundred yards down or so. It's an old place. It's a road that's not been used in years and years and years, and the kudzu has taken up in its gravel, woven through and around and over its edges. The vines are fast about luring in this land; inch by inch, stone by stone, they take it for their own.

"So this is the place," I say. "So this is where it happened."

My mama nods, steps out into the gravel, and studies the ground.

"It was there. Or over there," she says.

She sighs and folds her hands within themselves, turns her body slowly without moving her feet.

She says, "I don't know; there used to be a hole in the ground and some rock missing. I haven't been out here since you were born, Mavis. Not once in all those years. I guess I'm not one for a spot to stand and cry over something."

I keep thinking how I've been past this very stretch so many times, anytime I left or came back to Edisto, anytime I came out to the farm or swam in the river. I've lived beside this place my whole life, this road where my own father died, this place cured by fire and ash and kudzu. I just never knew what it was before.

I say, "I've been by here a thousand times, Mama, and I never, ever knew."

My mama comes over to me and pulls her arms around my waist, rests her head on my shoulder. She squeezes me so tight I am surprised, so tight my breath catches in my throat.

She says, "It's just a place, child. It's a place where something happened, and you can look around here all you want. You could've been looking here for years, but that man blew himself to kingdom come."

She leans back against her arms and smiles up at me. There are no tears in her eyes and her voice is strong and sure and true.

She says, "But you came out of it. You came almost like one of those birds, up from the ashes. Like one of those saplings from the forest fire. You're the thing to see, Mavis. You're the wonder."

❧

When we get back close to the parlor house, we can hear Punk calling to my mama and me from off the back deck. His words cross the distance, Punk's voice like no other man's.

"Elsbeth. Mavis. Shake your tail feathers, women. It's time for the light show."

My mama and I gather ourselves up and traipse around to the front side of the house. Files and files of vine stroke into the coming darkness, and there are children everywhere, white children and black children, dirty children barefoot and mostly naked catching fireflies. Men stand amongst each other with bottles of beer and women sit at the picnic tables Punk's set up, drinking last year's wine. I say hello to Tee, wave to someone's wife who still has her head, and make my way to where Punk sits ready to light some fuse.

"Pull up somethin' to set on, Mavis. I got a thing to ask you."

Punk calls Tee to take over the lighting of the fireworks and we step aside, find some lawn chairs with no kids in them.

"What do you know about this organic farming?" he says, and then he yells to Tee to not lean over those firework tubes.

I fold one arm beneath my head. "What'd you hear?"

"Les Shipley up the road got aphids in his peaches. Now, instead of spraying for 'em like any white man, he's crated in a whole fucking truckload of ladybug larvae, got the trailer parked up on the ridge ready to set them things to his orchard. Says he's waiting for just the right dark dusk to set them loose. Now why in sam hill would he do that?"

"Ladybugs eat aphids. They eat aphids and they told me up at Pickens Stock and Nursery if you irrigate and then set them out at dusk, they won't leave home. They don't like to be away from home after dark."

"Yeah, honey, but what about that? What do you think?"

I'm about to say I don't know, but I realize that I do. I think back on things Punk sent me through the mail up at school, articles and brochures he'd tuck in with a note and a twenty. He'd want me to stop by Ag Days in Chapel Hill and pick up stock samples for him, or run into Raleigh and look up a topographical map he had a passing interest in. And since I've been home, there's always something for me to read, to think on. It's not just facts to know, not just things I've been told anymore. I'm not picking information up like bread crumbs or backhand stories. Punk wants me to ponder and form opinion, pay out my education in more ways than one, and I can do that.

I tell him this: "Organic farming is still a new and coming thing in these parts, and it's not cheap. Say you get your ladybugs in there and if you've set them out right, they'll stay, sure. Or they might take over."

I pause, check his face, and he's with me.

"If they take over, you're back to the books to see what eats ladybugs, and your yield per acre goes in the shitter. It's a gamble, and when it comes to pesticides, you can afford to gamble. Not with your whole crop."

Punk smiles, smooths his hand 'cross the armrest of his lawn chair.

"Damn straight, Mavis. That's just what I told the man."

He sets a look on his face as if all is right in the world and he yells for Tee to let the tar outta them puppies. We sit together like two people who know what's going on and this is special. Punk's the kind of man who keeps the stories of things, their naming, and their details to himself. He believes in due course, due time, keeping people in the dark 'til the very last minute. He doesn't ask questions just to know the answer.

He says to me, "Where were you women this afternoon? I was calling you."

And I tell him about the service road and the kudzu and about how there was nothing to see, no sign that Wyman Jackson had ever been there.

He says, "Hell, he *ain't* there. Ain't one part of him in that ground. I figure on that boy like he's a spirit out of one of them foreign religions. I figure he's about everywhere."

We go to quiet. I think how my father might well be everywhere, like a spirit or part of the very air, and I think how I've come up in myself without his known presence, without even the where of him or the last place he was seen until now, and I've done just fine. It's as if I've been watched over. And then I realize my father is in Punk even, in how he's taken me to hand, shown and taught and provided for me in the most determined ways. I feel blessed to have Punk's sights about me and I wouldn't change that for anything. I wouldn't change it even to have Wyman Jackson here, and whole, and close.

Beside me, Punk watches his fireworks, ticks them off as they shower down around us: clustering bees, sky monkey, hovering swallow, silver, blue, and white, trident, wild geese, green, gold, something that fizzles, tiger soaring, fairy rain, red, red, red, whistling Jupiter, jasmine gun, chrysanthemum; he speaks these words into the lighting air and with each flash his face goes to solid, to liquid, and back again.

12

Morning brings coffee and biscuits at Punk's kitchen table, but he's left already for the farm. I've gotten used to his hours, rising before the sun and the two of us making the run to the vineyards in his truck, the early light enveloping, the very ground becoming opaline. It's a nice time in the morning, a hush time. I feel as though I must have done something wrong for him to have left me behind, like I'd forgotten an important date or slept in late, but it's not six A.M. It's as if I missed my bus.

Miss Pauline tells me, "Punk said you were cutting circles around yourself out at the farm, not enough for you to do 'til Sal and Hazel get back at the end of the week."

"Well, then, I guess I have the day off," I say, and Miss Pauline laughs.

"Don't get your swimming suit on yet, Mavis baby," she says. "I thought you could come straighten out the books at the store."

I finish my breakfast and go upstairs to get dressed in real clothes, good clothes instead of my boots and jeans, a silk blouse instead of a T-shirt. I put on makeup and some perfume of Hazel's she's left behind, perfume that smells like baby powder. I put on a pair of ivory stockings and high heels the color of chocolate. I think how this is nice to do every once in a while, fix yourself up for something like I did in that motel room coming home in June. It makes you expect good things from a day, sets a roil of prospect going through your insides, but I like that I don't get dressed this way all the time.

Miss Pauline calls from the bottom of the stairs. "My word, Mavis, don't you look pretty," she says, and I thank her.

We lock the front door of the house behind us and make our way up Sorghum to Main. Neighbors wave and gather their newspapers off their front porches, move their sprinklers over browning grass. Miss Pauline goes to work early, and most everybody else is still having breakfast at this hour.

She smiles and waves to more people on the street and I think how she knows about everybody in this town, probably knows everything that goes on, too, and I think that would be quite a thing to have at your fingertips. She keeps to herself, though, doesn't open her mouth unless someone's asked first, and when an old silver bus barrels up the street ahead of us I think of what I'd want to know from her.

"Miss Pauline, you ever hear tell of a little Asian woman coming through town? She would have gotten here about the same time I came home in June."

She wrinkles her forehead, squints her eyes up at the sun.

"I don't know. An Asian woman?"

"She rode the same bus as I did, got off at the Rexall's, and I haven't seen her around anywhere since then. It just seemed strange, her being here and me not seeing her."

"Oh, now that's because she disappeared. Yes, that woman was hired on to be Etta Shipley's cleaning girl and she got here at the beginning of summer just to up and disappear. Etta had paid her passage, bought her clothes, and everything."

"I can't imagine someone disappearing in Edisto. There's no place to go."

"Well, she did. You'd be surprised, Mavis. Stranger things have happened."

And I know she's right. Come to think of it, I know she's right because I saw that woman disappear, vanish from the sidewalk with her tear-tracked cheeks and her pillowcase full of God knows what. She was standing so painfully still beneath the Rexall's sign, and when I looked away for just a moment, she was gone. It was as if she'd been sucked into the ground or lifted into the sky, as if her papery bones had just caught the wind and been borne away.

Miss Pauline reaches her hand out and takes my arm, takes me back to the here-and-now.

"This is different from the times you used to come with me before you went away to school," she says. "You used to run late all the time, and I'd holler up the stairs for you to get a move on. You'd be hotter than a fish out of water, come scrambling down still spraying your hair or pulling up your stockings. We wouldn't speak for hours, like two people who hardly knew each other."

"Oh, yeah." I laugh. "I'm more used to mornings now."

"You're more used to yourself now, Mavis. It's a nice thing to see."

She holds my elbow and gives it a squeeze. "Yes, ma'am. Punk calls you a connoisseur of life these days. Nothing more, nothing less, he says."

"Really. A connoisseur of life. What a thing."

"Well, school was good for you. None of my own babies saw fit to go, and it would have changed them as surely as it changed you. They'd have come back home with big ideas they'd yet to plan quite through."

"You think I have big ideas?"

"Oh, Mavis baby, I count on it."

We tuck ourselves down the alleyway between Miss Pauline's Boutique and the Dixie Home Store. A connoisseur of life, as if life was a delicacy or a drink, a work of art. I like that. I like to hear the way other people think of me, the way I live, even as I don't do it on my own so much anymore. It's nice that even in Punk's house, even living with my family, they see me as different. I suppose it's what I've wanted all along.

I help Miss Pauline get the Boutique ready for customers, sweep out the dressing rooms and dust the front cases of scarves and jewelry and white gloves for church. When she unlocks the front doors, I head through the velvet curtains to the big desk and her books.

She's an excellent bookkeeper and her receipts are neat and filed, her ledgers complete for last month. I realize she didn't want me to work over her books so much as approve them, and I tell her she's a fine bookkeeper and she smiles. I notice she runs about a five-hundred-dollar account every month from Punk and I ask her about it.

"Oh, that's business," she says. "Punk has an account for the hired men to come down for coveralls and shoes for their little ones, whatever they need for clothes."

I know good and well that those men don't spend a hundred dollars apiece a month on clothes, but I can see how the money helps her through tight spots, tight times like the summer months and January. I realize Punk has his ways with her, too, helping her out even as she doesn't understand it that way.

For the rest of the morning I place her orders to Hanes and Polly Flinders, help a few customers when the front gets busy. I check the loss projections from last quarter, and they're low, but I start an inventory audit anyway. By noon, I'm almost finished.

With the mail for the Boutique there's another box I'd sent home after graduation. It has a postmark from Nantucket, Massachusetts, and RETURN TO SENDER stamped across the top. This I don't understand, because I'm the sender and the sender sent this box from Boone. But, then, I'm the sender and this box was returned to me. This makes me think the mail might be personal rather than locational, and I smile as I take the box into the back room to open it.

Inside are all my pictures from college, all my postcards and souvenirs from my trips. There's a squash blossom necklace from Texarkana, some Mexican jumping beans, and a picture of sunset over the Rio Grande. On the back I've written a note to myself: *Rain in Texas — you need a place you've never been.*

I remember that trip, the dry vineyards there and the rain on the dry, dry road and how it reminded me of Edisto and of Harris in almost inverse ways. It reminded me of people and things because it was unlike those people and things.

"Miss Pauline," I yell from the back, and she pokes her head through the velvet curtain.

"Do you think I could take tomorrow off, take a quick trip? I could be home for Punk on Wednesday."

She smiles. "Sure, Mavis. That'd be fine."

After Miss Pauline closes up, I walk to Burdine's Diner for a Key lime pie. It's the best Key lime pie in the state and Punk has quite a weakness for it. I figure it might ease my time off a little, tickle his sweet tooth and make him smile.

I push open the front door and Evelyn Metz is sitting in the back booth with a cup of coffee. I haven't seen her since the wedding, and she looks blue around the eyes, tired and disheveled, her hair pulled loose of her braid. She smiles when she sees me, signals the waitress for another cup.

"How's it going?" I say, sliding in across from her.

"Up and down, sugar. Like a top."

The waitress brings my coffee and she knows Evelyn and they chat a bit. She touches Evelyn's shoulder as she walks away.

"Look, I've been meaning to see you, Mavis. I'm wanting to know, I guess, wondering . . ." She trails quiet, her eyes slipping over my head, slipping out of focus.

I put down my cup, put my hands on the tabletop, but she stares around me still and her voice comes from someplace far off.

"You know, sugar, he used to dream about the desert. He'd dream about sandhills like blacktop in August. He'd talk about being so thirsty you'd think in water, like some people think in words or pictures or playing cards. He'd go all day without a sip to drink, just to see what it'd be like. Some nights he'd wake up jabbering away in Arab. Even I could tell he didn't know what he was talking about."

She stops and I can see her shake herself from the inside, sip her coffee. I know nothing about them really, what she was to Owen, what he said to her when no one was around. I don't know their state of fancy, their strings, their fixes, but I can't help the ache in my chest listening to her like this.

"I haven't heard from him, Evelyn," I say softly.

She leans back in the booth and takes her coffee with her, smiles a slow smile.

"You know what's funny? I'm glad you haven't. I'd almost rather he be dead than call you before me."

"I know he's not dead."

"Oh, he's not dead. He's not dead and I know he's been turning this trick his whole life, and he'll do it again. This is what I do know."

"Do you love him?" I ask.

She reaches into her purse and pulls out a cigarette, rolls it between her fingers, and the tendons in her hands ripple and tense. I shouldn't ask. I don't really want to know. Somehow love would change the way I look at Evelyn, at Owen too. It would make them soft somewhere.

"Don't answer that, don't bother. It's none of my business," I say.

She smiles and lights her cigarette, french-inhales a long loose drag. She sweeps her hair from her face, draws one knee up to prop her elbow.

"I suppose I could ask you the same, Miss Mavis."

"Do I love Owen?"

"Yeah."

She studies me through her eyebrows, tends her face into something like a smile, an expression vaguely related to dare. I think how loving Owen is like loving a gust of wind, something you hear coming and going, something that wraps around you and disappears, something that has no handles, no haft, no place to have in hand.

"Oh, Evelyn," I say, "you couldn't be further from the truth of it."

She smiles true now, shakes her head.

"I can't say I believe you, Mavis. I've seen the two of you, and there's a tune between you. I knew you in high school, and you thought he hung the moon. Now that's the God's truth."

"That is the truth."

"That's all I'm saying."

"But you're wrong now. You are so wrong now," I say. "I've changed about him; he's more than I can bear. Less too. It's as if he doesn't even apply to mortal words like love."

"Girl, there's not so much difference in thinking he's hung the moon and thinking he's hung it wrong."

She looks away from me and exhales, the smoke filtering away in the thin sunlight.

She says, "Last year Owen was in a gas station near Columbia and some collector was looking for a late-model Camaro. Well, I used to drive one in high school, but it was on its last legs even then, six years ago, and up until last summer it sat in my back lawn on blocks. I hadn't turned the motor over since graduation."

She pauses and draws off her smoke, raises an eyebrow at me.

"Owen sold that car for two thousand cash, sight unseen. Nobody could have made that hunk of junk sound better. We took the money and drove to Myrtle Beach for the weekend and stayed at the Xanadu Hotel. Owen bought me a pair of red suede shoes and a dress that fit like butter and we went dancing 'til four in the morning, drinking champagne and eating strawberries. It was the best time."

"Now that's hanging the moon," I tell her.

"Maybe so. Maybe so, but it was my money. It was what I wanted to do with it. I don't expect nothing more from him, and that's the difference between you and me."

"He's not for me, Evelyn. I know that."

And even as I say this, I think what an outrageous distinction to make. The difference is clear in Owen and me, even for all our curious affections and all our nearnesses, even for the way I did and still do love him. But then I realize such a line is not part of the way Evelyn thinks about this world and I remember her toes on my arm the night Owen took us to the remains of the carnival and I remember her saying how it's all skin, and skin is to be touched. Owen and I as lovers is not out of the question for her, and I'm glad I've cleared the air between us.

She smiles again and the waitress comes 'round with a fresh pot of coffee, fills us both. Evelyn pours three packs of sugar in her cup. This conversation has passed between us so calmly and she's said things that should get my skin to prickle, get me all worked up. But they haven't, and maybe that's because she's said the things I've been thinking of late and answering to her is like answering to myself. It's different to be with this woman. She's not quite a friend, but somehow closer to me than anyone I call a friend, closer to the parts of me I keep quiet.

"I've got an idea," I say. "You want to drive up to Boone with me tonight, go and see a friend of mine?"

"Oh, honey, that's a plan. That's a good idea, Mavis. Let's get out for a while."

"Okay," I say. "Okay."

I reach across the table and pat her hand. She turns palm up and takes my hand in hers and we are at that table in the light of day, holding hands like two friends, two women finishing a conversation.

Punk, Miss Pauline, and my mama are drinking coffee when I get home, dinner dishes pushed away. I set the Key lime pie on the table, get some plates from the cupboard.

"Hear you're heading out on a trip," my mama says, raising her eyebrows.

"Actually, Mama, I was just coming in to see what you thought about that."

I bend down and kiss her cheek, smile real pretty at her, and she laughs.

"You're your own lady now, don't have to ask my permission. Going to see that boy Harris?"

Punk clears his throat loudly, frowns up at me when I nod.

"I don't think that's right, Mavis," he says, dipping a finger into the pie's cream. "You cavorting around with some boy, staying alone with him for a night. It's just not fitting, not fitting at all."

"Evelyn Metz is coming along."

"Now is that supposed to make me feel better or worse? Good Lord, you two just go on and get a hotel room, stay the night there."

He lays a hundred-dollar bill on the kitchen table, checks himself, and covers it with his hand.

"You watch yourself now, girl," he says, reaching up and taking my chin in his thick fingers. "I don't want you ending up like that other one upstairs, gone stupid over a boy not worth it."

"That's my son, Mr. Punk," Miss Pauline says. "You watch your mouth."

"Don't worry. I'm not going stupid," I say.

"Okay," he says. "Okay then." He slides the money 'cross the table top and pats my hand.

I take the back stairs, full happy to be going away, and I don't think it's stupid. Driving in the night to Boone, I can't wait to be there of a sudden, that place for all its coolness and mountains. And there's Harris, too. I get all fleshed to think of the things we've done and these are things I haven't thought of for a while, motions that had worn away from us and now list back inside my fingertips and the ends of my hair like nerves.

My hands still clutch Punk's money and I realize he did not give me a hundred-dollar bill, but that there were two more hiding under it. I think how hard it must be for Punk to keep up with himself.

I pass Owen's bedroom at the end of the hall and Kat leans in the doorway, her head against the jamb. She's found one of Owen's black T-shirts from the Winston Cup series, letters 'cross the front in red.

"You going somewhere, Mavis?" she asks, all weak and listless.

"Yeah," I say. And then, "You want to come along?"

I have no idea why I'm asking, no idea at all. My head is someplace else altogether. It's an exciting thing, going on a trip to see your lover, cutting out of work and on the road. I'm thinking in wavy lines, yellow curves, and green lights. I'm thinking of my own stir, the things swelling and welling in me, right now. Still, I try to spread it out. I give invitations when I don't want to.

Kat chews on her lower lip, thinking. "I don't know," she says. "Where are you going to?"

"Up to North Carolina. Boone, near the mountains. Evelyn Metz is driving."

"Let me think. When are you leaving?"

"As soon as I can pack," I say.

"All right. Okay, I'll get my things."

She smiles and shuts the door and I think how she'll choose amongst her black clothes and Owen's blue jeans, how she'll not even bring a hairbrush otherwise. Kat's kept herself real plainly since the wedding. Days will come and go without her seeing a bar of soap.

Evelyn and Kat, all they have in common is Owen and now my trip to Boone. But three women together is never a good idea. It's like three witches, or three's a crowd, three women on the road to the mountains, these are things that will not work out for the best. This is stupid, this is what Punk should have worried about. It's as testable as long division; three women are always going to come upon trouble.

"Kat," I say through the door.

She pulls it open, a pair of Owen's jeans in her hands.

"Kat, listen. You can't be talking about Owen, now. He and Evelyn had this thing, and, well, you just better not bring him up. Understand?"

I'm looking at my fingernails, trying to be nonchalant and all, but when she says, sure, whatever, I catch her eyes.

"Okay," I say.

"Okay."

I head down the hall to my bedroom and pull a canvas bag from my closet. I pack enough for a weekend: a bikini and a long strappy negligee, shorts and halter tops and jeans. I pack a fancy dress, a pair of cowboy boots, and some panties. I pack towels, a stadium blanket, and the condoms from my jewelry box. It will be late when we get to Boone, and maybe I'll just be still and watch Harris sleep for a while. Get a beer from his fridge, wander through his apartment, and wait for him to wake and find me there, like a night crawler, a thief, or a vision.

Evelyn's Pinto honks from the driveway and Kat and I are ready. We kiss everyone goodbye and Miss Pauline whispers to me, tells me to cheer Kat up, get her back on her feet. She follows me out to the car and tucks three pieces of pie in a paper sack under my arm, as if it will do the trick.

For a single moment, I want to turn around and go back inside. I glance over my shoulder and I can see my mama still sitting at the kitchen table, laughing at some small thing Punk's said to her and only her, and waving to us like we'll be back in ten minutes or a year, it doesn't much matter. And right here, Miss Pauline. I take her in my arms again and I think of our walk this morning, the feel of her hand tucked in the crook of my arm, the sun on her face and her smile on me as if she was proud and pleased with me to no end. I have the feeling this is where I fit, amongst these women, and no matter where I go, no place will feel this sure.

So I do get in Evelyn's car and we head right out of town and up the highway, because I know I can come back to that kitchen in ten minutes or ten years and I will always feel to home.

I start to talking to Evelyn and Kat, because I feel like talk and their silence between each other is hard to listen to, and also because I feel favored and fortunate and part of a constellation. I feel big-hearted, magnanimous. I tell Kat she will love Boone because it is a town of dogs. I tell her the dogs are welcome in the bars, in the restaurants, in the dressing rooms of the shops if that's what you want, and all of them are friendly and none of them wear leashes.

"Dogs," she says, and I can't tell if she smiles or not.

So I tell Evelyn about Hobson's Knob, and how that mountaintop is sweet and undeveloped and you can see all of Boone from its overlook. I tell her about the hang gliders and how they poured a concrete runway in the crest of the mountain to drift out and into the valley when the air was just right, or the fall leaves just breathtaking enough, and how at least once a year somebody catches a draft in the wrong direction and gets dashed back into the mountainside.

"Jesus Christ, Mavis, do they die?" she says. "That's the awfulest thing I've ever heard."

So I go quiet. I always thought it was sort of a romantic thing about Boone, people getting lost forever in the mountains and the trees and the scenery, giving their lives over to a pretty view of the world. Apparently, I am the only one to think this way. Harris had plenty to say about Hobson's Knob in the falltimes himself. He'd tell me exactly why and how those gliders missed their marks in the air, telling more about velocity and wind speed than drama or beauty. I am glad now to be going to him in the heat of July, when his dissenting mind is most at rest, and when he will be happy to see me and just fine to let me go.

I hum a tune I can hear my mama singing, something about pine trees and lovers in Vermont and I try to think of something bright and cheerful, even if I just keep it to myself.

By the time we're past Columbia, I can see that nobody's going to be cheered up and I almost wish I'd come alone. Evelyn's scowled at me twice and Kat's the only one talking now and she's forgotten if she ever knew what I told her in Punk's house about not mentioning Owen. She just babbles on in the back seat, words coming to her like *lovely, adorable, cute,* words like *us* and *we.* She talks about how wonderful Owen is, how much she misses him, and when she says someday she'd like to marry a man like that, we are a hundred miles from home and Evelyn blows up.

"I don't know if you're aware, Kat, but Owen and I've been seeing each other for quite a while."

"Yeah, well . . ."

"Oh, yes. And I can guarantee whatever passed between the two of you was but a fleeting thing. Nothing but a pass in the grass."

This shuts Kat up for a minute and I watch out the window at the blackness going by. This is none of my business, none at all, and I will not get involved. I'm not even going to pass around some Key lime pie. Five hours and we'll be there, four with the way Evelyn's driving, and we'll all be out of the car. We can go our separate ways.

Then Kat says, "So I think I have a problem."

"You do, missy," Evelyn snaps.

"No, I really think I have a problem," and she starts to cry, caving into great heaving sobs, real tears. Her mascara runs black down her cheeks and she doesn't try to wipe it away, her breath in tremors, mewling like a gut-shot dog.

I look to Evelyn and I can see her hands tighten, knuckles white on the wheel.

"What's the matter now?" she says. "You wet your pants or something?"

Evelyn's voice is edged and hot, but Kat's really shaken, she's gotten herself all worked up. Maybe it's a real thing or maybe it's something she's prepared for the attention, but she's crying hard. She's young for eighteen. She's led a much different life from Evelyn or myself. I dig in the glove box for a Kleenex, a napkin, or something. I turn in my seat and hand Kat a dishrag, all I can find.

"Calm down," I say. "Calm down and wipe your face."

"I can't."

Evelyn starts to breathe through her nose, heavy bursts of breath like a wild horse, or a kettle run over.

She whispers to herself.

She whispers, "She's pregnant."

She slams on the brakes, and we must have been going over seventy, because the car fishtails and spins across the highway to the far shoulder, head-on to the southbound lane. She rests her head on the steering wheel, her eyes closed.

"She's pregnant," Evelyn says.

Kat doesn't say anything.

"She's fucking pregnant." Evelyn is yelling now, and her voice splits in my ears.

"Yes. Yes, yes."

Kat starts to whimper again and Evelyn throws open the door, shakes the whole car when she slams it shut.

"Oh shit," I say.

Oh shit. Oh Owen. Oh God.

Kat starts to mumble in the back seat, her voice thin and cracking. "I don't know. I mean, I'm not sure yet, but I could be. I feel like I could be, I feel different. I'm late and I feel different."

Her hands draw up to cover her face and she lies down in the back seat, her bare feet pressed against the passenger window.

She says, "I feel different."

She runs her hands over her abdomen, slides them underneath her T-shirt, and strokes her belly. She holds herself and weeps and weeps.

"I'm going to get Evelyn, I'm going to go see if she's okay and then we'll figure out what to do," I tell her.

It's all I can think to say. I have no idea how to soothe Kat, no words to fill in here. I'm witness to the truth of her, the fact of her and Owen, and I've seen her ways from start to finish. I've let it all play out before me. Now I have to find the solution, give the answer, and I don't have a clue.

"Don't worry," I say, as if this will tide her over.

I push open the car door.

Evelyn sits beside the right front tire, her back propped up against it, her toes in the road. I crouch beside her and I want to hold her hand, I want to touch her arm. I want to tell her not to worry either, but I don't think she'd believe me. I wonder why I know these things for her and not for Kat.

Evelyn hands me her cigarette, pulls her feet up, and a car blares past, horn and rush of wind.

She says, "I took a girlfriend of mine into Columbia last year to get something like this taken care of. I took her to a clinic and there were crowds outside, waving bottles and carrying signs, pushing papers in our faces."

I think this could be me, this could all be me.

I could be young and pregnant. I could be angry and sad on the side of the highway. I could have been aborted. All these chances have come into my life and they might've just as easily bloomed out the other end, at any moment. I feel on the edges of myself, someplace groundless and thin like the highest branches of a tree. There are times in your life when you step outside the here and now, and look back in from far away, through a lens, or a window, a pane of glass, a sheet of paper. This is that time, that moment.

Evelyn tells me how she and this girlfriend got inside the clinic, the girlfriend shaking so hard she couldn't hold a pen, hold a cigarette, hold her breakfast. So Evelyn filled out the forms for her. She tells me how, under religion, they laughed and wrote down "Catholic, lapsed." They laughed and wrote that down and it was funny.

She reaches into her jacket pocket and pulls out another cigarette, lights it off the butt in my hand.

I say, "She's not sure, Evelyn. She doesn't know for certain."

Evelyn looks me full in the face and I can see her eyes wide, her jaw set up tight. An eighteen-wheeler peels into the other lane to avoid us; I can hear him lay on his horn but I don't look away from her. I want her to get back in the car, I want to think this out. I want the three of us to say something decisive, something determining, and to never mention this night, this moment on the side of Highway 321, again.

Evelyn tells me about sitting in the waiting room of the clinic in Columbia and a family of people from India waiting along with her and her friend, two little kids with them. There was a young married couple, and a woman who sat next to them and cried for three whole hours.

"Three hours, and not like this; that woman wept," she says. "Mavis, I'm telling you, I will not do that again."

"Maybe you won't have to," I say. "Maybe it will never come to that."

"But it could and that's the point. This little girl, she doesn't know what she wants. What if that's her choice, she decides to go to a clinic, and where's Owen? What's she gonna do, tell her daddy?"

I had not thought about that and I remember Punk saying, just tonight, just at the dinner table, about Kat going stupid over Owen, and now this whole thing could be taking that road. This would shock the deal between Punk and Sal right out of the water, and I saw what Punk did when he was just thinking about how that might could happen and he was grave and dangerous. This not just between Kat and Evelyn and Owen, but now it affects Punk and Miss Pauline too, myself and even Harris. It would be as if Harris was right about my family, all of us crazy and stupid over men. I feel my stomach sink to bone.

"She might not be pregnant, Evelyn. We might not tell anybody."

I say this as though it's one thing to seize upon in a great course of things whipping by and I can only hope it sounds reasonable.

"She's just a kid, Mavis," Evelyn says. "She doesn't know him. She's just a kid, eighteen or so."

"It might be nothing."

"Yeah," she says. "Yeah, it might be nothing at all."

13

We drive to a twenty-four-hour place near King's Mountain for coffee and it's nearly two A.M., the place stark empty except for the waitresses. Evelyn is quiet and somehow she looks keen, wise like stone, wise like flame and gnarl. I'm amazed she's so composed in this face, that she's not dissolving, weeping and fitting. Some women just don't do that.

The waitress comes and Evelyn and I order coffee, Kat a blue cheese omelette and root beer. Kat pulls a compact mirror out of her purse, occupies herself with cleaning up her face. She dips the edge of her napkin in her water glass and daubs at her streaking mascara, pulls at her underlid and inspects the whites of her eyes gone veiny with tears.

"What are you planning to do?" Evelyn asks her.

"I . . . I'm not sure yet."

"But you have to be sure. You need to be sure."

Evelyn stares at her, but Kat won't look up from her compact mirror, won't look Evelyn in the eyes. I think this could get nasty, Evelyn hot and caustic, Kat sniffles and woe. I try to say something with resolution, try to smooth things out. There's always one in three who has to take this on, always someone keeping grace among women, like honor among cutthroats.

"Okay," I say. "Okay, we'll get a pregnancy test," and Kat starts to cry all over again.

I think of how Harris told me the word *hysterical* stems from the Latin for uterus, how hysteria was a woman's disease in the nineteenth century, and how it was thought to be the travel of the womb about the body. I think, how appropriate, how true right now.

I cover Kat's hand with mine, I tell her it will be okay, that pregnancy tests are nothing painful, but I've never taken one. Evelyn's never taken one either, but we go on and tell her what to expect. I remember that she grew up without a mother, and I wonder just how mysterious this all seems to her. Evelyn and I, we make things up to tell her, and they sound good and simple: pee in a cup and then you know. But she has so many questions about results and time and contact we can't answer, I'm amazed at how little we know about our insides, our workings and timings, all three of us sitting here not knowing.

But all three of us, carrying this beginning inside of ourselves that defies explanation and description, this part of us that's wise and prehistoric like light or ice. It's the prime number, the alphabet, yellow, blue, and red. How wonderful, women like elements, indivisible and multiplying.

The waitress brings our coffee, Kat's food, and she smiles as if she knows us from somewhere. She touches Evelyn's shoulder as she walks away, but Evelyn hardly notices. It's as if she has a connection with waitresses, some joining they recognize immediately in one another, a pact sealed with a touch on the shoulder. I don't know what to make of this, and I think I'm the only one who's trying.

Kat's wiping her tears, digging in with her knife and fork. She looks out the window, looks into her plate, pretends we're not even here. She eats as if she were alone. I watch her for a while, bewildered. I can't judge her swings, her highs and lows, her tears and smiles and tears again. I can't tell when Kat's really okay and I wonder if I knew her better, if that would make a difference.

Evelyn says, "I know the way luck runs. I know how luck

changes and it happens just like this, sittin' in a diner at two in the morning."

She says this as if it's an answer to someone, and we both know she's been carrying on a conversation in her head, talking for the three of us.

Evelyn looks across her coffee cup at Kat, but she's not noticed, not paused in her eating. She says she doesn't know what to do. She says she doesn't know if she's pregnant. She thinks Evelyn and I will work it out, fix things up for her, and she can pretend that nothing's going on, because soon nothing will be.

I push up from the table in a clatter of silverware, walk right out the door. There's an all-night convenience store across the highway and I bet they sell tests, Fact Plus or First Alert or something, a simple yes-or-no test, a pee-in-the-cup test. It's stupid to wait around on this, to try and have a vacation with such a weight on all our minds, tension tight in us like drums.

In the Handy Pantry, the woman behind the counter has tattoos on both hands, her fingers spelling out LOVE and HATE. She puts the test in a bag and smiles at me.

She says, "Oh, sweetheart, last time a body glowed like you, she was three months along."

I'm watching her hands as she says this, cat crossing rose, dagger to the wrist and a man's name inside a heart, her fingernails curled like talons on the paper bag. She smiles at me with the dragon on her pinky. This is my life in a Handy Pantry on the side of King's Mountain. She's talking to me. She thinks I'm the one.

I try to, want to say it isn't for me. I want to say this is not mine, I am still child enough for myself, but all I get out is a strange twisting in my face.

She shrugs her shoulders.

"Yeah. Well, like I said, it's in the glow that you know."

When I get back to the diner Evelyn is paying the check and talking with our waitress at the register. I toss the bag on the table in front of Kat and slide into the booth across from her and look at her closely. It's in the glow that you know. Kat's eyes are rimmed red and dark. She keeps checking her face in her compact mirror and running her fingers down her blood-bright cheeks, fretting at her forehead. She looks hopeless, like a levee, surge coming on to her fast and hard, and she's just found out she's lined with glass.

"I should do this now? Right now?" she asks.

"It says on the box, 'Administer any time of the day.' Now is as good as ever."

I know I sound cold, I can hear it in my voice. I can't help myself. It's in the glow that you know.

"Will you come with me?"

I look to Evelyn at the register. I don't want to be alone with Kat. I don't want to hear any more than I already have, know more than I do right now. I raise my hand to call Evelyn over.

"No," Kat says. "Just you."

She says it with those eyes, big and pooling, and I think how easy it would be to not like her for her weaknesses, but instead we walk to the back of the diner to the bathroom.

She dumps the contents of the test box onto the vanity. There's a little vial, a packet with a Handy Wipe, another with a tablet, some folded-up directions on tissue paper.

"This is really gross," she says, taking the vial from the counter. "This is way too small."

"Just get it over with, Kat."

She goes into the stall and closes the door. The vial *is* small and I'm not sure how she'll keep from peeing on her hands.

"Nothing's happening," she says.

"Nothing happens 'til you do the dropper thing."

"No, I mean nothing's happening. I can't pee."

She starts laughing, high-pitched laughing, and she can't stop. I push open the stall and she's doubled over on the pot, holding her stomach.

"I can't believe this. I can't pee."

It's funny, her squatting here, on this toilet, in this diner, in the middle of nowhere. There are tears running down my face, too. It's late in the evening and I'm so tired I'm punchy, giggles welling up in me so fast. The things we do, silly, silly things in the middle of the night.

"Coffee," I say. "You need some coffee."

I push open the bathroom door and Evelyn's still at the counter, talking. I go to her, ask the waitress for some coffee, and wipe my face with a napkin.

"Are you okay?" Evelyn says.

"Yeah, sure."

"What is it then?"

"She can't pee in the little cup."

"Good God, she can't do a damn thing by herself."

Evelyn is hotter than a viper in a stew pot. She takes the coffee from the waitress and huffs back to the bathroom, but I've had enough. I'm staying right here, and eventually we'll have to leave this diner. Eventually, I'll get where I'm going. This trip has come down to a few hours with Harris between his work and when I have to be back to Edisto, and strangely I don't mind. It seems the trip was what I wanted, the travel and the being in old spaces. Tomorrow, we'll all go to the Faire, and that will be something, I'm sure.

I flop onto a stool at the counter and try to stop giggling like a child. I take a breath and strain runs out of me like something artesian, coursing of its own accord. I'm left like skin with no bones. I rest my chin on the backs of my hands, folded on the counter.

The waitress wipes the space in front of me with a dishrag. She's got bottle-red hair and her name tag says Angeline. I think of a country-and-western song I know: *Angeline, Angeline, darker nights I've never seen.* I can't remember what the song's about, but it runs through my head as I watch her cleaning up.

She asks if everything is okay.

"Yeah," I say. "One of those nights."

"Your friend, the little one, she knocked up?"

"She might be."

Angeline looks back to the bathroom door as if she's studying it, sees through it, sees Kat in it.

"Nah," she says. "She don't look the type."

It's now Evelyn throws open the bathroom door, the test box in one hand and the vial in the other. She throws them both at me.

"That little cunt," she says. "That fucking cunt."

"Evelyn. There's pee in here."

I catch the vial like it's a raw egg and set it lightly on the stool beside me. I'm giggling again, but one look at Evelyn's face and I go stone cold.

"She wasn't pregnant, she knew she wasn't. She wanted me to know the chance was there, she wanted to make sure I knew . . . well, goddamn, like she's the first lily in May."

"Now. Now, now."

I smooth my hands down Evelyn's arms and her flesh moves and crawls beneath my fingers, drives of its own volition. She is angry like a house afire, like something monstrous has grown inside her to get out, solely to release itself upon this roadside diner at three in the morning. It's scary, seeing a body set upon itself this way.

"I could string her up with my bare hands. It wouldn't take a breath."

"Now. Evelyn."

"I could. Right now, I swear to God, I could. They tell you that's what boys do when they get riled up and that's a boy's job and all, beating the tar out of somebody, but that's bullshit. I could do it. It wouldn't take a breath."

Angeline comes out from behind the counter. She moves between Evelyn and me, slips herself beneath my arms, and whispers to Evelyn. She takes her wrist in both her hands and with great force she pulls Evelyn to her face, nose to nose.

"Get hold on yourself, darlin'," she says.

She whispers low to Evelyn, whispers things I cannot hear, cannot understand, soft sweet things that sound as if they come from inside a flower, words formed in a shallow pool or a dish of cream. Behind her back, Angeline shoos me on to someplace else.

In the back of the diner I push open the bathroom door and there is no Kat, no sound coming from inside. I push open the stall and she is doubled over, clutching her knees to herself, she is trembling and rocking. No tears now, just pitching back and forth, back and forth, her hair sticking 'round her cheeks and neck, clinging to her lips. I think of the Asian woman disappeared in Edisto and how she was just the opposite on that bus from Boone, all tears and no motion, no wrack to her pain. For the first time all night, I feel truly sorry for Kat.

"Come on," I say, taking her arm. "Come on."

I lead her out to Evelyn's Pinto and sit her in the front seat. I stroke her hand, her hair back off her face. I tell her it will be okay. I comfort her the way I should have before, and she closes her eyes and rests her head on the dashboard.

"Oh, Mavis," she says.

"Well, now. It seems everything's okay. It will be okay."

"Oh, Mavis, I am so dumb sometimes."

"Yeah. You sure are."

It is now that Evelyn drifts out of the diner and in seconds she's got the car started and a cigarette lit. She draws long off her smoke and looks upon Kat and me, looks down and through and behind the thin blue fume and the night air cool, Kat propped in the front seat and me in the open car door. I feel like a doe in the headlights, frozen on the spot and fascinated by something bent on running me down.

Evelyn says, "Get a move on, ladies. We got someplace else to be."

She smiles.

I climb in behind the driver's seat and we get back on Highway 321, headed north. The car is dead quiet except for Evelyn, who hums a tune under her breath, smiling to herself. She passes me a paper sack, chicken salad sandwiches and slaw, big deli pickles Angeline packed for us. I think we have enough food now to feed a whole family, and how strange to consider the three of us that way.

Angeline, Angeline, darker nights I've never seen, I don't love these East Texas pines.

I stretch out in the back seat, rest my head on my canvas bag, the paper sack on my stomach. The road is empty, the back seat cool vinyl. In minutes I'm asleep, lulled by the motion and the stillness of our passage.

And then Evelyn is waking me at the Boone exit for directions, nudging my shoulder lightly with her fingers. It's morning and we're almost there. She whispers, and I sit up to find Kat asleep too, bridged 'cross the center console, her head in Evelyn's lap.

I whisper, "Evelyn, what all did Angeline tell you?"

"She told me about the family of women."

"Family of women?"

"Yeah, some all half-baked shit like that, but it was the

chicken salad that brightened me up. Even the family of women got to eat sometimes."

She smiles and I can see she really has brightened up, and if I'd known chicken salad would've done the trick I might have brought my own in gallon tubs from Edisto.

Evelyn says, "In fact, pass that bag on up here and I'll take me a sandwich right now."

14

~~~~~~~~~~~~~~ When Harris and I met, he'd just moved into this apartment a couple of blocks from campus, and it's a lodge of a building with unwaxed pine floors and high ceilings that've been tamped down with fiber glass tiles. The rooms are tall and breezy in the winter, cool in the summer, the way a home is supposed to be. Before he lived here, he had another apartment up on the mountain and a roommate who kept his dead girlfriend's sneakers in their refrigerator, and this roommate also had his dead girlfriend's car keys, her prom corsage, feathers from birds she had owned, and a pair of her pantyhose. He kept a little shrine of these things beside the television set and at the end he would talk to the shrine while he watched TV. Harris didn't live with him long, only so many times he could explain such a thing and not sound peculiar himself.

He moved into this apartment when two college girls moved out. They'd painted every room a different color, fresh coats of sea green and tallow, pale purple, red and yellow.

Harris says, "I have no luck with apartments, no good sense about them. I never want to hang my posters on the walls. I leave things in boxes in my closet. It's enough to make my head ache."

But I liked his place when I was in Boone, I liked to wake up in the bed, nap on the sofa, drink beer on the windowsill in the summertime when everybody else was gone home from school. It was in the summertime when the ice cream truck would come around, late in the night, and all the kids long asleep; that truck would list down Harris's street with its bells going like a carousel. That was a fine thing, come midnight, to have a Sno-Cone. This is a fine place, and I liked it because I lived here most of the time, with Harris.

Evelyn, Kat, and I let ourselves in the front door with my key and I know Harris won't be home. It's early morning, and down the long hall I can smell the coffee burning out in its pot, hear the shower head dripping in the bath, and he's already gone. I don't even call his name.

"This is it," I say, setting my bag at my feet.

This is where I spent most of my nights the last few years and most of my afternoons and mornings too. Just inside the hallway to the right, there is a broad arch leading to Harris's den, with French doors to a balcony and floor-to-ceiling windows and so much light fallen in panes on the floors, the furniture reflected in the TV screen and this room is the color of fair skin and it's my favorite.

Kat pushes past me inside. She's all agitated 'cause we woke her up, pouty in her eyes, sitting low in her jeans. She crosses one heel over the other and torts around, looking, looking.

"Where the hell's the pee pot, Mavis? I'm about to burst."

She sounds like Evelyn, just the way she says that, the way she gets short and snappy and twanging in her voice. I think how Kat tries on words, ways of being, and I wonder if it's a form of admiration that Evelyn's her aim now. That's the difference between younger women and older women. A younger woman talks, tests out, does everything in front of the world. Older women hold more silent with themselves. They change, but they're quiet about it. I think I'm somewhere in between.

Evelyn nudges my hand and rolls her eyes at Kat. She sees it, too, and maybe she is flattered. They seem better, temperate after last night. They're together now out of necessity, like three-legged racers. They've played out their secrets and that alone trusses them up in each other and makes for easier company. It's as if they've seen each other naked and they know that about each other, or they've been on a long trip and mixed up their underwear.

I wave Kat down the hall, the bathroom small and out of the way like a coat closet. I think to tell her the light in there is broken, that it's been that way for months. It's a bare light bulb by the vanity mirror with a pull chain, but when you pull the chain nothing happens and Harris has yet to tell his landlord about it. I like that too about this apartment. I used to take long baths with only a candle to see by, with the walls soft as taffy coming 'round me and the water dark in the low lights. That was at night, though, and another time. I feel feeble with sentiment, weak about my tendons and bones as if I've come disconnected somewhere.

I don't tell Kat about the light. It's daytime and she won't need it anyhow.

I turn to take Evelyn's bag, Evelyn's arm. She drove all night to get me here and I want to show her this place, show her what's important about it. She might like it, too, might see the things I see to be of value without the memories, think this place wonderful without romance to tie her to it. There's a safe in Harris's bedroom that doesn't open and a dumbwaiter in the kitchen, a laundry chute that's been nailed shut with one tattered shirt cuff caught outside the drawer, monogramed with four initials.

I imagine Evelyn knows me right now, knows what I want her to see without my showing. I like that thought. I hold that thought and lead her 'cross the threshold.

"Lord, girl," she says. "Your man lives here? It's about as manly as a baby's butt."

"Come on, Evelyn."

"No, honest, did he do all this himself, or was it a ready-made candy shop?"

"Oh, Evelyn, please look around."

Sometimes I expect so much from people and I suppose it's not fair. I expect Evelyn to know this place, and me, instantly by sight, smell, and touch, and hardly anybody takes in things like that, by osmosis. Hardly anybody is like me. The great leaps I take inside my mind when no one else is looking, it's a wonder I keep up at all.

Evelyn wanders through the big front room. She takes things in her hands and smells them, skates her fingertips across the furniture tops. She flips the light switch on and off, on and off.

"Look at this," I tell her.

I take Evelyn into Harris's bedroom, and his bows hang on the wall. Harris is an archer. It's what he knew as a child, what his father did and knew as a child, what he'll teach his own children. He can hunt and he's shot deer and pheasant, running things and flying things. He knows the history of bows, the Zen of archery. He knows how to nock an arrow, aim and release between heartbeats.

He says, "It's like poetry or music. It's a study. I could write my thesis on this."

He's got a longbow he uses at the Faire, two compounds, and a recurve of his father's, wood arrows of pine, cedar, rose, and tamarisk. The recurve is the finest, handmade by someone in Arizona. I tell Evelyn how this bow holds sixty-five pounds of pressure Harris has to maintain himself, not like a compound bow which would do the work for him. I tell her how he has forearms sinewed and veined like marble. I tell her how archery is like ballet and karate all put together.

She takes one compound off the wall and tests its string.

"Sweet Jesus," she says. "And he can hit something with this?"

I tell her about holding small things in my hands at ten

paces, at twenty and thirty. I make Harris sound like Robin Hood, and this is silly, but he's very good. He's accurate to a fault. He doesn't hunt anymore, but when he was in high school he used to fly out to Pennsylvania for deer, Wyoming for antelope, Canada for black bear. This was how he spent his vacations, his Christmas and Thanksgiving. I've heard stories about chase and kill, blood in the snow, so often I can't remember the details of even one, but his parents speak of Harris's trophy room at home.

I think how this is such a woman's way, knowing all about what her man does in his spare time and telling, but I can't help myself. It's as if Evelyn had challenged me, and I had to meet her with something grand about Harris, something that would impress itself upon her besides the looks of his apartment.

She starts at a rustling in the corner.

"What sort of animal is that?" she says.

By the bookcase is Harris's she-cat, making a meal out of something she crouches over, a leaf of plant, an insect in distress.

"It's Venus. It's Harris's cat."

"That thing is one snack shy of exploding."

I laugh. This may be true. Harris got Venus spayed last Christmas while I was in bed with the flu, because the neighbors complained about her howling when she got in heat, and she sounded in pain, sounded so lovesick we couldn't quite stand it ourselves. She used to back into our ankles; it was awful. The thing is, now Venus has the same passion for food, and almost everything she comes across is food and Harris worries she'll eat herself to death. Her belly slaps the floor when she walks, tight and full of tuna fish, Purina, and whatever she can drag from the trashcan.

Kat finds us from the bathroom and spots Venus right off.

"Kitty-kitty," she coos and trots right over to pet and scratch, to cuddle with the cat.

"Don't get in the way of her mouth," I say. "She'll take a finger and not even know it."

Kat pshaws at me, and when she gets chomped, I don't even say I told you so.

Last winter Harris had a spat with his landlord, Maynard, for keeping Venus in the apartment. Out on the balcony was fine, but on a February morning Maynard showed up to caulk the bathtub and found her gnawing on the sofa cushions. He called Harris at the graduate office to chew him out.

He said, "The thing is, cats is related to skunks. I know they's not skunks, but that smell's awful related, cat piss smell stuck in every part and parcel of that place."

Harris told him she was a stray, showed up on his doorstep, a poor little homeless cat he couldn't turn away. There was no place else for her to go. Now surely he could see clear to that, just a little cat with no place else to go.

Maynard said, "Cats is small, sure, like skunks is small, but they's still big enough to charge the feline rent. When I come upon a situation like yours, I like to rent out to cats by the pound."

Soon after that, Harris had some friends over and we were thinking how best to go about such a thing. One scruffy guy offered a beam scale he had back in his apartment he stole from the science building for weighing pot, but we figured she might break it, and then we thought to take her down to the butcher shop in town and weigh her there, but it was late. Harris tried to hold her in his arms and weigh both of them on the bathroom scale, but she wouldn't hold still long enough for the needle to stop jumping, and by that time it was all a joke. It was one of those things we laughed about doing and never did and it seemed as if that was enough.

Harris finally agreed to twenty dollars extra a month, but

Maynard isn't real strict about it. He isn't real strict about much, like propriety and knocking first before he uses his passkey. One time, Harris came home from work to find Maynard asleep on the sofa, a beer from the fridge between his knees and dinner's chicken gone, the bones left out on the counter and a plate in the sink.

I wander into the den and flop down on the sofa. Evelyn follows, stretches next to me, folding her arms behind her head.

"Must've been nice." She sighs. "Your man with his own place for y'all to go. Sometimes I wish Owen and I had a place like this."

"Yeah," I say and we smile to each other.

"Yeah," Kat says, and we shoot her a look across the room like fire and tiredness.

We think it best to nap awhile, and Evelyn and Kat fall about the floor like orphan girls, curling up with pillows and printed Indian cloth Harris bought at the college store. They are asleep in minutes, but I'm not that tired, roused of a sudden with nothing to do, no one to talk to. I wander back through the hallway to Harris's room, Harris's bed still mussed and sleep-twisted with blankets and sheets. I lie back on his pillows, and the smell of him rises up, cool and blue like chlorine and some cologne in his deodorant. I feel restless and wanting. I'm so awake my eyes water.

There's a book of poetry amongst his bed things, a paperback called *Walking Distance*. I think about how that is always the way with titles, with the names we give things; there's what you say aloud, *walking distance,* and there's what you say to yourself when you think about it, why it might be named the way it is. So much is like that, twofold and doubled upon itself, and you can be trained to see both things at once, to hear both meanings in one word. I imagine that's quite a talent, like rubbing your stomach and patting your head.

I get sentimental again inside myself, drift off and think

about when I first came here with Harris. He made me dinner, and it took all night, eating carbonara and drinking jug wine until two in the morning. We were very close together when I said I'd better be back at the dorm. I had class in the morning. I was nervous in myself, not trusting, not solid but held together with vapor and light in my spine. He made me feel so pretty I could've cried.

He said, "You could sleep over. Just sleep, passively," and he smiled so, I kissed his neck.

It was our first kiss, me kissing his neck, and I think I took him by surprise. When we went to his bedroom, he set me out a pair of boxer shorts and a T-shirt, left the room for me to change.

This was a twofold thing, a suggestion within something else, and I could have left it alone that way, but I didn't. It was both of us asleep in the night, carefully uncomfortable and happy. In the night, my hands browsing across his thighs in sleep and he soft like something ripe, his breath in my ear and his breath like summer flowers, like sweet William and rosehip, lobelia, bleeding heart and buckthorn. His breath like the paint on the walls in his apartment. I thought of flowers as I touched him, and when we touched I thought of petals, stems, and soft, soft color in sunlight. I came out of sleep, touched him again, and drew him to me, and then Harris was over me, his shoulders, his mouth, his knees between mine and him soft like I thought, the way I'd felt with my eyes closed. Stroking against me his skin raised a means rare and delicate between us, something like air, something like petal flesh.

This is this place to me. This is the place that makes me think of Harris and me as something inevitable and runaway, sweet and cleaving to everything we touch. I think how this is the stupidness Punk means, how memory sugars everything, and how Harris and I haven't been these things to each other for months now. Lately it seems places can't hold on to the truth for very long, and I think this is okay. This is why there are people to go to, as well.

There's a statue in Rome, a sculpture by Bernini called *The Ecstasy of Saint Theresa,* and Harris has a postcard picture of this statue tucked into his bureau mirror. It's a woman in marble and the angel of God piercing her heart with a flaming arrow, the whole thing of marble, but seeming to be so light that it hovers in the air above the cathedral floor. It's a sculpture of God like an archer, like a hunter, like a man with one thing on his mind and it ain't holding hands, and there was a time Harris was this angel of God and I was made of marble, so heavy, yet so slight and weightless that I'd surprise even myself.

I take the postcard off the mirror and slip it in my pocket. This was another time, and there's no need to labor over its passing. Harris would die to see me do this. He's bothered if I have nightmares while sleeping in his arms, if I cry during a love story or lose something he's given me. He's concerned with the symbol making of things, signs in the world to be read if you pay heed. But this is a postcard picture, and I know there will be others. Other pictures, other times, other ways of being. There will be others.

15

Kat comes into Harris's bedroom to wake me around noon. She's put some music on the turntable, an old Supremes album.

She whispers in my ear, "Wake up, Mavis. Wake up and face the music."

She's kneeling next to the bed, humming along, and I have the feeling she's been watching me in my sleep, the feeling she's touched my face, my hands, without my knowing it, pulled some covers on or off me. Her face is very close to mine.

She says, "I'm sorry about last night."

I mumble something and wave her away. I say, "It's over now," but I think it comes out differently. I'm heavy with sleep, my limbs leaden, my head clouded. I have to focus hard to keep just one of her beside the bed.

She slouches down and folds her head to her knees, makes stretching sounds, with her back convex, her shoulder blades like wings.

"I get away from myself sometimes," she whispers into her knees.

She whispers many things while I'm on the edges of waking, things about how her dreams are fleeting and hard to remember, how even she knows the speed in which her fancies turn. She whispers things about Evelyn and me she would choose for her own, things like strength and secrets, things like control.

I have the feeling the things she says are the truest things she knows and I'm touched she's sought me out to hear them. I feel tender toward her in a sleepy way. I think she's a girl much like myself at her age, fallen to the same wants in this world, wants of Owen, wants of singularity and womanness, but she's been physical about seeking these out in ways I wasn't, and there's a certain courage to that.

I tell her we should take a walk to campus, we should leave Evelyn to sleep a while longer. I tell her time is not much matter anyhow, as I will only have a few moments to spend with Harris between his work and us getting back to Edisto. I tell her we should buy something, something that costs about as much as a hotel room. I find my shoes, and we step outside into the daylight and the streets of Boone.

She tells me more things as we walk, things she says without actually looking at me, without care as to whether I heed it all or not, and so I listen with the same carelessness. I follow her step. I listen without trying to make connections, make sense of her or for her. I don't ask questions. I don't give advice.

The air is warm around us, but the breeze makes it feel soft and cool, as if it might have just rained on this street but left the sky eggshell blue. There is no dust here, the air seeming too soft to hold it. Dust would just sift right through, like tissue. We pass the movie theater and a bookstore, and Kat keeps on talking.

She tells me she reads books she doesn't understand, books like *Lady Chatterley's Lover* and things by Salinger, and she tries to memorize lines that seem important in case she needs them to live by later.

She tells me there are solid weeks she wakes at three A.M. every night, weeks she can't tell black from blue, weeks she listens to the same music over and over until it plays in her head as she walks around, her mind playing music instead of thoughts.

She thinks about being Owen's girl. She thinks about him in pickup trucks and coming to her with dust like static in his hair.

She thinks about being at Wellesley in the fall and being a girl's girl there, someone who holds a lot of women together, like me.

She thinks about having babies and she tells me it's not just Owen's babies she wants. Lately, she's wanted to be pregnant, to feel something hard and growing inside her, and at the picnic on the Fourth she held Tee's youngest in her arms all night, kissed that baby like it was her own.

She thinks she thinks too much.

She doesn't say any of the obvious things, like *Mavis, I'm confused,* or *Mavis, help me,* and even when I buy her a cup of coffee at the BeansTalk Coffee Shop she doesn't say thank you. We walk. The day is bright. Kat has things to get off her chest, words she wants to swarm the air between us, and I let her speak without hindrance.

When she was a little girl she wanted to be a cashier with long silver fingernails, but someone told her she'd never make a life that way. It's something she's been concerned with for a long time, making a life. She thinks about it as making bread like Merrilee, or making love like Evelyn, making herself into a prize like Hazel at her wedding.

I think how there's a psychology behind everything she's telling me, ways a girl would look at life if she'd lost her mother, if her father took another wife, if she was going off to school away from home for the first time. But I only think of this because we are on this campus, a place where psychologies are talked about.

We wander in and out of stores, finger racks of clothes. I decide I want to buy her something and tell her such, and this makes her happy for a moment. She picks at jewelry and things for her hair, ball caps and silk scarves and barrettes with big bows attached. In one shop I see her run her fingers over a leather collar with silver studs, and I laugh.

"About what I said," I tell her. "There's no way in hell I'm buying you that."

"Just testing," she says and smiles.

We pass in front of Mast General Store, where I used to work. Kat makes a move for the door handle, but I just walk ahead, knowing she'll catch up. She does, and we go on down King Street. Something in me just didn't want to see the people I knew there, the people I worked for and with. I don't want to account for my time since I left school, don't want to exchange the nice words, pass on the safe details. I don't want to make that effort where it's not important.

Eventually, Kat picks out a pair of boots, black leather with red lizard skin on the heel and toe, and I pass over one of Punk's hundreds for them. They slip right beneath the legs of her jeans and she walks tall out of the store, her other shoes in a shopping bag. Then we buy flowers to carry and take back to the apartment, flowers like my mother used to collect from her garden, lacy and bright. They're not flowers for a vase, but such like a woman should carry, and this is what we do.

We pass men and women on King Street and through the winding campus, and Kat continues to talk in one unbroken ribbon of words looping about herself, asking questions then answering them, pausing then erasing her pause. She contradicts, she edits, she talks for a solid half-hour and we end up at the campus theater, let into the costume closet by a friend of Harris's I know.

It's only now she draws quiet.

"What are we doing here?" she asks.

"Costumes," I say. "For the Faire."

I push the racks around and find what's Elizabethan, the summer stock costumes, things we could wear to the Faire so as not to be just people passing through and stopping in, not to be just tourists. I take clothes off their hangers, pass them to her one at a time, and she holds each fabric to the light, tests the feel with her fingertips, feels them to her cheek. She casts things aside in piles: a court jester, a herald, a queen, dresses in brocade and velvet, dresses in sheer white. There are slippers of silver, veils, girdles, gauntlets, wreaths of roses for her hair, and soon she starts to smile. She stops talking. She strips to her underwear, trying things on, finding herself hats and gloves and crowns of gold.

I sink to the floor amidst these swamps of clothes, sink into myself. At one time, I too held all these clothes to my cheek and stripped to my underwear to try them on, but just now I don't feel as if it's something I want to do. The essential thing I feel is soft of heart. Kat is like a field mouse or a luna moth, something small and naked in this world with not enough fear to make her smart about it.

I know there's so much life out there already, so much sometimes I get lost in all the things I already am, let alone the things I could be. Like early this morning, when I got all yearnful about Harris and his apartment, about the parts of me that lived there with him. I've shed these things like so much skin, so much sweat or blood seeping into the floorboards. Even the newest layers, the things I was only months back and coming home, by the time I'd fleshed these out, I'd grown whole days larger. I think that's why I didn't want to go back inside Mast General Store. I never knew the people there well enough to explain the way I'm changing, not in a few sentences, and I don't much feel like reeling out the easy responses anymore.

I thought this trip was going to be something, the Renaissance Faire a grand occasion for us to attend, but now it's just getting down to moments of purpose and meaning, a few moments here before leaving. It's as if something of myself anticipates the rest, precedes, guides, and this is why I came this way, after all.

When we get back to Harris's apartment, Evelyn is up and awake. She's got on a short Oriental robe with a dragon embroidered on the back, and she and Maynard sit at Harris's kitchen table sipping coffee like old friends. Maynard is wearing some sweat on his forehead.

"Where you all been?" she says. "Oooh, Kat, I like them boots."

Kat models her foot around and everyone says how nice her new boots are, even Maynard.

Evelyn says, "Mr. Maynard here was just telling me how much he misses you, Mavis, and how much he likes your man, what a wonderful cat y'all keep."

I look to Maynard and his face doesn't seem so ratlike anymore, but full and flush and sweating from every pore. Evelyn crosses her legs and I think the man about falls out of his chair.

"How sweet," I say.

"You are, Mr. Maynard," Evelyn says. "You are so sweet."

Kat lays the costumes over the back of an extra chair and Evelyn stands to hold hers up against herself. She tucks the hanger 'neath her chin, stretches out her arm to hold a sleeve.

"I don't know, Mavis," she says. "I had something more in mind like a corset, something to lift up the finer parts of me."

She runs her hands down her body and cinches them at the waist, takes in a deep breath.

"Maynard," I say, "you look like you could use a glass of water."

❧

The Faire is on the grounds of a tobacco plantation in Lenoir, a great house of columns, porticos, stained glass, set back from the road, down a magnolia path. Evelyn stops the car, leans across the steering wheel to get a view. Her face fills with light.

"Sweet Jesus," she says. "This is better than Graceland."

I know the history of this place, been on the tour. When the owner signed the deed, he said, "Home sweet home for my Sweet Sixteen."

But come late summer, no doubt, he'd disappear from his Sweet Sixteen, down to Winston-Salem, to Greensboro, Burlington, north to Danville for the tobacco season. He'd go to call the bids, shoot the shit. He'd go for the corn whiskey, for the wild nights, for the sweet stacks of flue-cured leaves softening like velvet on the warehouse floors, while she did what? What all did these young brides do, alone in a dozen rooms with a dozen servants at beck and call?

This was 1929 and he was the highlight and the spotlight, people coming cross-county just to hear him spill line after line, the sound of his voice a heartbeat in their ears. He took in a percentage of the house, and when he stepped out, he made money like a king. And she, she took up with a young man, took sick, took off, took her life. She may have overseen, entertained, worried, and wept, she may have touched herself when she was all alone. The parts of a girl but sixteen that were not wife, mistress, maid, hostess, the parts she shed, loosed, and left behind; they fill that house as surely as her husband's straw hats, his white gloves, his cigarette advertisements in museum cases. They hang in the air. They haunt the high spaces. And this is something to see, too.

We drive through wrought-iron gates and park with the other cars in the grassy front lawn. Two token rows of his tobacco plants still stand, full flowering for July. I know these things, too, because when he was an old man, Punk was a young man and they traveled together for a time. It's how Punk learned to cure tobacco, how he learned to grow it, and he used to tell about the women he'd seen wearing bathing suits made from great green leaves and twine.

He said, "Pretty young things like they were fresh-sprung Mother Earth, and when I was a young man I thought all women should wear only tobacco and high heels."

I realized the link between Punk and this man's estate in Lenoir the first time I came out here with Harris and I thought to tell him about it, but he'd just had those things to say about my mama and her mind. I didn't feel like sharing such a family story with him, something that would connect him to my grandfather in a roundabout way, didn't know how he'd appreciate it, and I suppose up until now I just forgot.

Those tobacco plants by the gates, they tower taller than I can reach, taller than Kat or Evelyn can reach either, and we get out of the car, make a point of trying.

We're all decked out, the three of us peasant women in sackcloth and wide-necked blouses, bloomers, and leather girdles laced tight. I have a wreath of silk leaves in my hair, gold and red and orange.

It's so beautiful up here, green and mountained, and this afternoon is the kind of sunny afternoon that makes you think you're in a movie or a shampoo commercial. I pine again for Boone in the summertime, for this kind of summertime and the summertimes I spent here. And again, I think how it makes me feel old to feel wistful, old in a good way, changed wise and special from the girls in the street I saw this morning, at the theater, the girls with ponytails and cutoff shorts, backpacks and tan, tan colt's legs. The girls like Kat. That's part of getting older, I think, feeling special in yourself.

But coming to this Faire, my stomach doesn't thrill against my rib cage. Everything in me isn't so high and light and shining. Seeing a lover after a long time is most like waiting for Christmas, only you're the present. You're in the box, wrapped up in the bow. I want to see Harris and I want to surprise him to tears, but my legs have grown so tired.

He's a tournament knight for England this year, Sir Harris the Dragonheart. He does things with longbows, William Tell things with players dressed as jesters and idiots. He lofts flaming arrows at bales of hay set to blaze. In the end, Harris is the knight who dies in combat. He's been practicing since last year.

The only way into the Faire is through a maze, a weave of toothy shrubs, gnarled and wrapped to tunnels overhead. The path is dark, and there're false starts, dead ends, wrong turns.

"Through here," I say to Kat and Evelyn.

It's strange to take yourself from such sunlight to green darkness, and for a minute I can't see. Kat and Evelyn touch my back and I feel my way, my fingers snapping along the branches, no one ahead of us, no one behind. I think I hear voices seeping through in registers like echo, not from a direction but from the leaf walls themselves. This turns me around, pitches me differently and a bit off-balance. I hunch over, as if everything is closing in.

And when we unfold ourselves from the boxwood maze the feeling comes around me that something small is uprooted, some idea of abandon released. The plantation's old cure-houses are now open markets, cottages from the sixteenth century with Tudor fronts and striped awnings. They make a town laid out before us, and their cobblestone ways fill with people in costume: jesters and heralds, courtiers and courtesans, peasants, wenches, mimes and knights. Some of these people work here, like Harris, and some are just visiting, like us, but none so pretty as our own private family of women. Over all, there's sound of flute and kettle drum, weightless music in the sun.

This is one big thumping heart of people here to have a good time, to see things they could never see at home. In front of where we stand, a man blows a teardrop of glass, yellow and blue and green. To his left, a woman reads tarot cards, and to her left, a family chews four legs of roasted turkey.

We stand staring at each other, this family and I, and I think about what this place is, how strange it is here in the middle of the green, green mountains like a shire, or a hamlet out of England. I want the feeling as if I've tucked myself into a happening, as if there is entropy, kinesis, action here that might sweep me up, carry me off. But all I can think is how nobody eats a turkey leg in public.

A woman stands in the street with a gathering crowd, a woman round and busty, not much older than Evelyn, but not like Evelyn in any way, not curvy and graceful, but round and sturdy and ruddy with sun. She hollers about how wooing sheep is like wooing women. The press of people grows thick and happy.

Evelyn shakes her head, repulsed and staggered at once.

"Well I never," she says.

There're parts jokes and position jokes, the men forever handling themselves and their codpieces, kicking each other in the crotch, the women tucking things between their breasts. It's funny the way cartoons are; if you were alone, you might not laugh out loud.

Carts pass us on the street full of things to sell. There are herbs, rosemary, lemongrass, hyssop, cinnamon and marigold, handmade candles, leathers, baskets and fruit. There are women who will plait your hair into twists and crowns, weave it with ribbons and flowers. They'll cut a lock from underneath and braid it into a bracelet for your lover, a bracelet of hair for him to wear as a charm or a favor.

I tell Evelyn and Kat where they can get maps of the grounds, where the neat things are like the mud pits with people sunk to their necks and the human chess match, where they can get a cool drink and have their fortunes told. I give them each a kiss on the cheek.

"Go find your man," Evelyn says. "We'll meet you when it's time to go."

They go off one way and I go off another, toward the jousting ring and Harris. I weave in and out of people sunburned, people eating, people ready to go home, and then in the cobbled streets I am washed over with a memory of Harris and me, here, at this Faire, a summer ago.

He was standing in the shadows of an alleyway, watching me move toward him, coming to meet him in the afternoon in this improbable place, this village out of time. He winked at me, grinned as if he'd had a wicked thought, and I could see in his face a doorframe, a window, an invitation.

I make eddies in the crowd from the place where I've stopped still with this memory, people fluxing 'round me and pushing and pointing, and all these players in performance of their Faire things, calling and running and laughing, and me just standing there, thinking of things vital and blood-carrying, thinking of bodies and skin and closeness between people who know each other well.

I will say this: when Harris made that door frame, made his motion to me, I walked on to him and he smiled at me with his teeth so white, so full of himself, so pleased. I got right in front of him, nose to nose, my breath against his face, and I backed him down that alleyway, deeper into the shadows, and he still grinned upon me.

Stop doing that, I told him.

It was a test. If he kept himself a smiling man, he'd lose.

But he did stop and he stood himself straighter, swelled his chest a bit, and I came closer to him, as close as I pleased without touching. I fitted myself around his body so that every part of me was just away from him, and when he stepped back, I moved with him, and when he held up his hand, mine followed. My eyes did not leave his face and I could track his body just by heat, just by the distance and the closing of space between our skins, and he grew serious with me. He was a man pinned down and, I would almost say, awestruck.

And I rocked forward and he rocked back. I rose to my toes and he did too, and I began to wonder at touching him right then, wondering if he would start, if his blood like mine would flood through the thin parts of his skin, if he would go all hard or all hot or all soft.

And so I did it.

I reached down to his thighs and his hands went there and they ran alongside mine, holding mine when I touched his legs in tights, and I could feel his muscles leap and sweat and when I turned my palms on the flats of his hips and rode my hands up his body, his hands were there too along himself, his breath sharp inside his chest.

Stop doing that, he said.

I smiled. I leaned my face to his and I looked into his eyes and he was Harris, yes, but he was untimed and unbodied and I sparked my tongue along my own lips and then I was kissing him, full and reckless and tasting and our bodies still apart, connected only by my hands upon him, my mouth upon him.

This is enough, I thought. This was the passing moment in life that everyone should have. It was singular and wild and plenty and I would not find myself wishing for another like it. I thought to say this to Harris, but I didn't. Instead, I laughed, and he looked at me and I reached down to the edge of my skirt and lifted it to my mouth, my next kiss wiped off on my hem.

And now, I am full-flooded with that day, that time, that event between us, stopped still in a crowded lane of people, and all I am capable of is holding quiet and remembering. It's a moment stayed in time and space, a moment where I feel myself to slam together, to contract and crystalize. I'm intent on seeing Harris, off to find him, and still I'm held up on the way by thoughts of how he was and how he could have been, us like two mirrors with no image between. Suddenly I'm want of the sanctuary of my books and ledgers, the parlor house and the safeness of my air conditioning. I don't know why and I cannot seem to help myself.

❧

By the time I get to the jousting ring, the crowd is full and I am out of breath from a long and crazy run. I fold my arms across the fence top and watch. The knights canter around the ring, twentieth-century men with pennants and colors and feathers and chain mail. They are attractive men, dangerous-looking. They feint and posture. They call things to the crowd assembled. I trace my way around to the far side of the ring, away from the grandstands and the people, all the while searching Harris out.

"Harris!"

I cup my hands around my mouth to carry my voice, and he turns on his horse, a black gelding, and he's grown a beard. He looks different, so remote and particular, I have to remind myself this is Harris. *This is Harris.*

He says, "I didn't know you were coming."

I say, "I didn't know I was coming."

He reaches down for my cheek, and his fingertips are so light, so soft, I feel my skin span beneath them, my own self pouring out to meet him.

I close my eyes. *This is Harris.*

I open my eyes. *This is Harris.*

He has to go. I know he has to go, he has to do his job as the knight who dies in the final act, but somehow I expect this moment to be longer. I want this moment to be longer, and then his horse turns, and he is gone.

170

16

~~~~~~~~~~~ I drive Evelyn's Pinto in the late afternoon, down out of the mountains and the quiet and through the nightfall lights of the small towns along the highway. Kat sleeps in the back seat, and Evelyn, with her head propped against the window, sleeps too. We go like this because I have work in the morning, Punk and the farm, because that's what I've promised, and Evelyn has canceled appointments in her beauty salon she needs to reschedule. Kat has nothing waiting for her tomorrow, but twice before sleeping she mentioned calling her father for a plane ticket to Pennsylvania. I told her to do what she wanted, but I could use her help out at the farm now that Sal is sending down his side of the books. She said she'd think about it, and I don't really have anything for her to do, but something in me wants her around. I've begun to think of her as part of Punk's house too, part of coming home.

At the Faire, I watched the rest of Harris's joust, threats called and answered, attacks made and foiled, and then a run of blood bright against his chain mail. Harris reeled and splayed in the cinders, his face stitched and clutching, the wound to the center of his body. His horse quieted at his side, lowed its neck to nuzzle him sweet, and it was all sort of convincing. I even thought to go to him, to lift his head and cradle it in my lap, brush his hair from his forehead, but there was another woman to do that, a princess or a lady of the court, a woman who would do the same thing for him all summer.

We walked together when the Faire was over for the day, and Harris told me he'd have time off weekend after next. He has a professor with a place on Ocracoke and this professor offered him a visit anytime. The keys lie beneath the oleander on the front walk. We could go to the beach, go fishing.

Harris said, "Let's go away together," and I said yes, let's do.

I rode back with him to his apartment, Kat and Evelyn following behind, and we talked about the weather and his cat Venus, what sort of mail he'd gotten lately. He asked me if I saw the longbow shot he'd lofted through some flaming hoops, and I lied and said yes, yes, I had and it was great.

Then we were back in Boone and I gathered up Kat and Evelyn, our things, and we left, a kiss at the car door.

He said, "Thanks for coming."

Harris thinks of spontaneity as an unnatural force in the world, a way to arrange a closet, not a life, and I took him aback, coming up the way I did. Even for all my wild memories of him and thoughts of us together, I took him aback. He prepares for visits and somewhere in the back of his mind I think he makes lists of things to think about, points to bring up, ways to feel in a given space or time. His mind functions out every possibility for departure, every permutation of plan like a hummingbird or a steel trap. He narrates his decisions as if to set them down, says things like, I'm going to the kitchen and then I'm getting something from the fridge and I wonder if you'd like something too. It's a quality I used to find soothing when I was with him in Boone. I had the idea I was always somewhere in his thoughts, and I liked that feeling.

But there's no chance in Harris, no taste for cunning or wile. I don't think he'd know what it would be to truly risk his life, his head, his heart, risk himself for a good reason or a bad one. It goes as far as what he does, learns, studies, reads, takes in, writes down, observes. He doesn't grow anything. He doesn't do what Punk does, and I guess that makes a difference to me, makes me see him as distant from the heart of things.

It's not that I don't care for Harris anymore, because I do. I miss him even now, in this car, and I think about him, and I want him in my arms from time to time, but the urgency is gone. I'm not sure how long it's been gone, but I think clearly and reasonably about us now, and that could be good or bad.

And so, good or bad, it's nice to be on this road in the middle of the night, heading back to Edisto with these women. I feel certain of my place. I feel high and mighty and headed toward clear light and warm days. I might even say this aloud, because Evelyn comes out of sleep beside me and she mumbles something I can't hear but that is directed at me.

"What?" I say.

"Human hair."

She sits up straight and rubs at her eyes, leans over, and checks in the back seat for Kat, still sleeping. She does think about hair, even in her dreams.

"What about it?" I say, and I am truly curious.

"Well, at that Faire today, Kat and I saw all this jewelry made out of hair. Bracelets and rings and bits to tie around your ankles. There was a man who would cut a lock of your own and make it up into whatever you wanted."

"Did you do it?"

"No. But it looked easy enough. You know, my mama used to have this glass bowl on her vanity. She saved those strands that get caught in a brush for making hairpieces and such. I always thought it was kind of wonderful. Like collecting up spider webs, don't you think?"

"Jesus," I say. "How'd she ever get enough for a hair-piece?"

"That's the thing, you know. You lose an awful lot of hair just naturally over a lifetime. Like for instance, there are Indian women in Canada whose hair never sees the light of day. They keep it wrapped up from the time they're born and it grows and grows and whatever falls out just stays wrapped up with the rest."

"Don't they have to brush it, or wash it?"

"I don't know if they do. Well, they do now, because these days they all grow their hair for this shampoo company. They call it virgin hair, never seen the sun or wind. They rinse their virgin hair only at night and with rainwater. They aren't allowed to use shampoo, even their company's, 'cause everybody knows it's bad for you anyways."

Kat sits up in the back seat.

"Evelyn," she says, "what would happen if you just stopped washing your hair?"

Evelyn and I look at each other.

"Your hair, or my hair, Kat?"

"My hair."

And both together we say, "It'd fall out."

Evelyn and I go to laughing at this, partly because it's late in the night, partly because we were poking fun, and then Kat is laughing with us, as if it's no big deal, the joke's on her. She says she knows she could probably pay more attention to herself, and even this is funny. She makes a face in the rearview mirror, and Evelyn tells her that's not the way to do it, it's like this, and then they are poking and tugging and holding their eyelids in ways nature never intended, and before long I'm holding my sides, trying not to run off the road. We ride like that, laughing, and after a bit the laughter seeps away, first to smiles, then to quiet, and then to sleep, riding with us all the way 'til dawn and Edisto.

❧

Wednesday morning, the new Chisholm Ryder comes in and I am at the farm to take delivery. The dealer in California trucked it all the way to Edisto and now that contraption comes highing through the vineyards on a flatbed truck, the biggest piece of machinery I've ever seen. It's blue and oiled with road bugs from its ride, stands at least two stories in the air. It's more cage than tractor, more structure than equipment, more like the roller coaster up the road dressed out in kudzu than what they have around here. The hired men filter out of the barn, gawk around the flatbed as if they've been set upon by something beyond their ken.

And these days the hired men look upon me the same way. They duck their eyes and call me *Miss Mavis;* they come to me for small decisions and directions and paychecks. I smile and tell them the what-to-do and they thank me for their paychecks and I thank them back. It makes me feel capable here, more of a tradeswoman than an accountant, and I like that the way I like that I wear boots and jeans to my office, the way I could go out into the barn or the vines if needs be. But the ways of the hired men with me might have more to do with my resurrection of Cy Bertel's dog. I hear that story told and told again, making me out to be a mysterious woman with powers in my littlest fingers.

Now I stand here, outside in the heat and dust of Edisto, and watch the flatbed and its tractor come to a halt, and Tee comes to me for where to put such a thing, comes in on my memory. He seems taken aback by that tractor, as if it's so much more than he expected, as if he might want to consider the comfort of such a machine.

He says, "Where do you think would suit it best?" and I smile and tell him the barn will suit just fine.

Punk's been excited about this machine all summer, but he's missed the delivery, gone to town to see a man about a horse. I asked him where he was headed this morning and that's what he told me.

He said, "Goin' to town, sugar. Got to see a man about a horse."

I've finished auditing his ledgers and that man could buy a fleet of horses. He could buy a racetrack, jockeys to go along for the ride, fallow fields of grain to feed them all, but he's not making money like last year. There's the expense of the Ryder, and even with the cut in hired hands, it eats a chunk of profit. In fact, I'd say he'll bring in half what he did last year, and that's if his yield is the same. This merger with Sal, this was last-ditch genius for the vineyard. If Sal knows his wine, if he can produce for next year's competitions, if he can get a label started for this corporation, the two of them are made in the shade. If not, Punk's got some trouble ahead. For too long Punk's run on the idea of cash flow, cash flow, without realizing a little more was flowing out than flowing in. You can play that way for a long time, but if the interest rate ticks up a notch all the sudden, your ass is in a sling.

I've never thought of Punk this way, never seen the exposed in him. He's always been a gambling man, someone taken by the seat of his pants, and sometimes that's what it takes to make it in this world, but now I know the details. Now I know how thick it can get and it makes my brain go all atingle with fear and hope, a girlish feeling, a mindless, powerful wishing very close to prayer.

The men cluster around the Ryder, Tee right up front and explaining. He's got them underneath its carriage and on top of its drive box, has them inside clearing space in the barn.

"Okay," I say, and Tee gets behind the wheel, and everybody runs for cover as he backs the thing off the flatbed at speed to suit a drag race.

"Watch your heads, boys," I yell, and I have to laugh at myself for my poor humor, but the men go to laughing, and thankfully Tee can't hear me from inside the power of the machine.

The delivery man from California follows me to the parlor

house and I go to my desk to cut his check when the phone rings. It's Sal, calling from Pennsylvania.

He says, "How's tricks on the home front?"

I tell him about the arrival of the new Ryder, about how Tee is so excited we can hardly hold him. I talk about the cuts in labor costs, the possibilities for more acreage now the fruit can be picked in machine time. I tell him things I think he'll want to hear, things about business and the farm. I want to sound competent. He pays my salary the same as Punk.

Finally he says, "How are you, Mavis?"

"Fine. Yes, I'm fine."

"Well, that's a good thing."

He asks after Kat and I tell him we're putting some weight on her and she's starting to mind, starting to sit up straight. I tell him she's out running errands for me now and keeping the coolers full of ice water for the men. Keeping icewater for men in weather like this is job enough for anybody. Sal doesn't say anything, as if I've just surprised him with such news of his daughter. Then Hazel's on the phone, her voice echoing in extension. She sounds breathless and tinny like a tree full of wind chimes, full up with stories of Jamaica.

She says, "Oh, Mavis, it was wonderful down there, crazy in the streets and hot, so hot you'd walk around all day mostly naked. I was all the time sweaty and getting tan. All the time sticky with sunscreen and sweat like I was swimming in honey."

I think of Sal and Hazel down in the tropics, near the ocean where it's bluest, near the sun where it's hottest. I think of the things newlyweds do in water and heat and I find blood flushing through my body even as I stand in the air conditioning of the parlor house. I want to be near these things too, heat and water and love and salt. I want to be mostly naked in the sun with a man as certain as oxygen, as essential as the color blue.

Hazel tells me she felt so good. Every day at lunch she'd walk to this Cuban neighborhood and buy huge Cuban sandwiches that they'd make with a press so they were sort of flat and grilled and she'd squat on the sidewalk and eat them right on the street. She tells me how one day she went to pick up sandwiches and the old Cuban man who made them set a green fruit in front of her and said something in Spanish and pointed to the fruit. Hazel picked it up and held it in her hands and the Cuban man said papaya, that's a papaya, and it will be ripe in three days.

She says, "He could have handed me a pot of gold, it wouldn't have meant anything more or less."

I wonder where you get fruit like papaya, exotic versions of apples and oranges, mangos, pomegranates like precious stone. I wonder if they're worth a pot of gold. Hazel sounds so overwhelmed, something in her voice like a schoolgirl, as though everything in this world is beyond recognizable definition, everything a thing to marvel at. I wonder if this is being married or if this is being in Jamaica.

Sal says, nearby the phone, "Mavis has to get back to work, Hazel. Let her go."

And I do. I tell them both how happy I am for them. I wish them the best.

I hang up the phone and Kat gets back from the post office. She is red and sweaty and she has tears in her eyes, some new tragedy, some new problem welling there. But for one time it looks as if she's trying to hold herself back. She skulks the corners of the room and taps her feet around as if there's something inside her skin she wants to shake out, but quietly. I don't want to, but I ask.

"What's the matter this time?" I say.

She tells me she was stung by a bee, and I feel sorry I judged her so quickly.

"Come here," I say.

She bites her lower lip and closes her eyes, peels her sleeve off her shoulder and there's a welt growing there. I can see the stinger still embedded in her skin. I sit her down in my chair and go to the bar sink to wet a tea towel, fill it with ice.

"Sit still, now," I tell her.

"It just crawled right up there," she says. "It crawled up there and latched on."

"Because you're so sweet," I say, and one fat tear streaks her cheek.

I hold the ice to her shoulder and tell her how it hurts, I know it hurts, but the kick is those little fuckers die and all we get is a lump and an itch, and she laughs a little. I stroke her hair back from her face. It's long and blond, and down around her shoulders there's something sticky in it, something that feels like wax.

"I got into something in the barn," she says.

"What?"

"I don't know."

"Well, come here. Let's get that out."

I get a bottle of dish soap from the kitchen and take her into the main room, bend her over the sink at the bar where the faucet is highest. She gets the water going hot and her hair wet down, but she's trying to balance the ice on her shoulder and soap her hair with one hand and she's doing neither well.

"Here," I say. "You're not getting anywhere."

I take my hands to her head until they're white with suds, until her hair is thick with white, and I scrub my fingertips over her scalp hard, the way I like to be washed myself when someone gets their hands about my hair, like when I was a girl and my mama would do it, or when I would go to the beauty parlor. Who knows what Kat could have gotten on herself in the barn, which is full of fertilizer and chemicals and oil. I let the water rinse over my fingers in webs of clean, the smell of lemon soap and her hair so that it squeaks to the touch. I twist her hair tight, wring the water from it, and take a stack of tea towels, walk her back to my office to pat her dry.

Punk slams the front door now, comes in the office, and Kat's in my chair, her head wet and her shoulder welted and me standing over her with a flurry of towels across my desk. He has a half-empty bottle of bourbon and rests it down right on my ledger books.

"Mr. Punk Black, Esquire, requests the presence of you two ladies in the front drive," he says.

We follow him outside and there's a brand-new Mustang convertible parked front and center. The convertible is white with red leather interior and it's hot and sleek and low to the ground. Kat squeals and claps to see it, forgotten already about her bee sting. She jumps over the door and into the driver's seat, runs her hands 'round the wheel. Punk tosses her the keys.

"You go slow, honey, and drive the lanes," he tells her. "Have a big time."

She starts the engine with a gun of gas and we stand watching her pick her way down the drive, about as fast as I could run. We watch until she is no more than a billow of dust, and I take Punk by the wrist out to the barn to see the new Ryder. He pulls me up the outside and we sit on top, a sort of platform near the rafters and the mourning doves. He's on the edges of his alcohol, something in his voice unbaked, doughy and thick.

He says, "Well, look at that. All new toys."

We look down through the grill of the platform to the pith of the machine, its gears and steering column, its knobs and levers and lifts exposed from our angle.

He says, "This is the Cadillac of tractors, Mavis. I'll bet there's a goddamn TV set in here somewhere."

"You bought a new car," I say.

"Yes, ma'am, I did. I'm too rich and too old to drive a goddamn farm truck around anymore."

He takes a slug out of the bottle and sets it between us. I can see his eyes roaming through his fields, threading 'cross the rows like a needle. Punk is not a drinking man. He goes to the liquor store when he's frayed down or full of life, when he's got something on his mind. There's something weighing on him, and I draw my legs beneath myself, draw a breath, as I know he will pass it on to me.

"When you were just a little thing," he says, "Owen fell into some puppy love. She was a farm girl."

I sit back on my heels on the roof of the Chisholm Ryder, get myself comfortable. I reach over and take a small wet-lipped sip from that bottle myself, just enough to cut the dust.

". . . he was all over himself getting her to look twice and he joined the 4-H Club just to hold her hand a little longer. He had to have a project, grow something or raise something that made a profit at the end of the year. I gave him a cow, but something happened. He lost interest, or, no, the damn thing died, threw herself into the river or something. But this girl was the cutest little thing Owen had ever seen."

I knew of this girl. Her name was Mayella. Her daddy was in hogs. She'd tell how Ike Timms came down to castrate their hogs, how she'd never seen a white man do such a thing. She told that story all the time to Owen and I can't count the times I heard it.

She'd say, "Ike comes down with his jar of pine tar and sharpens up Daddy's hawkbill. My brothers hold the pig and Ike finds the balls under the skin, makes a slice and they just pop out, like grapes outta skins. Ike tars the spot and lets 'em go, takes home all the hog balls he can eat."

And then she'd laugh and Owen would want her to tell it all over again, about the knife and the tar and the man who ate the balls of a pig. I can't help but smile now, thinking of that girl from so long ago and the way she turned Owen's ear.

Punk goes on, "And because of Mayella, Owen bought a

sow from her daddy, already in season. She had ten little hogs, and then she ate every last one of her babies, bones and all. But you see he still had to do something to make a profit, or they'd send him to 4-H jail or some such goddamn thing, maybe kick his ass out. So Owen sent away to Pickens Stock and Nursery in Minnesota for vine stock, only needing a space in the back-yard and some rain for a vineyard. Well, time moved on and Owen got a car of his own, and that farm girl moved on, replaced by a cheerleader named Babs, who just loved Owen's car. He forgot all about his grapes; never watered, pruned, or trellised them, even. But I took an interest in them and that's what I'm trying to tell you. So one day I just flat told him, boy, those grapes you insisted on are rotting before our very eyes. You're shittin' on your mother's backyard, son, and sometime soon, you and your car are gonna wish you hadn't."

I reach over and take another sip from the bottle, and Punk laughs.

He says, "You likin' that?"

"Yes, I am."

"Well, don't like it too much."

I shift my legs out from underneath me and let them swing over the edge of the tractor alongside Punk's. He doesn't mind my sipping with him. In fact, I'd not be surprised if that's what he had in mind all the while. I remember summers ago when Punk sent me out to Pickens Stock and Nursery, not far from Saint Paul, and I took an airplane. It was one of the first times I'd ever been on an airplane and those lights coming up through the darkness when we landed, those lights looked like stars to me and I remember having the thought that we were going the wrong way, that we were landing up instead of down. And when I made it out to Pickens itself, I walked through all those greenhouses like a whole city of plants, learned about grafting and pruning and trellising, but I didn't hear about Owen Black and a 4-H order years and years ago.

It's now that I realize Punk was sending me back to the beginning to go to Minnesota. He was starting me where he started, letting me watch what he watched when I was too young to care about grapes and wine and business ventures.

I look over to Punk's face and it is tired and worn like a good piece of leather. He takes another swig from the bottle between us, rubs his eyes with the flats of his hands. Wedged beneath his nails is a flat blue moon of his land and his grape and his oil for his machines, a rim of his dirt coloring his skin like a tattoo. He's had those fingernails for as long as I can remember.

He goes on, "And of course Owen needed money like always, money I sure as hell wasn't givin' him anymore, and one day he went out back and picked every grape out there. Ripe, green, and rotten, he got eleven bushels and sold them all to the Dixie Home Store for sixty-seven dollars and nineteen cents. I watched him count his money on my kitchen table. That was in 1967, the same year I sold the cows for stock, the year we started buying beef and tobacco at the Dixie Home Store like everybody else."

We look out the barn doors at that hot little car, Kat just now stepping out the door of it, looking at this moment more like a woman than a girl far from home. I think about how space lies in stories and how it gets filled in. Punk didn't have any more to say. What he was wanting to tell me was in that story and in his head and heart and in that little car like Owen's, and if it was to be misunderstood it'd take a fool to do so.

Later, I will think back on this day and I will know he'd been to the doctor and I'll know what he'd heard and why he'd bought that Mustang and I'll be honored that he came to me. He didn't tell his news, but he came to me and he told other things and we sipped on his bourbon, and it is a moment I remember all the time.

$\iota \mathcal{J}$

~~~~~~~~~~ Ten days later, I take the farm truck and drive on up to Boone for Harris and my weekend away. At first it's very still. We are quiet with each other, quiet as if to soothe something over, quiet as if to brood. I drive Punk's truck down I-40 to the cape of North Carolina, and we hardly speak at all. The sky's blue-dark and it grows late in the evening, less and less in the car windows, everything close in black. It's nice. We're hush, and hush seeps in around us.

I think about silence and travel. I think about going places I've never been, places hot and salty. We stopped at a shop up the road and I bought a bottle of lotion scented like guavas, bought it because it smelled like something I couldn't name, and now with it on my skin I think it smells like where I'm going to. I've never even seen a guava. I think how I wear this lotion like a slip of the equator 'cross my back, the imaginary edge of an imaginary fruit filling up the air between Harris and me instead of sound.

I think about what we don't say here in this truck on this trip and I wonder if this is the not wanting or the not needing of words. I've spent this much time quiet with Harris before, comfortable silences over the newspaper on a Sunday morning, studying, or listening to music. Sleeping we are this quiet, but it's been long whiles since we've done that together.

Harris is tired. I think how I'd like it if he'd touch me, if he'd reach across this big bench seat and rest his hand inside my thigh or against my knee. But that would look funny, a woman driving and a man sidled over next to her, and he'd get tangled up. A man should slump against the door and close his eyes, snore and hang his mouth open, hold a beer between his knees and not talk when he's tired, when his woman drives. This is as it should be.

This quiet reminds me of West Texas, of this time last summer when I took a bus across the country to Odessa, on to the vineyards out there in the plains and then up to Truth or Consequences, New Mexico, for myself, just to go away. I could travel my own way on Punk's errands. I trusted it was okay.

On the way to New Mexico, I sat next to a blind man who was quiet, like Harris, and older, like Punk. He had a yellow Lab with him and wore dark wraparound glasses. His socks didn't match. He held his hands on his knees as if they rested on a pillow.

I think about going blind in the night and listening to our quiet, Harris's and mine. I close my eyes for an instant even as I drive and there's so much flux and course around us. I separate the sounds: the mouth of wind around the truck, the breath of air conditioner, the slow throb of my own lungs, in and out, in and out. It's a meditation, closer and closer to the center.

This blind man on the bus, he liked to play cards and we played gin rummy from Odessa to the New Mexico border. His cards had Braille numbers beside black and white ones, and he always let me deal so as he couldn't cheat. He taught me how to win with a knock, how to bluff and hold a card across the fan of my hand, how to look as if I was interested when I wasn't. He taught me these things without saying them; he did these things himself without seeing them. Ace, queen, king, and jack of hearts. A spade is a spade is an imprint on a card.

He said, "You're a sweet thing, ain't you? Sweet things break my heart."

This blind man got off the bus before Truth or Consequences. He was met by a woman in a red dress, and she and I watched each other as I pulled away from the station, going on.

We go on now, on across North Carolina through the tobacco belt, through furniture country, through High Point and Kernersville, Graham and Durham, through universities, through Chapel Hill and Raleigh and north on 64. Sign after sign, name after name, these places are known for things, they know things, and some of that comes with us as we drive on. Some of that always comes with us.

I have a friend at N.C. State. She graduated this year, with me, and when we were freshmen I visited her for a weekend. I brought snacks with me, Japanese crackers that were her favorites, Patsy Cline records that we knew by heart, and a goldfish in a Mexican glass bowl. We ate crackers in her bed and sang long low songs until late in the night, when we got sleepy and crawled 'neath her sheets. We whispered stories back and forth, her life and mine in small detail, both of us drifting off with the lights on. It was early in the morning when her friends burst in, waking us together and laughing, a pack of wild boys. They serenaded us, an old song from the fifties that my mama used to hum to herself, a song like "Chantilly Lace" or something by the Righteous Brothers.

I find myself thinking of that moment as something romantic, something playful that happened to me before I met Harris. I don't know if that's how it really was or if that's just how it is now. These things that stay with you, things that follow you without your asking, they walk on their own two legs.

It's not long before midnight and I pull off the highway to a motel somewhere near Rocky Mount, this quiet still between us, sheer like glass. Harris checks in at the lobby and I wonder how he puts it to the desk clerk. Up at Appalachian, we used to do this sort of thing every once in a while, check into the Starbrite Rest for the morning, before classes or research, and it was a wild, secret thing to do. Harris would give someone else's name, a professor's, or he'd speak only Italian and pay in cash. Tonight seems heavier than that, more serious and real than mornings in a cheap motel, mornings when very little mattered.

Harris carries my bag up the outside staircase and he unlocks the room for me. He is formal, courtly, and intent. He is different. Something's settled out in Harris and this idea makes me feel slighted, left aside. It's different than something settled out in me. Want comes over me and I can't balance it; I can't tell if it's want of food, of beer, of cigarettes, of lovemaking. I feel my vices to be many. I feel the need to be wicked like I know I can.

I stretch my arms, my legs, run my hands along my limbs, and stretch out along the bed. I toe my shoes off and cross my feet at the ankle, cross and uncross, cross and uncross, the only sound in the room the sound of my skin upon itself.

Harris leans against the bureau and scratches his new beard. He says, "I missed you until today."

"Until today?"

"Until now. Now you're here."

"Yes. Here I am."

He looks out from beneath his brows, looks to me laid out across the bed.

"The thing is, Mavis, you left. We had a good thing in Boone and I thought something would come of that. I thought we'd be together. I saw you gardening. I saw you skinning peaches in the sink and driving my car around."

"Harris, what all is this?" I say. "You don't say a word for four hours and now you talk about peaches?"

"I know you have things you have to do, but we didn't make plans. Didn't end what we had, or start something new. Now I go to work, I go to the kitchen, I go out in my car, no one else."

"I've been lonesome too," I tell him.

"I'm not lonesome. I'm disconnected, and I'm getting used to that."

Harris says this to sting me, and I find myself wanting to snap back at him, say something with barbs in it, too, like *you'd better*, but I don't. I turn away from him, the sparks falling away from my belly, my whole mood changed to sulk.

"What brought you here?" he asks me.

"Missing you, wanting to be with you."

"Mavis, it's not the same."

"It is. I missed you and I missed the way we were."

"Me, the way we were. I've felt alone and you've wanted to be with me. Listen to yourself, Mavis. It's not the same thing. It's the opposite."

"Set it up however you want, Harris. The fact of the matter is, here I am. Here we are, and this is it."

I drag my bag off the bureau and take it to the bathroom, slam the door, and it bounces open so I have to shut it with calm for it to latch. The light is bright and white and I think of reckless things I could do. I could sleep in a separate bed, not sleep at all, could trot down to the front desk and get myself another room just for spite. He can't play those games with me, tearing me down, paraphrasing us to nothing. *He feels disconnected*. I wash my face and brush my teeth.

I wanted more tonight, much more than this.

I wanted to be on my way to someplace hot and exotic like the ocean and to be filled up with wild things. I had the thought we were going to Jamaica like Sal and Hazel, Harris and I reckless and lusty like people newly together. I thought we might be like that because we've been apart so long, as if we might be fresh and strange to each other. But we're not. And it's not Harris's fault.

I don't know how long I stand there looking into the mirror, but when I come out of the bathroom, Harris seems fast asleep. The lights are dim and I lie atop the covers in a straight line. I could make this seem like anger, as though I'm still dressed because I don't want my skin to touch his on purpose or by accident, but in fact I'm just tired. Too tired to take my clothes off, to slip beneath the sheets, to make the effort of smoothing things between Harris and me. And I can hear him breathing deeply, evenly, as if this is okay with him, and then I seem to fall asleep too.

It's dark in the room, in the night, when I wake to the sound of running water in the bathroom, steam licking out from under the door. For a moment, I can't sense where I am, the bed misplaced and strange, and I stand as if in sleep and go to the sound of water, the lick of steam. I place my palms against the door to feel for heat, and the doorlatch opens to the white light, the white tiled floor, and the black marble tub. Harris kneels on the tile, his clothes puddled in the corner. His body is lean and earth brown, so dark as if he is made of walnut, something polished and oiled and grained.

Seeing me, he turns from the bath water, trails his wet fingertips down the inside of my thigh. I reach to unbutton my shirt, but he shakes his head and moves my hands away, fans his fingers across my hip bones, his breath flat on my stomach. My head sinks back on its stem; it has been a long while since I felt him this way. He slips his index finger inside the neck of my shirt and pulls me down to kneel in front of him. This is the finger with the ring, and it's still cold against my chest.

He says, "I want to tear these buttons off with my teeth and chew them for a while. I feel senseless to be with you, Mavis."

I raise my arms up and he skins the shirt over my head.

And then he is behind me at the clasp of my bra, his tongue hot-slipping at my shoulder and along my spine, a bite at the nape of my neck. I am fascinated with his movement, the way he moves, the way he moves me. He parts my legs with his knee from behind, his hands skimming and cupping, the still-running water lapping at the tub edge.

We make love on the floor and everything is water. Bath, bodies, steam, me, Harris: we are wet from making love, our fingers pruning from each other's skin, from so much touching, from suffocation, from drowning. It is not beautiful love, but more like survival. The air is so thick with steam it hurts inside my lungs.

And afterward, Harris holds me in his arms while we languish in the bath, everything run out of us, all the want and spite and sadness gone the way of the bathroom floor. We are like swamps or reservoirs, holding water above all else. I circle a sliver of soap about his knee, sinking back onto his chest.

Slowly, his hand moves to cover my lips.

He says, "The thing is, I love you."

He tells me he has for a while, hasn't told me before for fear of things great and small, and he doesn't want this to be some moment that marks us forever. He tells me it's not a gift or a promise, just a fact, and of a sudden he wanted to say those words aloud.

He lets his hand lag down my neck, resting 'cross my windpipe, his cheek laid atop my head. His voice comes out over me, seems to hover and toll through my whole body like shock or paralysis, and I imagine I hear him best with my rib cage, with the fine bones around my heart. It is with my chest that I listen to Harris.

He says, "It's not completely true, what I said earlier about feeling disconnected these weeks. It hasn't been the way it sounded."

He'd grown used to us being together and he knew it'd be hard when I went back home. But that was him, that's how he felt and thought and looked at us, and he only knew himself.

He says, "You're not with me, but without me."

And I am. I'm outside of him, unknown to him, beyond or behind or beside him, and this is what leaves him feeling disconnected. I think how Harris's feelings are in his head, and how mine are physical, residing in my bones and tissues, feelings in my vital parts.

He says, "I love you, Mavis. And I don't know what happens next."

I reach my hand to Harris's face, his cheek still laid on the crown of my head, my hair still wet and mingled with his beard. I roam the pads of my fingers across his features, his chin beneath his beard, his lips, the sharp bones of his cheeks. He is so rough, so soft, all at once. Gently, I brush his eyelids closed.

"Okay," I whisper. "It's okay."

But nothing leaps and sweats or trembles in me. I don't have those sensations in my body the way I think I should, no ache, no longing. Maybe this way of feeling, this physicality I have, is a fleeting thing, shorter lived than the feelings of thought, and I expect too much. I expect a sustained tone inside as if I were a tuning fork and I want to feel the pitch of Harris and me even when I can no longer hear us, when we are no longer words between each other.

I think one sane thought: I don't have patience for such labored hearts. I wonder why it was so hard for Harris to say those words to me when his feelings are in words, why it took such heaving and quiet, such preparation. If it's truly this hard, can it truly be love he's talking about, and if it takes this long for him to say it, will he ever say it again?

18

Harris and I dip south in the morning, picking up 264 in Greenville and winding down along the Pamlico Sound. Something passed by us last night and I don't know what it was, don't even want to think on it.

As soon as I see the ocean I say, "Tell me again what you told me last night," and I swear to myself if he gets it wrong I'll push him out into the highway. But he doesn't get it wrong, he tells me again he loves me, says it clean and clear and without hesitation, and I think this is good. This is a good place to start.

The shores are just beyond the blacktop flats, lacings of loblolly pine, beach myrtle, egrets, gulls, yaupon bush, and black needle rushes. We have ferry reservations at one o'clock out of Swan Quarter, a big boat that will hold the car and us for forty minutes across the shoals to Ocracoke, this place, the graveyard of the Atlantic.

Harris says, "Just out there, ships have run aground. Edward Teach used to run these islands with blood and death. He used to weave his beard with hemp fuses. Imagine that. A burning beard."

Harris rubs his own, a Renaissance man's instead of a pirate's, as if to say this thing, this piece of a man, on fire.

"How romantic," I say.

And I think it is romantic, these reefs and banks and shoals with all their wild past, with times upon them that held pirateering and naked women, beheadings, buried treasure, sunken gold, and foundered ships. I've learned these islands migrate and erode, land taken by the ocean, deposited in the sound, these islands rolling over themselves, ocean taking, inlet giving, and back again. I wonder if our histories are like that too, rolling over themselves and seeming to disappear, only to emerge in another place, someone else's ears, all the better and more fantastic for their time below the surface. Harris and I might be able to do that. We might be able to do that here, by the ocean and in the sand, and such a thought gives me cause to smile.

In Swan Quarter, we park the car in line for the one o'clock ferry, park behind other cars loaded down with bikes and luggage, sun umbrellas and bags of groceries, beach balls, rafts, and inner tubes for vacation. I feel myself to be suspicious, like checking into an airline ticket counter with only my pocketbook on me, or a hotel without a change of clothes. We lock up, head back down the block to an oyster bar for lunch, some fresh shrimp and a beer or two.

Across the street from the pier, there're people carrying signs, picketing with NO DRILL, NO SPILL printed 'cross their T-shirts. The sun is bright off their long blond hair, they wear mirrored sunglasses and sandals, bandannas tied 'round their sweaty necks. They seem to be in front of a gas station, broken-down and dilapidated in its sides, a trailer with a front porch and an old man in his rocker set out to watch the show. Every once in a while he slaps his knee and seems to laugh, chews a blade of grass, the spectacle of activism.

Over everything there is a Mobil Oil sign attached to an ad for Pepsi-Cola.

Harris says, "Good Lord," and a man hands him a flyer, tells him to increase the peace.

The flyer tells about consortiums and exploration rights, mentions Greenpeace, departments and interiors, disclaimer and risk. The point is natural resources versus nature's resources, natural gas versus nature's wildlife. Money is reeled about in hundreds of millions, and beneath the text there's an artist's rendering of Moses parting the Red Sea. The caption reads "Moses Parting the Dead Sea."

Harris tosses the flyer into the nearest trash barrel.

When I was on that bus in Texas, the blind man sitting next to me told a story he knew from when he used to see, from when he sold fiberglass pipe in West Texas in the fifties.

He said, "There was once an old dirt farmer in Sealy, Texas, drilling for water for his cattle, and around 1905 he came up with a shallow pool of crude oil. Well, he struck and struck again, sold some cattle and struck again, and before too long it was time to incorporate. This dirt farmer and his wife rode two days in a wagon to Austin, set on meeting the secretary of state and filing the necessary articles. Two of them, two days in the Texas sun, and the secretary of state looks them in the face and says, 'Where's your third party?'

"Well, there weren't no phones back then in West Texas, so they sent a Western Union telegram on horseback to fetch their only son, a senior in high school back home in Sealy minding the ranch. The Western Union rider flies up to the front porch and says, 'Get your britches on, boy, and come with me.' This son and the Western Union rider shook their horses back to Austin, two days for the boy, four for the rider, just to sign a name.

"And names was the next question, what to name the corporation. See, this old dirt farmer was a romantic and he looked 'cross those high state offices to his wife and her tired, dust-dry face, and he said, 'Call it Magnolia, after my beautiful magnolia woman.' They did. And that's the biggest damn oil corp in the world today, that dirt farmer's son upwards of ninety and latched to a beautiful nurse and an oxygen tank last I saw him."

I think about how that's natural resource, a man and his

family crossing hot, hot Texas for some piece of paper, a man looking into his wife's face and saying, *for you, for you.* Bad things happen to good land, I know, but nothing is black and white, nothing can be so simple. And it shouldn't be.

At the oyster bar, everything is covered in fish nets, the ceiling, the walls, the salad bar. Harris and I order a peck of raw oysters, a half pound of boiled shrimp, hush puppies, and beers. The waitress spreads yesterday's newspaper across the table and brings our food in baskets, heaping high and smelling of ocean water. I look to Harris and he's grinning down at everything, his knees against mine beneath the table and us all ready to go away, and I think how this was what I wanted last night, and how if we don't look too hard, too soon, Harris and I are okay with each other.

After we eat, Harris and I take the ferry across this piece of ocean and find his professor's house right on the beach, close to water like everything on Ocracoke. The island's only two miles at its widest, and from everywhere you can see the waves, the ocean or the sound moving in and out against this trace of land. We find the house key beneath the oleander, just as Harris said we would, and the house is beautiful, stilted and glassy, lone on the beach for yards and yards in either direction. Inside, there is lots of wicker furniture and tiled floors filmed in sand. There's a fireplace, and up a few steps, a bedroom with the biggest bed I've ever seen, a bathroom with a garden tub enough for three.

In the fridge, there's a six-pack of Dos Equis, butter and horseradish, chopped spinach and chicken backs in the freezer. We take the beer and chicken, and downstairs in the carport closet there's net and line for crabbing. We dig out a washtub and an old Styrofoam cooler, Harris gets his bow and quiver from the truck, and we carry everything down a mile's sandy path to the sound to catch our evening meal.

The sun is clear and the currents of breeze off the water so soothing I feel cool in spite of the sweat that rolls off my elbows and down the backs of my knees, the sweat collecting in my belly button, in the waist of my shorts. It feels so good, as if I'm breathing with my whole skin, my whole skin to the air and the sun and salt that hovers everywhere. As Hazel said when she talked about Jamaica.

The tide is out in the sound, low tide in a half-hour, and the sea smell heavy in the heat like sap. We scramble over beds of oysters, sharp even through my sneaker soles, and I'm careful not to cut myself because of hepatitis and oyster shell, one of those true facts or wives' tales, I'm not sure. I wonder how you could get a disease from an oyster shell, from a dead thing made by a living thing. It seems to me like catching a cold from a house and I think illnesses are probably more personal.

I tie a chicken back on about fifteen feet of line and cast out with a splash in the olive-dark water.

Harris laughs.

"What? What's wrong with that?"

"Nothing, Mavis. Just isn't that far out."

"It's fine. I bet I catch more than you anyway."

Harris ties his own line to a broadhead arrow with red fletching, catching the knot with his teeth. He has the recurve with him, his father's bow, and when he nocks the arrow I can see the veins in his forearms pulse. He tells me to hold a chicken back thirty paces out and I decline. I've seen him do such a thing before but it takes a steady hand and I'm tired in the sun after the drive. He smiles at me, turns, and baits the arrow himself, arcing it over the top of the ocean.

"All the fatties are out there, see. I'm catching dinner crab, and you, you're just first course."

"Apéritif type, the most delicate," I say.

"Yeah."

He laughs and the sunlight catches in his teeth white and in his hair and his new beard and in this moment he seems relaxed and easy and I can feel the turning parts of me rousing 'round inside my chest. This is how he is when he's having fun, and it's not something I've remembered often in these last months. I soften to him, and I smile more.

It's not long and I get a strike, crabs being not so subtle. Slowly, slowly I nudge in my line, and Harris waits in the shallows with the net. I can see my catch, waving and blue, before he even snaps out of the water.

"He's small, but he's feisty," I say, and Harris kisses the back of my neck, runs a cold beer down my spine.

"You watch," he says.

The afternoon passes this way, Harris catching big blue claws, big as dinner plates, with his arrowed bait, and me with smaller ones but many more, filling the washtub and creeping over. We turn each crab over and check the shell bone bellies for egg sacs, rusty against pearl. We throw the mamas back, make a big show of watching them scuttle away into the sound.

Harris folds a beach towel over the top of the tub of crab, and I carry everything else, lugging back to the house tired and sun-brushed and hungry. The sand kicks up behind us, sticks to the backs of our legs, and we have to hose down before we can go inside. Harris finds a kettle and he takes the crabs out on the balcony to cook them over the gas grill, so as not to stink up the house.

I take a quick shower and run to the store. When I get back, Harris stands out on the balcony over a pot of boiling water, watching it go.

"You know," he says, taking my hand, "I could do this all my life."

"This is vacation and if you did it every day, it might lose what makes it special. You might get listless, or even bored."

"I can't see it," he says.

"Yeah, but that's 'cause this is temporary, a short time in something bigger."

"But see, it could be the something bigger. You and I could make it bigger time."

Harris strokes his hand up my arm and cups my elbow, pulls me close against his chest. He draws my eyes to his, scans and looks deep, but I look away.

I say, "It was real fine with you today, Harris, real fine."

The waves break and foam on the shore in the fading light, blue, then brown and green, white like teeth or feathers as they course over themselves. The wet trails cursive on the sand, in and out, in and out. In and out.

We cook the crabs up red, make big bowls of drawn butter and spicy cocktail sauce. We feed each other, Harris and I, spread on the tiled floors of his professor's house with loads of newspapers and pencil-thin asparagus grown wild on this island for the roadside market. Harris opens a champagne and we drink right from the bottle, smacking another crab with a hammer, sucking meat from its claws, picking delicate backfin, and licking each other's fingers. An oldies station plays over the radio out of Norfolk, Elvis and the Supremes, Jerry Lee Lewis, Hank Williams, the Temptations, Sam Cooke, good music for dancing. Before too long, Harris and I are up and hand to hand, shagging 'round our dinner in our bare feet.

Harris sings along and whirls me 'neath his arm, knocks back some champagne from the bottle in his hand, holds it to my lips for me to sip. We are out of breath, a little drunk, trying to tango to the Motown music in the next set with slight success.

"You are so much, Mavis," he whispers in my ear. "So much."

"I'm too much for you, I think."

I say this with a laugh, but right now I know it to be true. I think, in the end, I will confuse Harris. I will not consider him enough, I will wander off at times in myself and he will think himself disconnected again. But maybe I need that distance and its closing, the sweet feeling of coming together again after a long time apart. Maybe everyone does this rising and falling in their own ways, their own lives. Maybe this is romance and how it lasts.

"Too much," I say.

Harris reaches his hand to the nape of my neck, tugs my hair back to make me look at him.

"I can handle it," he says. "I'm just waiting on you."

It's late and I've had too much to drink. My stomach and my head bring me out of sleep. Harris lies beside me, his arms 'round my arms like a ribbon, but I'm awake and I hear the waves outside the open window, the water so cool and soft at night. I get up carefully, quietly. I take an unopened champagne bottle, go down the balcony stairs to the boardwalk, to the ocean in my nightgown, and I sit on the beach in the path of the bright moon, the clean stretch of sand and water, always moving. I lie back at the water's edge and let the waves tide 'cross my body, soaking my nightgown with salt and sand, and I think wild thoughts of taking and giving. I ask for things. I promise others.

I stand and wade out into the breakers, kneeling down to keep warm in the water, out of the breeze. My nightgown swims around me, more a part of the ocean than myself, swirling with currents and eddies. It's heavy like hair, a covering of platinum blond in the moonlight, and I hold that champagne bottle to my side, heavy like a rock.

I imagine Owen drives his Mustang across wherever he is, someplace hot and talcine, someplace where the ground is sand of limestone, chalked like bone, and he drives across this place with foreboding and want. He feels within himself a heart of stone. There's glass still in his wrists and palms from the wedding and soon it will begin to rise in his scars to his skin's surface. The body repels what it does not want. He'll think, this is constance, prudence, and chastity. He thinks his thoughts in names of women he has known.

I imagine he's got the top down, the sun going down, the air slow and heavy in the seat. He's slicing down the highway in his Mustang, the engine hot and barreling and floored. He's got an old man from a blues band stretched out in the back seat, a beautician set to drive all night long.

I sink the champagne bottle between my knees and strip the foil down, twist the cage off, pop the cork. That bottle is cold and the champagne is cool and the water around me is no temperature at all, the same temperature as me. I drink off the neck of the wine and taste it with my lips on down through my skin as if it's more gas than liquid and just seeping into me.

This bluesman, he stretches his long blue skin over the edges of the back seat of Owen's Mustang and he hums a tune taken up in the wind. He is coolness and smoke, larger than life. He has a harmonica in his breast pocket which he will bring out somewhere down the road.

The beautician drives Owen's Mustang across wherever he is, and she holds the wheel with her fingernails, long and curling pink, which catch the ebblight in small points like faceted stone. Owen sees this and he thinks, *within myself, a heart of stone.*

He thinks, *Mavis.*

From the wind, he hears a song, something low and lone about girls and back doors, about what he is and things he'll never know.

He says, well now, how about that.

The beautician reaches down along her leg and trails those nails over her fishnet stockings to scratch an itch beneath.

Owen follows her hand back up her calf, the inside of her knee, and back out, inside and back out. He turns in his seat to face her, his back riding the car door, his foot propped on the seat. He thinks her legs to be rivers of net and seam.

He says, do that again, and she does.

Dust blows up behind the car and trails their path: Owen, the bluesman, and the beautician. He watches it settle over them, veil after veil of limeish dust in the setting sun. He thinks of home, the dust like that of home. He thinks this is what you see in life and where to say you saw it.

I take another sip of that champagne bottle, wet my lips, and let it fill my mouth, run down my chin, and onto my chest.

And when Owen returns, he'll bring me a pair of ostrich-leather cowboy boots.

He'll say, "There's nothing like the way a woman rides her ass in a pair of genuine boots. It gets me weak in the heart just to see you put those on."

But I won't care to hear it.

I feel myself to be true and wise to the ways of the world, charmed beyond belief here in this water, which is constant only to itself. I think, *for you, for you . . . and over and over for you.*

And then I can hear Harris calling me from the house and I am running back up the beach and I am calling him too. He's on the balcony and I stand in the sand, looking up, and I am wet and I am cold and I hold my hair back from the wind.

I say, "Get your bow. Get your arrows."

"What in God's name are you talking about?"

"Get your things, Harris, and bring them to the beach."

He shakes his head. He says, "Mavis, it's late. I'm half asleep still."

"I will not go back inside that house until you get your bow and bring it here."

He turns and disappears and I run up the slat boards to

where we left the bait from crabbing. There's a bucket half full of those chicken backs, slick and white in the moonlight, and I take them with me, follow the moon's path back to the water. I walk backward with that bucket heavy at my side, watching my footsteps fade out in the wet, watching the house for Harris.

And then he comes out of the dunes in his jeans and his open shirt, his quiver slung over his shoulder and that recurve in his hands. He's walking toward me and rubbing his eyes, the moon so bright like daylight and his eyes still full of sleep, I am sure.

I reach down into the bucket and take a chicken back, drop my hand, and then toss it high, as high as I can. I call his name out, but he's already nocked an arrow and released, and that arrow splits at the air and through the heart of the chicken and sends it feet and feet out into the ocean.

He's stopped in his tracks. I think I can see his own heart beat itself beneath his shirt, but that may only be the wind.

I throw another and he nails it midair, and the next one he misses, another less high, another and another, and his aim is sure and clean for these. He is steely and polished in the moonlight, with his arrows shearing by me, each one closer to its point of release than the last. I think how I could snap my hand from harm's path if need be, I could step aside at the last possible moment, hold up my arms and arch my back and his arrow would just graze by. Lower and faster and lower, and then I'm just flossing the thing out of my hand, barely letting it go its way into the air.

"Shoot," I yell to him. "Shoot."

He nocks that arrow and I can see the veins in his forearms pulse under this swath of moonlight, this mirror of water, and the chicken heavy and slipping in my hand and I am steely, too, and sure, and without a care but for this moment and the belief that I can do this, that I can escape hurt. Harris aims right at me and I think I am steady and quick and faster than light and then he's not there. He's dropped his sights.

"No, Mavis," he says.

"I can handle it," I say. "Goddamnit. I'm waiting on you."

"No, Mavis. I can't. It's too close."

And then I am running up the beach to him and I feel him pitch in me like heat, like tremble, and then I have my arms about him, my legs wrapped 'round him, and he holds me close, too, us fast against each other as if it's our lives we've just let loose for a moment, come snapping back inside us with the pull of the earth, and that of honesty, of mass and fear. It's now I realize we are both trembling and deliberate, we are willful, we are even-matched.

I whisper to him how amazing he is, how strong and true, and he's come open like me, come soft and shaking from what's happened. He made a decision just now, and I am not someone he wants to risk. He values me over his skill and yet the moment was there for him to nock and aim and set free. I can see he's scared himself. We have scared each other here tonight, and how very foolish we've been to test each other like this, to be so hard on this thing we have that is full of distance and its closing, that is full of real space and real time apart.

19

~~~~~~~~~~~~~ August comes banging at the front door, a Saturday off before the thick of the harvest, and there's a thunderstorm. It's not rained to speak of since I've been home, and now I wake sticky in my skin beneath my open window. The breeze highs and whips the curtains from my windowsill and it's the sound at first, the crack of the air, of water coming through the air. There is nothing quiet about this storm's coming, and then the rain is a taste in my mouth, like white flowers and talc, things thirsty and pale and atmospheric. I kneel on my bedcovers and there's lightning and thunder, rivers in the street outside. The ground won't hold water, as if it's been baked in a kiln, thrown like a pot.

Evelyn lives with us now. When I was away to Ocracoke with Harris, her trailer burned to the ground, her home, her beauty shop, everything she owned up in flames while she'd been down at Burdine's Diner having a cup of coffee. That's all the time it took, too, a cup of coffee and some bad wiring to her curling iron, then her with no place to go. She stood on the side of the highway next to her Pinto and watched the Edisto Volunteer Fire Department hose everything down, the smell in the air like a charcoal grill.

She said, "It smelled like somebody was cooking goddamn hamburgers."

And her beauty shop, nothing but blackened tubs of ashwater and shapes of charred appliances. She couldn't clean it up because there was nothing left to clean up, the whole trailer exploding as if it was made of gasoline. Miss Pauline offered the extra bedroom right off, Hazel's or the guest room, and Evelyn chose the guest room and a job at Miss Pauline's Boutique until she gets back on her feet.

She says, "What I really want is a spa, Mavis. Someplace where girls can go and put their whole bodies in my care, or maybe a tanning salon and stress center."

I have the idea she and Miss Pauline are dreaming something up. She still has the land her trailer sat on. They speak in low tones over the dinner dishes and I saw Evelyn with a measuring tape and graph paper last I was at the Boutique, her eyes gone to laying things out in her head.

And this morning, my own mind harbors the strangest edges of a dream, just a feeling now, but it was a full dream. It was in color, had taste, other people, and a place of its own. It had something behind me, waiting for me to turn around, to move my body like a helix and catch it full. It had a river and land and a woman with her heart grown outside her body.

I think of Punk's Niagaras, already picked and on a truck to Pennsylvania, the Concords almost ripe, the Catawbas and Scuppernongs waiting to carry the farm into October and first frost. I think of the rain on his grapes like condensation, his grapes out at the vineyards, his grapes as they go on up the highway. I want to feel the rain over my skin like that, as if it comes out of the air and forms there, or it comes from inside, sweats out from glass.

I slip on a T-shirt and a pair of cutoffs. I get a cup of coffee from the kitchen and head out the front door to the porch. The rain falls off the roof in great cascades and splashes, sounding itself like a waterfall, and the air thick with ozone and tar smell. I've been different since I got back from Ocracoke, something inside gone quiet and cool, and I have the idea this is the cause of such a storm, the cold parts of me coming full slam into the Edisto heat. I have the idea I control the weather.

Harris and I left everything the way it was between us when

we came off that island, and after all, what could be said? I spoke of distance. I spoke of choices and decisions and the future and I think I said things like *who knows* and *we'll see*, but these aren't sufficient words. These are the words you begin with.

I once heard the only gracious way to respond to *I love you* was to say *I am honored*. I thought to speak to Harris of honor, but that's a thing he understands, a thought he can hold and turn over in his mind, and a thought like that would tell him nothing. It would teach him nothing about us. When you talk about love, it's only important to put things into words that can't be understood in thoughts, feelings that have no formula for the brain, no names like *devotion* or *want* or *longing*. There should be talk of things that live inside the footsoles, things that line the kneecaps, and the migrations of these things about the body.

But I didn't talk this way. Neither did Harris, but it's not his fault, a way of talking he doesn't know to exist. But he felt such things that night on the beach. I know he felt them because I could feel underneath his skin, the pumping and pushing and knocking against my fingertips as if he was barely inside himself, and that's how I felt too.

Sometimes I feel cool about him, though, and there are days I don't think of Harris at all. But then there are days I think of him coming down this way, of us being together, different from how we were in Boone, and that keeps me up smiling when there's nothing funny around, secretive and happy and wanting to hear his voice in my ear telling me he loves me. It's confusing. What I do know is we scared each other that night of our showdown. We are neither one of us to be taken for granted, to be allowed in harm's way. We came off that island respectful, came away with new places to begin again and an undeniable tangent between us, a relation between us like blue blood and red, or ice and steam. Harris saw all of me that night, the parts that are kind and the ones that are frightening and cold, and I like to think I saw all of him. These are not sights you can walk away from, not things you can separate from what you know about yourself and what you know about your lover, and I know we won't try.

I step off the porch and into the rain and I expect the drops to fall on me like a shower, but they are far apart and hard like June bugs on a windshield. I wander down the front walk pelted by this rain I might have called up, and I hold my hands out as if to collect the water for a later use. It's as warm as the air, but chills my skin as the breeze rims across, a twofold thing, an opposite and its complement. I think of movements that are the same backward and forward, like spinning or dancing, the opposite and its complement the same. I close my eyes.

I open my eyes and there stands Hazel. Aunt Hazel, Vuitton bags at her feet, lace from her wedding gown trailing out her trench coat. She's appeared in the driveway in the rain. She smiles and she has lipstick on her teeth.

"I thought I should return the way I left," she says, hands me a suitcase, nudges past me up the walk and into the house.

I heft her bag inside and follow her into the kitchen, pour her a cup of coffee, and get us both some towels to dry with. I'll wait. There's something to tell here and I can wait for her to get it out. I have a patience lately in me, a calmness and a shrewdness, an understanding of space and time. Last Sunday, the hired man W. G. Marvelle ended up in jail come morning, spending his paycheck on a Saturday night bar fight over in North. I had to go bail him out and I didn't chafe to do it, even as it was a town I didn't know, a town where Punk's name means a lot less than here in Edisto. There was a story there too, a reason I had to go and no one else, and I still haven't gotten it, so I can sure wait on Hazel to pull herself into a talking mood.

She flops into a chair at the table and hangs her trench coat off her shoulders, mounds her dress in her lap. She drips puddles on the parquet floor, holds her coffee cup in two hands like a bowl of rice, and we consider each other a full thirty seconds.

"So. How are you?" I say.

"Half dead for coffee, sugar. I am tired to the bone."

Her eyes are red and webby, shadowed. She rubs at them with the flats of her hands, drums her fingers on the top of her head. She looks road dusty, the train and hem of her white dress gone near rust. She's tired, but I wouldn't say she's in pain. She's worn clean and fatless, she has come a long way home, but I would not say she is in pain.

"How'd you get here?" I ask.

"Plane. Cab. Bus. By air, land, and motorcar."

"How long you visiting?"

"Forever," she says.

She reaches into the bodice of her dress and pulls out a pack of Chesterfields and kitchen matches. She flicks a tip with her fingernail and touches the flame to her cigarette, clenched in her mouth like an old woman. I think they must have had an argument, her and Sal. I think this is what newlyweds must do, being as they are like forest fires, things subject to the moods of wind and water and heat. They must have fought, and Hazel would think to come home to Punk's house, because that's how she is.

"Hazel, what happened?"

"Dollbabe," she says, "nothing happened. Quit your fretting, nothing happened."

She smiles, exhaling smoke through her teeth and nostrils at the same time.

"Okay, then. Can I fix you breakfast?"

I fuss around the kitchen, peer into the fridge. There's food here. There's sausage and pork chops and pale cheese, milk and blueberries, stewed apples, gravy and biscuits left over from Punk's breakfast.

"What do you want?" I ask.

"All of it. I've not eaten since yesterday."

I lay some blueberries in a bowl with some sugar and milk, bring Hazel a jelly jar of orange juice. The stove is on. Meat is frying.

"Hazel, what's happened?" I ask again.

"Plain as day. I had my wedding and now it's over. Plain as day."

"What about Sal?"

"Sal's a good man," she says. "But, then, having a marriage is different than having a wedding. All's I really, really wanted was the wedding."

She goes to stub out her cigarette on the sole of her shoe, but she's not wearing any. She looks stumped at this for a moment, as if they were there and now they're not, as if they'd walked away of their own accord. Then she pinches off the butt and tosses it into a plant pot behind her, ash misting over the floor, slight smell of burnt hair hovering.

"It was a beautiful wedding," I say.

I feel I should say this, that it's important to her that it was a really great day. But all I remember of it is white and crystalline. I was tired. It was months ago. This is the difference between Hazel and me, one day enough reason for her whole life and the same with my mama, one man enough for always. I'm not built that way. I don't have enough saint in me to live the way they do, to be content or at least composed enough to give myself away for one moment of time. This is what makes me patient. This is why I'm here and not with Harris.

I crack an egg on the side of the counter, fry it over light in the fat of the sausage, slide everything over some grits. Biscuits and gravy, a bowl of warmed apples, some cheese if she wants it. Out the kitchen window, I can see the gutters spilling over, my mama's garden bending 'neath the rain. I want to tell Hazel how it hasn't rained like this since before she left, but it wouldn't mean to her what it means to me.

Hazel eats with her fingers, hand to mouth and back again. She pokes the egg yolk with her long red nail and trails yellow across a biscuit, shovels up a bite of grits. She licks herself clean, starts all over.

"I'll go get Mama up. She'll want to see you," I say.

"She can see me anytime," she says. "I ain't going anywhere."

But I wipe my hands on a dishrag and go anyway. Hazel watches me down the hall with her badland eyes, licks grits out of the hollows of her nails.

"Mama." I tap on her door. "Mama. It's raining and Hazel's here."

My mama opens her bedroom door, rubbing her eyes and still in her nightgown and hair curlers, the smell of her like steam in the hallway.

"Oh, my," she says, "and me looking such a fright. Hazel's home."

She grabs my arm, yells over her shoulder on her way to the bathroom. "Be right there, honey!"

My mama cups both my elbows in the palms of her hands, pulls me into the bathroom with her. She looks at me all serious.

"Okay. Now. Is he dead?"

"Dead?"

"Men disappear. They melt away, they go away, they die. Now is Sal dead, or did she just leave him?"

"Mama. What in the hell are you talking about?"

"A woman takes up with a man, and the woman comes home to her family after just a few short months. A few things could have happened, one of which the man turns up dead."

"She didn't say Sal was dead."

"Well, did you ask her?"

"I can't say I knew to ask her, Mama. She didn't mention that herself."

"Of course not. Of course not."

My mama rubs her hands up and down my arms as if she's trying to warm my skin. She takes a deep breath, lets it out. She thinks on something for a while. She watches the rain outside the window, sheets and sheets of it.

"Okay, sugar. Run along," and she scoots me out of the bathroom.

I look down the long hall, and there's Hazel in her wedding dress and her breakfast plate, and behind the bathroom door, my mama and her thoughts on men. Sometimes I wonder if I'm kin to these women at all. But then I'll feel myself ticking like a bomb, ticking the way I know they do, and I'll go out to the barn and lay low in the hayloft, or snatch up the keys to Punk's farm truck and drive absolutely nowhere with all the windows rolled down. This should frighten me, but it doesn't. I can see both sides of the world, the view from within this house and the view from without. It's as though I can pass through a mirror, understand the reflection and the thing that makes the reflection, understand my mama and Hazel and still understand myself to be different. Rounder. Warmer to the touch. Colder, when it gets down to it.

I take it up the back stairs to the guest room where Evelyn sleeps. I knock on her door and tell her Hazel's here.

"Hazel Black?" she says.

"What other one would be in our kitchen?"

Evelyn follows me down the stairs still in her thin nightgown and peeks around the corner to where Hazel sits, finished with her eating and smoking another cigarette.

"Hazel!" she says, and passing by me, under her breath, "She ain't even took the dress off."

They hug and kiss and my mama comes out of the bathroom and they hug and kiss some more and I watch. I have the feeling they should be together, these women in this house. They share things I don't have and I begin to think there's something to this family of women talk. They know things I don't know, but I can walk among them as easily as air, and what a gift that is. I feel myself to be lucky right now, privileged and mighty like a ghost.

Punk comes hustling in, comes in amongst these women at his table with grease on his hands and wrenches in his pockets, a chain slung over his shoulder. He's heard the news. Kat's behind him like his shadow, her face smudged, carrying more wrenches and a fistful of screwdrivers. Punk stops and looks at his daughter, bedecked in her wedding dress, sitting at his table. There's a hush fallen over the air. He bends to kiss Hazel's cheek. The storm has about ended.

"Mavis," he says, "pack up. Throw Miss Kitty-Kat here in the bath. We're about to head north."

Punk continues through the kitchen with his grease and wrenches and chain, down the back hall, leaving prints across the parquet. I can hear his footsteps stop, a boot heel tapping on the stairs.

"And for God's sake, Miss Evelyn," he yells back, "you put some clothes on while you're in this house. I may be old but I'm still a man."

20

The road to Pennsylvania dips and sways across the Appalachian Mountains, down into Virginia's I-81, which we crest near Fort Chiswell and high noon. Punk and I've been driving since morning, and I feel his new Mustang glide along beneath us like milk, like something cool and smooth in the early August heat. Punk sleeps now, his farm hat pulled low over his eyes to shield the sun out, his head resting on the red leather, and in the back seat Kat is only half asleep, lagging her hand out the window, letting the wind do to it what it does to the wing of an airplane.

But this car, our passage, keeps me wide awake. I picked up a whole mess of brochures at the last gas station. They have just enough writing to read and drive at the same time. I smooth one at a time across the steering wheel, pin them down from the wind.

This is the road of the Shenandoah Valley, the road to take to the Luray Caverns, great caves underground enough to ride a tour train through, see the stalactites and stalagmites, the black silences that fill up the inside earth. And there are other caverns too, the Dixie, the Shenandoah, the Indian Falls, and I'll bet they are all pretty much the same. They might even be the same, separated out by some buckle in the land that covers them. Up the interstate further is the Natural Bridge, an arc of stone left by God knows what force, and if I took this exit, Virginia Beach, this one, the Blue Ridge Parkway.

The movements of the land are tourist attractions here, the color of the mountains, the breeze off the ocean, the paths made through the ground we pass over. People come to see, they print up papers to be sure others come to see, and this is the same pride Punk has in his land. He says, *here, watch this. Here, feel this, taste this.* I think he's worried Sal will back out of their deal now that Hazel's left him, and he'll be caught with tons and tons of grapes and no one to use them. I think he's worried his fruit will go to waste, go to rot, and I don't blame him. I see the need for this trip. I see it the way I see my own eyes. And in that same moment I know it isn't just Punk's fruit, but it's all of us. It's the hired men and my mama, it's Owen gone far away and Miss Pauline's Boutique, Hazel and now Evelyn and all her plans. We all depend.

Brochure after brochure I spread across the wheel to read. Some of them make it back to a pile on the floor at my feet, some get whipped away in the wind before I can even see the pictures. There's history, this valley the road of General Thomas J. Jackson, Jeb Stuart, and Longstreet. Custis, Fitz, and Rooney Lee, the road of their father, Robert E., and of their undoing, Little Phil Sheridan. My mind latches on to such trivia of information, delivers up these details of men and war. When Sheridan took the Shenandoah Valley, he took with him hundreds of horses and mules, thousands of beef cattle, sheep and swine, hundreds of thousands of bushels of oats, wheat, corn, and hay, pounds of tobacco, fodder, yarn, bacon, and straw. He took women and girls, arms, legs, eyes. He took tanneries, furnaces, and barns. He took everything he could think of, everything I can see in this valley now.

I notice I'm doing eighty miles an hour. I slow down and wipe the sweat from my forehead.

Back in school I knew these boys who used to hang the Confederate flag outside their fraternity house on Robert E. Lee's birthday. They used to have a party on that day, as if it was the Fourth of July or Easter, every last one of them dressed in white, with string ties and plugs of chewing tobacco because that's the way they thought about Lee, like Colonel Sanders on a horse. I had a statistics class with one of these boys, all decked out in his cavalry hat and a bow tie that played "Dixie." The professor was from Vermont, not too forgiving of ignorance and computerized songs.

He'd said, "Valorization is the closest thing to rot and ruin. You people frighten me beyond belief."

The things I remember about history are few and fleeting, small things I read or overhear. I feel there to be something wrong in that, a debt of knowledge to the horror and evenness of what's past. And yet as I make this trip through this land, so much beats familiar, a name, a place, a detail. Stuart's Draft, Appomattox, Waynesboro, and New Market. Harper's Ferry. The Birthplace of Stonewall Jackson. Gettysburg. Antietam. And so I get the feeling this interstate is like a path cut through time, a place where things happen and have happened, a valley like a funnel of events I should know about, moments of importance kept alive in their places.

But then, if anything, I know the ground itself doesn't hold a single breath of any man who passes over it, just like that shoulder of road beside Punk's farm holds nothing of my father, Wyman Jackson. Maybe it's the memory that's important then, not that I stop Punk's car, get out, and walk these historical sites, but that I pass by them and remember the little that I do. People's history has small tie to the land; it's not something you can watch and feel and taste. It lives someplace else altogether.

They say all this is to teach us, and there are lessons here in this valley to be thought upon, taken down. This is the battleground of a lost Southern cause, a fated idea given up to its ghost, and I cannot help but be afraid that Punk and I are two more Southerners, coming north for some different but just as fated purpose.

Kat leans up in the wind and asks me to speed up again.

"Speed up?"

"Yeah," she says. "This trucker is flashing me signs in his window and I can't read them."

And then a tanker pulls in front of me and throws his brakes, slowing down so much that I just have to pass him, and when I do he's looking in his rearview mirror and checking us out, even as Punk sleeps in the passenger seat. The sign in his window reads SHOW A LITTLE LEG PLEASE, and I'm suddenly conscious of just how much these men can see from way up there in their cabs. I think of Wyman Jackson way up in the cab of his truck years and years ago and maybe there weren't any such convertibles or women in shorts and T-shirts, but I'll bet he wished for the same taste of skin as he passed on by.

I check my rearview mirror, and Kat's hiked her T-shirt up around her rib cage and tied it there and she's reclining in the back seat to suit a woman in faint, her black sunglasses and her hair in a ponytail. That truck driver's grin breaks about as wide as this damn valley, and he's pulling on his horn when he passes us again. There's a new sign in his window that says THANK YOU, and I'm figuring these must be signs he has ready and prepared for such occasions as convertibles and vanloads of cheerleaders, tour buses, and the likes of Kat. I have to wonder if he gets lots of women to flash him a little something. He was certainly polite about his asking.

Miles down the interstate, we see signs for the Mason-Dixon Line. Punk is awake now and has things to say, things about all hell breaking loose and God save this automobile. He's never been north of Staunton, Virginia, but once, and that was the first time he met Sal and how this whole thing got started. Somehow he's tied the Mason-Dixon and questionable circumstances together in his mind, correlated them into a reason for prayer.

He says, "Back in the war I got trapped in a bunker for

three weeks and I won't eat tuna fish to this day. I didn't have to cross the Mason-Dixon to get that done to me."

I wonder what Punk's not going to eat that will mark what's happened between him and Sal, and I'll bet it's wedding cake. Being in World War II is the only thing Punk Black doesn't talk about, and I don't ask. I think of him young and on the front lines in France or Germany, and the Mason-Dixon Line is like that, just something out there in space, not geology or geography. It's the thing that lives in the head and not the body.

But as we cross into Pennsylvania, Punk holds his breath.

We exit at Route 34, take it through Carlisle, Mount Holly Springs, and on to Tagg Run, because that's the way Punk remembers to Sal's place, because that's the way he knows and Kat is fast asleep in the back of the car, still lying down and tied up.

Punk tells me, "Sal came by this property up yonder at just the right time, and Mavis, it's something else. A real story."

I thread the car along the mountain roads, the turns sharper, the blacktop rising up ahead. Punk tells me of Sal's wife, Merrilee and Kat's mother, and how she was pregnant before they were married. He tells me of how things didn't work out for them in Utah, and how after Merrilee was born they moved out to California, and how Sal helped build Martini to what it is now, working with U. Cal–Davis, working with the other winemakers. Sal saw the big picture, how California would never be France or Italy, but what it could be, how it could taste, and folks listened to him.

Punk says, "He told me, yeah, you can take the grapes and stomp on 'em and you'll get yourself some wine. But it won't stop there. Naturally, it'll make vinegar if you leave it up to Mother Nature, and he don't trust Mother Nature, says she's a mean old bitch."

Punk's story goes on, some words lost to the wind and rush of the car, some words so loud and clear they seem to form inside my own ears. When Sal's wife was pregnant again, she hopped a bus down to Baja and took the girl Merrilee with her, left one harvest moon when Sal was in the fields, without even a note like a good woman might. She was down there two weeks before Sal found her, enough time to have the baby in a back alley like a whore, enough time for her and the baby, the little girl all so sick with the Tijuana curse they all about died. It was then he took the girls back up to Utah and hired himself a lawyer.

They don't like divorces, Mormons don't, and after Sal and his wife signed their papers, he took the girls and left town, left his own parents, her family, behind and moved out here to Pennsylvania. This was in 1972.

Punk seems to drift off, closing his eyes to the wind around the car, laying his head on the back of the seat. He watches the green green trees pass beneath the sky, and I drive the car still down Route 34 past the Toland Mission Church and public lakes with brown young skin laid out along their beaches. This is a vacation area of sorts, everyone on holiday in the late summer sun.

I say, "I bet those lakes are cold," but Punk doesn't answer.

We cross the Appalachian Trail, the trail that would lead right back down to Boone if I had the time. I've never hiked that trail, but I remember seeing its bits and pieces when I was at school, off the Blue Ridge Parkway, settling back into the country. I think it strange to see the same thing in different places as if it makes lives connected somehow, makes my life connected somehow. I think about Harris and I know myself to be so very far away from him now. This is the only thing that seems important, this drive, our land.

Punk says, "In 'seventy-three there was a great flood in

these parts. The Susquehanna rose up, the creeks ran over on themselves."

This was when Sal bought his land. The property had once been an iron furnace, almost a town itself near Caledonia. There was a brick works and a water wheel, a charcoal house, cold-blast furnace, and hoisting planes for ore cars. In the flood after Hurricane Agnes hit the coast of Pennsylvania, the ore pit filled and ran over, washing out a cemetery, coffins over a hundred years old finding their way to the surface. The couple who lived on the seventy-five acres hit the high road and put the land up for sale to anyone who would see to the coffins. Sal had to arrange for the identification and burial of almost twenty-five different boxes from pine and oak and even some of mahogany. And when the coffins were opened, he found himself with near to thirty bodies, some of the coffins from paupers' graves or criminals', some with two rib cages and no skulls or three left feet, and he had no idea what to do about such extras. He could get this land for a song, less than fifty thousand dollars. He had big plans. He had dreams of grandeur.

I know some of this story, the parts Kat told me at Hazel's wedding, and the parts Hazel filled in herself around the edges, and still it's a real story, a legend, and one to be told on a trip through strange mountains, driving to meet a man who's been left himself this time, the ground itself more important to the telling than the man who owns it. This land's made Sal what he is. This story is his geology, how the ground he works has given him up.

Punk says, "I reckon those old grave bones might be any-where on his property. He is I-talian, and that being so, he is also unpredictable. Moreover, he is a divorced Mormon I-talian. I do not know what all we will find when we get there."

He tells me he called up here to Pennsylvania the minute he

heard Hazel was home, and Sal had sounded vacant and down-hearted, that he hadn't said much of anything, and that's what got Punk worried.

"The heat's not on," he tells me, "but we got some serious cleaning up to do."

Punk points up to the right and I make the curve into a wooded drive, long-twisting and smooth into the side of the mountain, as slender as a reed.

"This is it?" I ask.

"This is that."

21

When Punk's grapes get to Pennsylvania they're processed, stemmed, crushed, separated seeds from pulp, as seeds and stems are bitter and the pulp important. That's the secret. The pulp, just juice and skin of grape, is the secret to red wine or white, vinegar or something to serve with dinner. Sal uses an Italian basket press to get about thirteen hundred gallons of juice per ton of our grape. Then that juice goes into casks or stainless steel tanks, depending on what he's making, and these are airlocked in order to release CO_2 that accumulates without air actually contacting the future wine. Air with juice produces flowers of bacteria, eventually vinegar, and not any sort of vinegar you'd use, either.

In primary fermentation the grape's natural yeast is very active, feeding, frothing, digesting sugars, and, within the first few days, forming the skins into a cake which floats the surface of the would-be wine. The longer the juice is in contact with the skins, the redder the wine, and they must be kept wet or they will grow bacteria all their own. When skins are removed, it's the wait, two, three months.

Sal has his arm around Kat. He can't help but keep looking into her face as if she's new, as if she's something lost been found. She stands here in her blue jeans and her T-shirt, the cowboy boots we bought her up in Boone, and her arm around her daddy too and she's glad to be home, glad to see she's been missed in her daddy's eyes. They look well together.

We stand inside the barn where Sal keeps his tanks, his presses, and his filters. The barn is warm and smells like old wood and sweet grape ferment. Everything looks as if it's been touched recently, as if people have been through here with their hands and their mouths, with their senses about them. When I was up at Taylor Winery in Fredonia a while back, Punk's friend gave me a tour, and their operations were much larger, much more stainless and sterile. You couldn't smell a thing at all.

Sal has a way about him of relief, as if he's just let out a deep breath, and I can only conclude that he's forgotten about Hazel's leaving, or is building up steam from a ways off, building up to being hurt and bruised and sad sometime later, but not now. Not standing with his little girl. He wears a pair of cutoff Levi's and a red pinstripe oxford, his feet bare and blackened on the soles as if he's been walking hot coals or tar just laid. There's a look about his eyes of hard work, long work, work that takes both day and night.

"When the wine is ready," Sal says, "the dead yeast cloud has to be filtered out. We try to do this in late winter, early spring, when it's still below freezing outside and we can just funnel the wine from the barn over to the cellar for first filter. We let it rest, then filter with a fine grade before bottling. We're talking about two million gallons of juice here, one point nine from Black Vineyards and another hundred thousand of French Columbard and Cabernet from N.Y. State for balance."

He takes us into the cool belly of his house, down underneath to his wine cellar, sweet-smelling like the barn and humid and walled with stone. It runs the entire length of the house, with racks and racks of bottles, whole rooms of California wine, Italian and French, bottles he made in Pennsylvania, bottles he made in Napa. He walks its corridors with his fingers outstretched, feeling the air as if it holds something to be read, direction, maps of placement and wealth, and Kat seems to hover in the crook of his arm, close but not touching.

They are steps ahead of me, and Sal's body seems to work as if from inside a space too small for him, a certain punch to his limbs, and Kat right in his steps, her legs as long as his. I can see the tendon that runs up from his ankle taut and flex like a cable, a chain reaction of muscle inside his skin. Kat asks after Merrilee.

"She's home," Sal says. "Run and see her. She's missed you."

"Merrilee's missed me?"

"Of course she has. Go on; my keys are in the house."

Kat leans into him and kisses his cheek and he seems moved by this; he smiles and his eyes burn up a little. There is such a charge to him and I begin to think his movements are not from strain but gladness. He's raised Kat much on his own, and I'll bet there are things between them like what's all between my mama and me, things that could lift you up out of a time's happenings. Things that could make you forget hurts you might have. He watches Kat pick her way through the cellar to some stairsteps leading upward.

He turns to look at me. "What do you know about wine?" he says.

I glance to Punk, standing beside me, and I feel there should be something said in the way of negotiation, the less that looms in the conversation the better, as Sal is an unpredictable man seeming in a good mood. But Punk's rolling a bottle of Zinfandel in his hands like a cube of ice or a bar of soap, something that might need catching on its way to the ground. He doesn't have anything to say here and maybe he doesn't think talk necessary.

"Not much," I tell Sal. And then, "I know what you've told me."

He laughs and says, "That's something."

He takes a bottle from this rack, another and another, and leads me into the heart of the cellar. Punk walks behind us, his hands in his pockets. We come upon a table laid with linen, set with glass. Sal pulls out a chair for me and I sit beneath a small window, the light filtering in the air as if it comes through fog, and Punk comes to stand behind me, shoulders up the wall and crosses one boot over the other. Sal uncorks the first bottle.

"I've known men who treat wine like a wife," he says. "They are as careful with it as if it's mercury."

"I don't know about these things," I say.

And I don't. I don't know about wives and how they get treated, but I imagine it to be a fragile process, something like the way glass is blown. Miss Pauline is the only wife I know, besides Merrilee, who I don't know well, and Hazel too, Hazel a sort of wife. I think how wives might be like mercury and how Sal might see his Hazel beaded and silver and poisonous, see her as something to be scooped up with a spoon.

I imagine Sal feels himself to be different as a husband, different from your average man at home. Maybe in fact he wants someone to be careful around, someone that could break or burst or run off. He's been left now by two women and I wonder what his end of these leavings holds, what he might have done when the door slammed or the bed lay empty. I wonder if he ran down the road after a trail of dust, if he crawled into his cellar and worked like mad, if he sat down on the edge of himself and cried. He is a husband wronged, but I wonder what he's done about that fact.

I've crawled all inside his brain now and I feel strange for it, as if I've crossed some line like the southern hemisphere or the time zones and felt the shift, felt an hour fall away from me and the sun beat harder. I presume a lot with this man.

He hands me a glass, the wine red like raspberries.

"How it feels in your mouth and down your throat," he says. "How it feels when it's gone, that's what it's all about."

I take the glass from his hands and raise it to my lips. I try to taste all the things in this wine: the bottle, the barrel, the grape, the way it smells, the way my face reflects upon itself in its surface. I try to taste all these things at once because I know that's how it should be. I close my eyes and Sal laughs and Punk laughs too.

"It's different when you think about it," he says. "Like tapping your foot to music and chewing gum at the same time, or something. It's easy and hard all at once."

Sal uncorks one bottle after another. He tells me about Beaujolais and how it's light, Fumé Blanc and how it tastes like figs, Rieslings like apricots, Zinfandels like anything else. He teaches me to hold the glass by its base, not its bowl. He teaches me to inhale as I drink, to hold the wine to the light, and then to close my eyes and remember if it was clear, if it jeweled in the sun, as I taste it. There is so much here. There is so much to know. I wonder if this is how it went with Hazel, that first night they met and Sal had her and Punk in this very cellar. I wonder if he taught her these things before they went out riding in his Cadillac, before they struck up to be married. I wonder if Hazel listened and learned, and somehow I doubt it.

Punk pulls up a chair and leans back in it, spraddles it on two legs, and smiles. He's kept his silence for a reason; he's let Sal become comfortable with him again and now they are friends drinking wine, a young woman between them, just as before. I feel myself to be part of the negotiations, as surely as Hazel was, seasons ago.

Owen was with them then. I remember this with realization, as if I'd just remembered he'd said he'd go away in the summer, and for truth, he is gone now. I have the idea Owen and I are forever coming across each other, overlapping and walking in or around or above each other, and I think we will be this way forever more. My mind spans us, him to me, no matter how far apart we are. Even as simply as sitting in this cellar and thinking of Owen sitting in this cellar once too, we are connected up. Even if I'm never to see him again, we will travel all across this world and we will leave traces of ourselves like blazes for the other, on the walls and on the air, in Paris, France, and in that far-off desert sand. I realize I don't miss him, because he is everywhere I go.

I look to Punk, and for the first time in my life I can see Owen's face there, the face of a man who pleasures in being a boy from time to time. It could be the light or Punk's winsome mood, but the likeness is there. I think that's why Punk was so hard on Owen, because he knew what his son could make of himself with his mind put to it strong and true, knew from inside his own skin out. I listen to him talk to Sal, and from phrase to phrase I have the feeling that Owen really is here, that Punk speaks to him as much as Punk speaks to anybody, and when I enter in the conversation, it's as if I'm speaking with and about and over Owen, too. It's not the words we say; it's the way we say them, casually and with charm.

We talk on about everything except why we've come here. It's as if we live down the road and we've just stopped over for a glass of wine and a bit of conversation, chit-chat. What do you think about the weather; what do I think about the weather. Sal opens more bottles and after a time we go upstairs and Sal makes dinner, a salad with fried potatoes and sweet sausage. There's rice pilaf and thick cuts of fresh mozzarella cheese, London broil, cantaloupe, and fresh tomatoes. There's more wine, and sparkling water with lemon. Kat's come home. She wanders into the dining room and takes a place at the table. She's changed her clothes and she wears her black things again, wears her face dragging almost in her lap. She does not look my way and I think we should have forgotten to bring her home. We should have kept her where she was, following after

Punk and me, and brought Hazel back instead, just pulled up the drive and pushed her out the door.

Punk and Sal and I are famished, and everything looks beautiful, all things I love to eat, although I can't imagine eating them together. I try to eat each thing separately, but fall to trusting Sal's taste more than my own. Punk leans over and whispers in my ear. "Greens and potatoes. Wonder if that's an I-talian thing."

Punk's not a man who eats many salads in his lifetime, and one with meat and potatoes probably strikes him just about right. I tell Kat to go ahead, honey, and have something to eat, and she makes an effort. Talk at the table turns to grapes and air currents, micro-climates, seasoning oak, and something called the come-hither factor, something important to the wine Black Vineyards will produce. It's mostly between Sal and Punk and I let it be that way, watching them cage and circle each other, testing to see how much change has occurred.

Kat sits at the table, pushing food around the rim of her plate. She's welling up and I can see it.

"What's a matter, Kitty?" Sal asks.

She starts to cry, opens up her napkin, and covers her face. She's shaking, shaking her head, and then she pushes away from the table and runs from the room. We can hear her foot-falls in the ceiling, hear her door slam. Sal just keeps eating.

"Sometimes she doesn't even know," he says.

Sal shrugs his shoulders and that seems that, the conversation turning away and more wine poured, but I know what's wrong with her. I know how she's expected a homecoming party, expected to be the center of attention for a few days, and that's what I expected when I came home from school back in June. But I was glad for my path out of such a thing, for the cover of the wedding and something more important than me in everybody's head. Kat's scared about going away and being forgotten. She wants to be sure she has something to be re-membered by, some sway or fit or start.

Now with every comment at the table there's a slam or a thud overhead, a thumping sound on the stairs. I think I hear whimpering. I think I hear opera, and it's distracting. I find myself watching the ceiling, waiting for the lights to flicker or the chandelier to crash upon the table.

Punk is saying, "What do I know about all that," but Sal is looking overhead too, looking helpless and distracted, as if something in his spirits is about to rend open and it won't be pretty. Punk leans toward me and says softly, "Mavis, you please go and see on her."

I take some bread from my plate, my glass of wine, and go upstairs, just as Punk asked. I think how this has very little to do with why I came to Pennsylvania and even less to do with accounting, but I don't mind so much. I have a job here you can't learn in a book or a class, something that tests out in real life, and sometimes that involves keeping quiet when it's needed, checking on small things when something big's to be discussed.

Upstairs, Kat's room is pale pink and she has collections of small glass things in boxes on the walls, small fragile things like animals and birds, small chairs and tables, babies and fruits. There are sets of glass shelves with larger knickknacks resting there, carvings and seashells and china plates. I think of her moving among these delicate things, sleeping and thinking around all this glass, and how it must make her careful about herself. Maybe it's quite a thing she's told me about what goes on inside her head. Maybe she's trusted me with something more than she would reveal during one of her scenes, more than she would reveal to just anyone.

She kneels in the middle of her room surrounded by steamer trunks, angora sweaters, wool and cotton and blue jeans and lacy underwear, and I see she's got lots of different colors here, lots more ways to clothe herself than like a widow. She's packing for school, folding things neatly and not so neatly, and I can see the clothes she bought at Miss Pauline's Boutique in a pile on the bed.

"You're scared," I say, and she doesn't even look up at me.

"Oh, Mavis. Just leave me alone," she says.

"No, come on. You're scared to go away and come back home and not find things as you left them."

She sits sullen on the floor with her legs crossed and her arms crossed over them and she holds on to her feet and does not look up from the carpet. I don't care if she wants to hear this or not; she's cried at the dinner table and I'll be damned if that means she wants to be alone.

I sink down onto my knees and finger through her stacks of clothes. I start packing things up for her, stacking all her T-shirts and her sweaters, folding her blouses and laying the trunk out like a nest. It's nice to have someone help you pack a trunk, and I remember how my mama helped me pack for college. When I unfolded those things in my dorm room days later, I could still see her hands in them and I felt good and safe and right in a way that I can't completely account for.

So I fold Kat's things for her and talk while I do it. I tell her that she'll go to school for twenty-eight weeks a year and there will be twenty-four weeks left over, tell her she can come to Edisto in the summertime again whenever she wants. Punk will let her drive his Mustang and maybe she and I will drive places in that car with the top down and the truckers rolling by. I tell her crazy things, too, things about ladybugs and how when you set them out in the dusk, they'll make a home on your land and it's not a home they'll leave for very long. She almost laughs at this, but rolls her eyes instead, as if to say *so what, Mavis,* and *big deal.*

So I say things about timing, how there's a time to go away and a time to be at home. I tell her how I used to travel in the holidays from school and how I didn't come home for two years but went other places, and when I did walk through that door my mama's arms were as sweet as they've always been.

"You know, Kat," I say, "you're always going to fit the crook of your daddy's shirt sleeve."

I talk around what I think she's scared about, about how she can go away for years at a time, how she can travel and think those thoughts she doesn't understand and see those things she's never seen before in Pennsylvania. Every once in a while I can tell I hit upon the true thing that bothers her. She's uncrossed herself and now she helps me pack up her trunk, layering in a sweater over a sweater I've folded, weaving clothes like a basket. And then she tells me what happened at Merrilee's when her little niece Anna said how she'd miss her and things wouldn't be the same again, how she'd be whole weeks older when Kat got home again.

She says, "I knew that she was right and I'd miss her too, and I'd be weeks older too when I got home, weeks that nobody else would know about but me."

I want to tell Kat how this is a good thing, a private thing, and how it's what I am most pleased about when I think about my time at school, the weeks nobody knows about me. I want to tell her how that time made me thick inside myself, the same shape as when I left Punk's house, only that much denser and layered and knowing in the most simple and important ways, that time like a lining or insulation I made for myself, and how it keeps on growing, even now that I'm back in Edisto, like a covering, a skin's skin.

Finally, it's a feeling she'll either have or she won't, something she'll pick up or she won't, and I can't tell her about it and expect her to understand, so I'm quiet. And she's quiet too. We pack her things for her to go away again and I hope that she will figure out her world before she gets too far away from home.

22

We sit in Merrilee's kitchen drinking coffee, she and I in the afternoon. Sal and Punk have gone off with first light to gad about the countryside, and outside Merrilee's kitchen, Anna and her Aunt Kat are playing in the big backyard. Kat and I drove over the mountain after lunch in Punk's Mustang for a visit. Merrilee lives in a gingerbread house with lots of lacy woodwork and lead glass windows that wave in the sunlight, board shutters with curlicues cut in. Inside the front door the walls are the color of toast, and everywhere there are baskets of flowers, fresh and dried, and braided rag rugs and piled pillows cover the floor. Things are soft and enveloping, and I think of what Merrilee said at the wedding, that she liked being a housewife. It shows.

I want to appreciate Merrilee's house more than I do, maybe nap in the room that takes the sun, curl up with one of those pillows on the floor, but my mind is riding through the hills with Punk and Sal. I would rather be with them, driving them and taking the turns fast or just riding in the back seat as quiet as can be and listening. They are talking important things, things lots of us hinge upon, I know, and I must admit I was disappointed when they did not ask for my company.

The kitchen where we sit is comfortable, though, and large; copper pots hang overhead from a black iron grid, Mexican tile underfoot. Merrilee wears a sheer blouse, and her skin shows dark through. She leans on her butcher block table with her coffee mug clasped in her hands, her eyes constant on the window by the sink, her eyes trained to the small shape of her little girl playing in the backyard and her sister playing with her.

She asks after Hazel, tells me right up front it wasn't easy at first or even later. She loves her father and she does not want to see him sad or hurt or made a fool. She tells me how it hurt her to see him after Hazel left and how she felt so helpless. Hazel is older than Merrilee but has never raised children. They just weren't in synch.

She turns from the window to watch my face as I answer and I can see she is truly concerned. I think before I say anything, wanting to be true to Hazel, wanting to be true to the question. I think of how she looked when Punk and Kat and I left just yesterday and she stood on Punk's front porch with the rest of the women left behind and waved us on with the train of her wedding dress. At that moment, I came to have huge doubts about her prospects, her intentions. I wondered if she'd all come back to us, or if it was just dabs of her with skin about them sitting in our kitchen, standing on our porch.

"She's getting on," I say. "She's well, but I think she's broken up a bit."

"You know, Mavis, I so wanted her and Daddy to round out."

She tells me how she thinks Sal needs a woman out at his house, how he just plain needs a woman, not to do things for him, but just to be there. The night before Hazel left, Merrilee drove out to talk to her, finding Hazel down at the lake, taking a swim. There was no reason for her not to use the swimming pool, and Merrilee hiked over the bluff to find her lying on her back in the green water of the lake, not a stitch of clothes on.

Merrilee turns her coffee cup in her hands, trying to make conclusions again on what she'd seen.

Myself, I don't know what the big deal is. Who wouldn't swim in a lake instead of a swimming pool, and if I had the choice, I'd always swim naked. In my family, you do something and it's done, and maybe later you go and do something else, and just because Hazel does crazy things does not mean she's crazy. She may well be, but there are other things to look for. With Merrilee, though, I expect the actions of a life add up to some sort of whole; parts should all fit together, make some meaning, and just now she's trying to decide what exactly that is about us Blacks.

She says, "I was in awe of her, really. I watched her float and I think I was jealous."

Some of what she says I don't believe, and some of it I do. I look around her house and what first seemed scattered and spontaneous now seems placed, more constructed in its comfort than I first thought. She's no better off than the rest of us, understanding things the way she does.

I think of Hazel with her long woman's body, fleshed and simple in that lake. I think of the water falling away from her limbs and what that might have meant to Merrilee, to Hazel herself. I see what it might be to be married and in love, and what it might be to watch another woman be married and her not feel the same.

"Merrilee, I don't think they'll ever be together in any normal way."

"I know," she says.

She turns back to the window and Anna turning handstands in the summer grass, her T-shirt falling away around her chin and Kat holding up her feet. I wonder what she must feel seeing Anna, knowing she will stay this way, small and playing, for but a blink of time. I think this is what keeps her home in the mornings, what would keep me home, the pale fear of missing some part of Anna's turning, one moment there on the grass, the next a teenager, an older child, someday perhaps like Merrilee herself. It must be something to watch.

I say, "It must be something to watch her every day."

Merrilee nods. "She's quite a lady now."

I realize she's watching Kat and thinking her to be something else too, and I think how Merrilee was the closest thing to a mother for Kat in Sal's house when they were growing up. It was as if Merrilee had already raised one daughter by the time Anna came along.

She tells me she was always so scared to be a sister, so scared she'd say something wrong in front of Kat, do the wrong things, and Kat would learn life in the wrong order and be all messed up because Merrilee was a poor role model. But Kat's not fearful and that makes Merrilee glad. She knows every child is sad or angry or scared some nights in the dark, but being fearful is like being sickly or deformed, worse probably. It's irreversible and it's carried forever.

"I always thought there was less of Kat, herself, than there is. She's really maturing."

Merrilee's just come upon this thought for herself, but such a thing's been true to me all along. She has a way of picking things out of the air to be said with weight and purpose, and these things lie still for her to do it. They can be picked up, checked over, and put back down, but I get the feeling when she says them she believes they are new discovered. I see both parts of Kat, the eighteen-year-old girl and the eighteen-year-old woman, and I don't think Merrilee does. I think Merrilee sees her for what she isn't.

I know what Merrilee is talking about, but I cannot rise to this conversation. When I see Kat I think of the time she and Evelyn and I stole down to the river weeks back and stripped down our clothes in the moonlight and the heat. We said all nature of things, the three of us so smart in that night, and Evelyn declared there was no man alive good enough for her, and I said I could in fact bring dogs from the dead and sometimes they smelled like hell and sometimes they didn't, and Kat said she in fact owned a leather collar with silver studs and had no place to wear it. We laughed and laughed and swam clustered together in the water, three women cooling off and making it up as we went along.

And when I see Anna I think of the time at the wedding she asked where I was sleeping that night, and my mind being someplace else, I said I didn't know and she told me that joke about the dark. It makes me smile even now.

Merrilee stands from the butcher block and stretches her arms overhead, checks her watch, and yawns. She checks her watch a lot. We wander outside to fetch Anna because Merrilee wants to head into town to the store and run errands before Anna's ballet class.

Anna's collected mushrooms from the backyard and laid them out in some order on a picnic table, by color or size or delight, I'm not sure. Kat points to one and Anna reaches for it and lifts it to her nose, breathing in and closing her eyes. And then Kat points to another, and they do it all over again.

She tells her mother this is the best smell in the world, and that she knows if she leaves them out to dry in the sun on the picnic table, later she can come back and the smell will have turned, gone away, and she will have been the only one to smell these mushrooms when they were good because Aunt Kat left all the smelling parts inside for her.

She says, "Dried-up mushrooms smell like turds, especially the big ones."

I toss the keys to Punk's Mustang over to Kat and tell her there's a full tank, maybe a few friends she'd like to show off to. I tell her I'm going to ride into town with Merrilee and she'll drop me off at Sal's when we are through.

Kat tells me she'll wax it and vacuum the interior, take it to the car wash one last time. She'd been washing the Mustang since Punk brought it home, every other day, whether it needed it or not.

We drive to town in Merrilee's Aerostar. It's a blue Aerostar with woody trim, like a station wagon, and the inside's like a van.

"It's a minivan," Merrilee says. "Like a regular-person sort of a van."

"It's a spaceship," Anna says from the back seat. "Want to see my paintings?"

I turn in my seat and Anna has a folder of watercolors on expensive paper. They are paintings of smears and color and textures. They are paintings, not pictures, not her family or her dog or her friends, and in each right-hand corner someone has titled them for her and she has signed each one.

"This one is *The Clockwork*, then comes *The Messy Trashcan*, and after that *Footprints of the Cat*."

She doesn't read the titles; she knows them. She named these paintings herself. It must be rare to spend a day with this girl, to hear all the things she thinks while the things she thinks still run hand to mouth.

I look at Merrilee. "Anna, she's a clever girl," I say.

She tells me about Anna's nursery school, about her teacher who takes the children around town every day to teach them something outside, something real. This teacher shows them things up close so they can recognize them later. She'll stop her car on the highway to pick up road kill and she keeps it in the school's freezer until the children may be interested.

"Anna's seen a hawk, a possum, and a fox. She's seen a human heart, touched it inside a plastic bag."

"That nursery school teacher would be pretty busy in Edisto. She'd be stopping her car every five minutes."

When we drove into Pennsylvania I noticed lots of deer on the side of the interstate. I wondered just how big that woman's freezer was.

"A heart's not all that big," Anna tells me. "It's not that big, but you can fill it with a lot of stuff."

Anna's ballet studio is across the street from a pastry shop, above the bank. Merrilee parks the Aerostar in one of the metered spaces out front.

She says, "Anna's been doing this since she was four, and she's really amazing. The Mademoiselle says she can go up on toe before she's ten and that's quite a thing."

We climb four flights of wide steps to the ballet studio, a lofty room with Palladian windows and mirrored walls, so much light and reflection across the hardwood floors. Anna kisses her mother's sleeve and bustles off to the dressing rooms, her dance bag clutched to her chest. Girls are already milling around, already dressed for dance.

We stand in the corner, in the shadows, and out of the way. There are no other mothers here and I get the feeling it's a privilege to be non-dancers in this room, not something allowed very often. The girls are so comfortable and clannish, giggling and calling out across the room the way any young girls might. They help each other, pushing on a back, pulling an arm, acting as balance or weight where necessary, stretching their slight bodies over themselves like bands of taffy, seeming to grow longer, taller, older, right before my eyes.

"I never did anything like this when I was small," I tell Merrilee. "There were no places like this in Edisto."

I remember again being six years old and sitting tight on an irrigation pipe in Punk's fields, the sight of my mama coming 'cross those fields to me, the sunlight from behind her as if she was her own angel and I was her baby child and she was coming for me the very way she said she would. How beautiful she was, and still since I've been home I will look into her face and see her beautiful like that again, her arms coming 'round me and sweeping me up and taking me to the parlor house, which was still a shack then, and hosing the dust from our feet. For my own little girl, I'd like for her to know both, ankle-deep in earth and dancing 'cross hardwood floors, but either way I want her strong and sure and pulling her own weight.

I wonder where Punk and Sal have got to, if Punk thought to call the farm this morning and check on Tee before they took off for God knows where, but I imagine them to be so far removed in their talk that I doubt it. Maybe they are back at the house, even now, both of them with all their plans laid out over a bottle of wine. Of a sudden I am no longer worried about their conference anymore. I have the feeling they are like versions of the same businessman, different but related enough to understand each other's smarts.

The Mademoiselle enters, claps her hands, and the girls grow dour-faced, coiled like springs lining themselves at the barre. This is a workplace, and they are here with direction and purpose, here for critique and aid. All the girls wear the same pink tights and black leotards, Anna on the far side of the line, away from us. Class begins on the dot.

Merrilee leans into me and whispers over the music, tells how the Mademoiselle uses French forms of theory, styles of movement, which are more complex than Russian ones. She names each step and exercise: relevé, plié, tendu, dégagé, frappé, small whisks of the foot against the floor, as if the body is a hinge to be opened and closed at lightning speed, with delicacy and control, with great concentration. I am lulled for a stretch of minutes by the sound and rhythm of their steps and then startled to hear Merrilee's voice again in my ear. She tells me she's going to take a minute and dash off to the store to run some errands. She tells me I can come along or wait here, and I decide to wait here.

I watch the faces of these girls, and they know themselves so well, what they're capable of doing with their joints and tendons, how far the knee can extend, how tall the spine can stretch, how fast the muscles in the thigh can contract. They know these things so young and so well.

The Mademoiselle moves the girls to the center and they practice strings of turns and jumps. Anna stands in the falling light and she is confident, aware of where she is at all times. I realize this is where she gets her old face, the eyes that turn down slightly, the concentration, the lines at the corners of her mouth. She knows her gifts, at only six, almost better than I know my own.

I realize there is an echo of her movements in my own body, the slight tension of her leaps in my legs, her spin in my shoulders. My nerves seems to be firing off in tune with what she's doing, and even as I stand here, I sway slightly to the music.

After class, Anna is tired, and Merrilee goes straight to Sal's house to drop me off. Before we're even in the drive, Anna's fallen asleep in the back of the Aerostar, her leotard pulled down to her waist.

Kat sits in the driveway on the hood of Punk's Mustang. She's wearing shorts and she has her legs crossed at the ankles, her hair tied up in a red bandanna. There's a young man, more a boy, and he stands beside her in baggy shorts and a slouched T-shirt, a skateboard held under his arm like a book, some dozen whiskers he's nurturing out of his chin. His head is shaved above one ear but still long everywhere else so that it hangs across his eyes and he must hold his head to his shoulder to see.

I stroll over to where Kat sits and the boy stands, and I can hear her talking to him. I say howdy, drag it out to be long and Southern. I brush my hair away from my face absently with the backs of my fingers and I catch the boy's eyes gone to me. He blushes and I'm flattered, feel as though I'm something he'll think about later and blush again and then go to thinking about Kat too, because that's how boys are.

He mumbles something.

"Say again?" I ask.

"You really talk like that down there, don't you," he says. "Kat told me."

"What else did Kat tell you?"

Kat says, "I told him about the farm and the grapes, that big tractor we got and Punk's new car, how we all lived together this summer in Punk's house."

"We did," I say, and I put my arms around her, pull her close to me, and the boy blushes again.

Last night I worried about Kat, worried that she might not find her way to be, but her way to be is thousands of different ways, and she just chooses between them like so many possibilities. Right now she is the farm girl, and it's nice to see the vineyards delivered this to her. I have this sense that she's coming off an adventure and she's charmed by that. She could have gone to Europe and this boy would not have been more impressed than he is with Edisto. I know I have no cause to worry. She will be fine.

I wander inside the house and there's a note from Sal and Punk on the kitchen cupboard. It says they're away for the night and won't be home for dinner. I don't quite feel like fending for myself, all alone in this big house, and I'm a little put out that I was not included in whatever they've planned. I run back out the side door to catch Kat and her skateboarder standing by his Jeep Wrangler, and I think she was about to give him a kiss. I feel sheepish interrupting, but I just plow on through and ask them if they have any ideas for dinner.

Kat tells me, "When my father has something on his mind, he drives it out. He could go all night, it just depends."

She tells me not to worry and that he will call after too long, that he is safe and never falls asleep at the wheel. She tells me it's how he thinks, and I imagine he and Punk have been thinking this way for most of the day.

We decide to order some pizzas, and Kat and her skateboarder call up a few more people, and before I know it this is something of a party, one last gathering of Kat's friends before they all go off to school. They are boys and girls and they bring beer and beach towels and cassettes of music with no intelligible words. I am only four, five years older than they are, but it feels like a lifetime to me. The pizza delivery man shows up and I'm there with a hundred-dollar bill like a den mother, all Kat's friends wet and running in the pool, diving off its sides. I yell off the balcony to Kat, tell her the pizzas are here.

"Thank you, Mavis," she says, the way you'd say, be right there, or don't wait up, or trust me, Mom.

I grab a slice with anchovies and fold myself into a patio chair, out of the way. Kat's skateboarder comes up to get the pizzas and take them down to the poolside, and he stops to talk. He's had a few beers. He's through with blushing.

"Gonna come swimming, aren't you?" he says, and I shake my head.

"Come with, Mavis. It'll be cool."

He goes to grab my hand and almost loses his stack of boxes to a topple, and I tell him maybe in a little while, but I don't intend to go down there. It's not for me. I watch from the balcony because this isn't how I think about swimming anymore, not a pool filled up with kids and splashing. Maybe later I'll go down when things are quiet and dark, and maybe there will be one or two people still left around and we will talk, tell things about each other that sound good and smart and true.

I watch the boys as they run past the girls and it's as if their bodies spread out into spectrums of color, the shadows of their wants of young women just now coming together. And the girls cluster up and giggle; they issue dares and ask to be lifted upon shoulders, thrown out into the air by strong arms. I admire all this, because I am at the point in time where I don't like to be picked up and weighed, don't like to be held vulnerable that way. I keep what I would be dared into doing far inside my own head, and if there is daring to be issued, I will do it myself.

I wonder where Punk and Sal have gone for the whole day and into the night, and I feel I would be better suited in their evening, to their conversations. Maybe I should go down there to the pool and be unconcerned with all their dealings, but I won't. Instead, I go inside the guest house and call Tee down at the farm to check up. The Concords should be started tomorrow.

"This Mavis," I say.

"This Tee," he says, "and I know whatcha gone to ask. Those Concords are yet another day away."

Then something else. He tells me Deputy Cy Bertel showed up right after Punk and Kat and I left yesterday, and I am to call him immediately. Tee is relieved to have finally been able to deliver the message.

I get Cy Bertel on the phone and he makes no bones about the news he has. He tells me Owen's car was dragged from a saltwater swamp down on the coast. It'd been reported stolen off a used car lot up around Norfolk. He'd been working the phone that day and found out Owen had sold the car near the wharf and in turn it had been sold again and then stolen and then sunk and Owen probably shipped right out of that port, or he could have been passing on through.

Cy Bertel tells me Mr. Punk should know before anyone, and telling me is as good as telling Punk. And then a niceness comes over him, so strong I can almost hear him smile through the telephone.

"I know you will, but you shouldn't worry, Miss Mavis," he says. "That boy's got more lives than a tomcat."

23

In the woods, everything is green and running, and I hike until I'm too tired to hike anymore. When I got up this morning, Punk and Sal were still gone, and I was beginning to feel wrought up with curiosity. I took cheese and some fruit and bread from Sal's refrigerator and left a note of my own, a little something for them to wonder on when they did get home. I feel myself to have something at stake here, too, and I just want to know what's happening.

I hike along a slow creek with lots of shade and still pools of water lined with last fall's leaves. These mountains and their trails make me think of Appalachian and Harris down there still. Being outside in such a countryside is enough to make me glad for how we are right now, respectful of each other and clean like these streams. We've found it hard to say the things we know about each other's company in the past months, but I know he will come around more than a once in a while when I get back to Edisto. The feelings are all there, and we will be closer now that we have seen them. There will be times I will eat a ripe fruit and I will think to reach for him and run its juice along his chest. He will be right there beside me, or maybe he won't, or he will be there but we will not be saying much to each other and I will check myself, and that's okay too, as I will do and say and be the same for him. There is still more of my life left for him than I've already lived, and that is quite a thing to offer someone. This is as close as we will get.

Along this trail it grows dusky and I stop to pick some wild blueberries the birds have not gotten yet. I basket them up in the corner of my T-shirt and before long I have more than a few handfuls and my white shirt gone blue, my belly full with heat and walking, the food I've found and the food I've brought with me. I've spent the afternoon with myself in the out-of-doors and I feel calm and good and at ease with what's to come.

When I return to the guest house, Punk and Sal are back, and Punk looks a little bleak around the eyes.

"Where have you been?" I ask him.

"All over this goddamn state and another one, Mavis. We went to New York City."

"New York City?"

"I swear to God, like it was just down the road. We went to a ball game. We saw the old neighborhood. We drove past the Empire State Building and the Statue of Liberty."

"Punk, you can't drive past the Statue of Liberty."

"Well, it was off a ways."

He rubs at his cheekbones, closes his eyes into his hands, but when he speaks again he sounds full of favor.

"Mavis," he tells me, "Sal drove that city like it was Edisto, like it had one fucking traffic light, and I've never been a city person but I must admit I took a liking to the place. It seemed about big enough for me."

"And?"

"I don't know," he says, his hand back to his eyes. "We've been full cycle. He started off talking about getting out all together, but I think it's okay now. I tell you, he's a terribly, terribly complicated man. He thinks more than anybody I've ever met in my life."

Punk tells how Sal was down about Kat's leaving home, his life falling apart, and his wife falling apart. He spoke of the stock market and friends he had in Chile. He said things like, I don't need this, and that worried Punk. Then he started talking about his dream, his dream to have his own label, something long after he was dead they'd be selling for twenty-five, fifty dollars a bottle.

This is his last shot at such a label. This corporation is unusual in the prospect it has for boutique-type wine, a one-to-one relationship between the grower and the vintner. Such a thing could make great waves in small circles like the ones Sal runs in, and Punk suspects that would be special to him. He does need something to be special right now, and Punk thinks he needs not so much to be calmed as to be collected up, set right again. He doesn't know why Sal just can't be content to make a lot of money.

And then Punk tells me again how *terribly, terribly, terribly* complicated Sal is.

But I know Punk isn't telling everything. It's not like Punk to leave out his own wisdoms, to not tell how he had put Sal back on the straight and narrow. If he spent a day and a night with someone and their troubles, he'd want to tell how he was the hero, how he set them right.

I get cleaned up, and dinner is sweet sausage and basil, plum tomatoes, garlic and red peppers, tagliatelle, still-warm baguettes, and then dessert, a cheesecake with Frangelica and ripe strawberries. Me and Punk and Sal alone, as Kat's gone off with her skateboarder. Sal has wine and cigars he's brought back from New York City. He uncorks the bottle and asks me to pass judgment on his fine and expensive and rare buy. I sniff the wine and give it a sip. I look at him.

"Well?" he says.

"Well, it depends on how much you paid for it."

"I like you, Mavis. I like you a lot," but he doesn't let it rest. "So how much? How much would you pay, Mavis?"

"Wholesale, retail, or at auction?"

I smile at him and he smiles right back.

"Fair enough," he says.

Then he sits down and goes to arranging himself in the chair. I see what a handsome man he is, how tan and silver and full about himself. He runs a hand through his hair and that hand is square and clean and looks as though it might hold a feather and a stone in exactly the same way. He clears his throat.

He says, "First, I want to apologize for you making the drive up this way for nothing. I didn't even realize your concerns or I would have said something sooner."

Punk smiles at me, big enough to beat the band, and Sal goes on.

"There's business and there's affairs of the heart," he says, "and the two are forever separate. I would not make a deal I didn't trust, even for the truest of all loves. What's between me and Hazel is between me and Hazel. And the second thing is, I hope our business affairs last a long, long time."

He raises his glass to our partnership and we all laugh and toast and feel relieved. I think back to when Hazel came home and told me being married is different than having a wedding. She saw the two as separate events in her life, one she wanted and one she didn't. Sal wants to work our grapes because they are good and fine grapes, and that fact lies independent of everything else.

But then Punk and Sal are toasting each other and lighting each other's cigars and there's a decanter of brandy on the table and I can't help feeling I've heard an abbreviation of their story in New York City, true things hard arrived upon made to sound so simple. A real decision made to sound like principle all along. I think to tell Punk about Owen's car, but I trust Cy Bertel and let it wait.

❧

I slip into my bathing suit and a T-shirt come night. Punk is asleep because we will be leaving in the morning, but I've decided I'll not miss a swim in that kidney bean of a pool. Our business is done here for now, and I know there's more to tell. I can only trust Punk to have said and done the right thing.

I steal out the sliding door of the guest house, and Sal is right there, in a lounge chair. He sits with his decanter between his knees and looks as though he's been this way for some time, drinking into the late. He didn't hear me at the door, and even now he doesn't know I'm here. He rubs his lower lip, rolls it back and forth between his thumb and forefinger, looks toward the balcony and the house behind.

He says, "My girls are gone, all up and gone," and my heart breaks.

I go to him and kneel down in front of his chair, take his glass, take the decanter. I rest my head against his knee and I think how sad for him to miss his girls, to miss Hazel and now Kat going away to school, to miss Merrilee, married with her own girl to think about, and maybe even Kat and Merrilee's mother so long gone now. Maybe he misses her too. He looks so far away and sad I think to rest my head against his knee, a touch I might have made to Punk or Owen if he'd been sad.

He says, "All my girls are gone."

I sit back on my heels and study him for a moment, and he seems to realize who he's with, seems to back away from what he's just said.

"Kat had a good time with you in South Carolina," he tells me.

I smile. "She didn't get underfoot too bad."

"No, she's changed some way now. She said she had a good time and now she seems like she could have a good time about anywhere. Thank you."

He looks earnest and grateful in a most serious way, and I get the feeling he finds such a change in her to be just shy of miraculous. He looks upon me as if I have talents black and in need of deference, and I almost think he'd bow if he were standing up. I think of Cy Bertel's hound dog, months ago, how I brought her back to life, and the look on Cy Bertel's face was much the same. It's a nice thing, men thinking you can do things like an angel or a priestess, and I smile up at Sal as if he's figured out something I've known all along.

"She wants to work like you do, Mavis. She could come down next summer and you could teach her, if that's all right. I would appreciate it. She's never shown any interest in all of this," he says, sweeping out his hand.

"Of course," I say.

But there's still a sadness in his face, a sense of being replaced, that I have accomplished something he could not, and I worry he'll fall back to missing women. I say things to fill up his head, tell him he should come down to Edisto and see the harvest one year soon, tell him I could show him around, and he smiles.

"I thought I was dealing with Punk," he says, "and today he tells me I'm dealing with you from now on. I respect that man. I understand the choice he's made."

Sal stands a little shakily and pulls me to my feet, holds me by my shoulders.

"You feel like swimming," he says. "You go swim."

The lights are not on in the water and the pool looks as black as any lake. I stand at its edge and strip off my T-shirt.

"Go on and get yourself wet," he calls, and I jump in and I am swimming.

The pool is so black I lose where I am, forget to look for the bottom, forget there is a bottom. I hold my breath in and settle. I let my breath out and I rise up and I feel weightless, bodiless, a waft.

Sal watches me.

He lies out in a lounge chair with his fingers tented at his chin. He surveys all that is before him, me that is before him, and my swimming self that is part of his blackwater pool.

"Hey, Mavis," he says, and he is laughing now, "just how far were you willing to go for this deal?"

I tread out far enough away from him so that he can only hear my voice, the rest of me disappearing into the deeps. I'm larking in the dark water the way my mother might have with Wyman Jackson years ago, my skin young and light and catching in a man's eye.

"Well, now," I say. "I suppose we'll never know."

In the morning, standing in the drive, Sal gets between me and Punk and gives me a letter, says he wishes I'd give this to my Aunt Hazel for him. He tells me he was up all night trying to convey his words onto a piece of paper, and he's not sure if it will mean anything, but, well, it was all he could think to do. I tell him I'll be happy to give it to her, and then Sal Arceldi does the nicest thing. He looks me straight in the eye and shakes my hand.

24

~~~~~~~~~~~~ Punk says for me to buy a dress when we get to D.C., the most beautiful dress I can find, and I say, thank you, I'll do that. Stopping in D.C. is Punk's idea. Overnight he has become a connoisseur of cities, and he wants to see all the sights, the Capitol and the Smithsonian, all the famous monuments and statues and memorials. We stroll in the National Gallery because it is cool and lofty and Punk is delighted by everything he sees, the paintings and the sculptures and the women passing by, and when we step back outside he buys us hot dogs and piña coladas off a cart because that's how people eat in the cities, quickly and on the sidewalk.

Late in the day, we find a mall with a blue million shops and there are all sorts of dresses for me to choose from. Long ones and short ones and red and black ones. There are dresses cut down to my navel, dresses that cover me neck to ankle, dresses I could wear again and again, and dresses with so many sequins I can barely lift them over my head just once.

Punk says, "Get yourself up like a New Orleans tart or the Virgin Mary, whatever your heart desires."

And so I choose a long black dress that fits like mercury, comes high around my neck, and disappears down my back to the hollow of my spine, and I turn 'round and 'round in the mirror of that shop as if I'm dancing with myself. I buy long black gloves to go with my new dress, high-heeled shoes, and earrings that graze along my collarbones. We buy Punk a suit, too, something dark and slick, because he's never owned a suit and he wants to flatter my arm for our night out in this town.

We take our boxes of new-bought goods and we go to a tobacconist and step back into the humidor to choose Punk some five-dollar cigars. He buys me some too, pencil-thin ones as long and graceful as straw, and I tell him I don't smoke. He tells me just for tonight, I should turn some heads, and he buys me a gold lighter so expensive I am embarrassed to tell.

Some stores down we go into a stationer's and Punk buys a dozen different kinds of paper, a dozen different envelopes, and a fine book with blank pages bound in vellum, and it's not until evening when we get to our hotel I realize what he has in mind for those envelopes.

"I just got to read that letter, honey," he says. "I'm dying to know what's in it."

Sal's letter to Hazel is in a steady hand and calm. He does not beg, and he does not get passionate, which is what I expected. He wants her to come see him, tells her she could stay in the guest house. He says if this is going to end, he just wants it to end differently. He tells her Punk is a great man, as if she didn't already know, as if she wants to hear it again. He says he doesn't know what he did. Maybe he didn't do anything, but he's willing to take responsibility.

We match up the stationery and reseal the letter in its brand-new envelope.

"What were you expecting?" I say.

"I don't know," he says. "I just don't know now. It was a foolish and desperate thing to do, almost against the law," and for the first time in my life I think he may cry.

"Punk," I say and run my hand down the side of his face, "what is it? What were you looking for?"

"I don't know, Mavis. I'm as confused at what I did as you are."

"Maybe something to eat will help you feel better."

I say this to him like he's a little boy with an empty stomach, a child fallen off his bicycle. He shakes his head, wanders to his room for a shower and his brand-new suit.

The hotel is big and fancy and there are thick white robes hanging in the bathrooms so that you are never naked and without a change of clothes in Washington. After I shower, I slip into one of these and fix my hair up big and full, shade my face and eyes with makeup I've not used in a long while. I dress myself up carefully in my new stockings and my new dress with no back to speak of, pull on my new black gloves finger by finger. I want to look just so for tonight, look as if I am with the man who knows all the secrets, and in my heart I half believe this to be true about Punk. I sit on the edge of the big red bed to wait for his knock at my door.

When it comes and I open the door, he whistles and says my name and I take his arm and we drop down through the floors in an elevator made of glass. Down there, the lobby is full of Arabs, and I think to ask them about Owen, ask any one of these Arab men, think of asking some Arab women. I would say to them, if you see him, that Owen Black, you tell him Mavis said hello.

We go to dinner at the Watergate Hotel, and Punk orders for both of us, orders course after course as if he wants a taste of everything, and the waiter is bowing and scraping and bringing fine champagne around. Punk raises his glass in a toast.

"To Punk Black, Esquire," he says, "and the lovely Miss Mavis."

And after the toast he tells me he's got the cancer.

He tells me how this isn't average cancer but real fine and sharp cancer, and sometimes he thinks he can taste it in his mouth, coming through his skin. He tells me how he got the news and went out to buy that hot white Mustang because he wanted it and why the fuck not. He tells me if it wasn't for his cancer he might have toyed with Sal, he might have let him sweat it out a little, but there wasn't time for that.

He says, "Sal got his heart broke. That's all well and good, but a year from now I ain't even gonna have that. I had to know, then and there, you'd be slick. I told him so, too. I said, man to man, I got the fucking cancer. I got to know what's what, what's over and under and 'round and through."

He tells me how he's not going to get any radiation or be pumped through with pesticides and the like; that is not for him. He tells me there's a little Asian woman on the edges of town who does things with long, long needles and pillowcases full of sea sponge, and he's been to see her once already and it's almost like a day in the sunshine.

Most often I have three or four feelings on everything I see, everything I hear, but when Punk tells me he's got cancer, I go cold in my brain and I don't feel a thing. I go clear and cold and I see my mama, Hazel, Miss Pauline, and Evelyn too. I see them at the screen door, on Punk's porch steps the way we left them just days ago, coming out into the yard, into the garden, coming down the driveway rivered in a thunderstorm like women sheer and frightless and needful of a dying man.

"When I die, Miss Mavis, you take it all," he tells me.

"Punk," I say, and my right hand is in the air and my fingers are silken and black inside their gloves and opening and closing, opening and closing. "Punk," I say.

"And about Owen," he says. "I fear I'm a better grandfather than father. Every time I step into a room, I take up all the air in that room, and most times he's been right behind me, and so when he steps into that room there ain't much left."

He tells me it would take Owen too long to settle into his own; it could take him five, ten years, and Punk doesn't have time like that. Tells me Owen is flesh and blood and that won't ever change, but I had to see him go out the way he did at

Hazel's wedding so as I could recognize it later, know for myself when he'd be any good to me. He tells me he spoke to Cy Bertel too, and Owen wouldn't die in any salt swamp, not on his life.

He tells me he was glad to see me away those two years at school, glad I could come home big and full with myself, glad I could come home and see clearly. He tells me there are so many things to see clearly in this world and he knows a few of them he can still pass on to me. He tells me this deal with Sal is the only one that man's ever made on just a handshake, and that alone will keep it together, but the fact that Punk is dying will make this tie thicker than blood. He tells me Sal will appreciate the theatrics of the coming months, and when he sees me coming out of such a fire, he'll appreciate me too.

He tells me all such as I sit there in my expensive dress in this expensive restaurant, crying like I am absolutely alone.

"He'll be back around, that boy," Punk whispers, "and you'll have a head on your shoulders about him. You will," and I don't know if he means Owen or Harris.

I bring my hand to my chest and hold it 'cross my heart and the tears just run down my cheeks and my lips and my chin, and soon I'm not taking any breath, just gulping at the air. I go still and soundless and I cry to turn myself inside out, to run my tears into a river that flows beneath these tables and out the big hotel doors to the Chesapeake Bay.

"Those I-talians are dramatic people," Punk says, winking at me. "Dramatic heart-felt people. You aren't a little bit I-talian, are you, Miss Mavis?"

I realize that Punk likes knowing the circumstances of his death, feels omnipotent like no other human being, and he's not scared to go out this way, sees it as no more pain or less pain than any other way to go, and he likes that he won't have to die in some hospital away from Edisto. A lesser man would be angry, but Punk just feels he's got yet one more thing up his sleeve now. I imagine him telling Sal he's got the cancer. Was it in the Lincoln Tunnel, at the top of the Empire State Building? Was it on the way or coming back, was it noon or midnight or just sometime early morning when Punk got his face in Sal's face and told on himself like that?

He tells me how there is anger in this world, eyed or eyeless like a hurricane, and it's best to steer clear of the eyeless sort in others, but he tells me to keep a bit up my own sleeve for myself.

He says, "I know you have that in you, Mavis, and you might never have to use it. I just want you to trust it's there when called upon."

Punk tells me the difference between a wet moon and a dry moon, tells me never to trust a man in a green jacket. He tells me that before I was born and my daddy had gone up in flames, he thought Elsbeth might just follow that Wyman Jackson into the fire and become nothing but ash herself. He tells me I kept her here, and he thanks me for it. He tells me us Black women are bred to be on our own, and not to forget that, because he fancies it comes straight from him. He tells me he owes nothing in this world to no one except for Miss Pauline, who he owes for a life of misery and heartbreak, and this makes him smile from ear to ear.

He tells me he likes the handbells, and he'd go to church every Sunday if they played the handbells in Edisto, but they don't and he doesn't and he won't.

When we leave D.C., I will thread Punk's Mustang down through the flats and the orchards of the southland, through the smell of peaches and wood smoke and pasture thick with cows. We will cross rivers glassing in the heat and tangled to the west and sometime later on, when it is cold and raining, they will tell him he has six months, maybe a year, but Punk won't care. He'll take his vellum book and Miss Pauline will buy him smooth fountain pens and he will set to writing himself down, the memoirs of his life's wisdom, pleased by his fine penmanship above all else. He'll show his words to Harris when he comes to Edisto, and Harris will praise them up and down, and Punk will touch my shoulder as if to say he knew I'd take a good man all along.

And Punk himself will take a thick white bathrobe from our stay in D.C., because he's never owned a bathrobe, and he will wear it all the time after long because it is as thick and white and plush as anything he's ever seen.